What Reviewers Say About F

"Zedde's explicit erotic scenes keep no secrets, and her tender, masterful storytelling will keep readers spellbound and squirming."—*Publishers Weekly*

"Fiona Zedde is a culinary artist with words, cooking up spicy, flavorful tales [to] satisfy the appetite of a malnourished audience."—*Washington Blade*

"Fiona Zedde conveys the helter-skelter speed of [her character's] chic lifestyle with sharp prose, fast-moving actions, and erotic interludes that are intense, shocking and arousing."—*Erotica-readers.com*

"Fiona Zedde's portrayal of a black lesbian love affair is exquisitely written and described."—*Femininezone.com*

BROKEN IN SOFT PLACES

Broken in Soft Places

by

Fiona Zedde

2013

BROKEN IN SOFT PLACES

ISBN 10: 1-60282-876-8
ISBN 13: 978-1-60282-876-6

This Trade Paperback Original Is Published By
Bold Strokes Books, Inc.
P.O. Box 249
Valley Falls, NY 12185

First Edition: May 2013

Credits
Editor: Cindy Cresap
Production Design: Susan Ramundo
Cover Design By Sheri (graphicartist2020@hotmail.com)

Dedication

To Angela.

For believing, encouraging, and always reading.

WHAT WE ARE

STEPHEN/ATLANTA

Stephen watched Rille walk past him in her rock star underpants, shirtless, and whistling an Otis Redding song. Her breasts bounced gently as she rocked out to "Dock of the Bay," swaying like a belly dancer in front of the bathroom mirror. He lay back in rumpled sheets, enjoying the rare pleasure of having her to himself. Their lover, Sara, had abandoned them, gone back to the office because she forgot something and had an important case on Monday she needed that particular *something* for. On a Saturday, for heaven's sake.

Rille came out of the bathroom with a wet towel held between her two fingers like it was contaminated. "Whose?"

Stephen knew she found it on the floor, miles away from the laundry hamper. Right where he left it after his shower earlier that morning. With what he hoped was a penitent air, he claimed it and she chucked it at him, sending the damp towel whooshing into his bare chest before going back in to tweeze her eyebrows. She left the bathroom door open.

From the bed, Stephen watched her. Barely paying attention to his book, a history of the bicycle in America. He watched her. The way her breasts sloped in that universally beautiful way, the lean lines that led to the soft swell of her belly and those ridiculous panties. They were shiny and pink with sequined stars and a guitar stenciled on the ass. The words "rock star" flashed across the pubis. Not the expected attire of a tenured physics professor at Emory. Her students would be shocked to see her now.

In the bathroom, she finished tweezing and began to shave her armpits. After being with these women for almost three years, Stephen thought he'd get used to rituals like these, but they were still endlessly fascinating to him. Sara had had all her body hair lasered off. And her already perfect eyebrows arched over perfect eyes that matched her perfectly lean brown body and the dreadlocks she wore in a thick black fall down her back.

"Stephen, let's go out for dinner tonight."

Rille emerged, still shirtless, from the bathroom and gave him a soft, lingering look. She walked past the windows with curtains that had been pulled aside to let in the sound and sight of rain tapping, a curious visitor, against the glass. Like Rille, the day was beautiful. She climbed into the bed with him, pulled his book away and crawled into his lap.

"Kiss me."

Rille's beauty was the most awful kind, Stephen thought. The awareness of it grew on you, sneaking into your consciousness with each passing day until, years down the road her loveliness hits you like a whip every time you see her. But by then she has lost interest in you and it's time to move on. By second semester, all her students were in love with her, mesmerized by the tangle of brown and blond flyaway curls and the changeable eyes that crackled with energy as she walked back and forth in front of the classroom with fractals and chaos theory on her lips.

He touched her the way he knew she liked to be touched, gently, with the roughness growing by turns until he twisted her nipples hard, dug his fingers into her skin, and she hissed, dragging his shorts off, rolling on a condom, and mounting him with quick ferocity. A brief moment of fear, of the rubber breaking, of Rille forgetting herself somehow, snared Stephen's attention from their lust. But her heat engulfed him, like always, scorching away the habitual terror. She was tight and wet, a snug satin glove. Her panties still clung to her hips, just shoved to the side for convenience.

Stephen lay back and let her set the pace. She rode him with skinned teeth, breasts bouncing, eyes fierce. Sweat flushed to the surface of his skin, her skin, and electricity lanced between them, shooting up from his hips into her hips. The whip of orgasm began to uncoil in his cock.

"I see that you're enjoying your weekend off."

He turned at the sound of Sara's voice, still grasping Rille's hips. She slowed her pace, but did not stop. A grunt rose in Stephen's throat as the orgasm retreated.

"You could be too," Rille offered in her sex-roughened voice.

"True."

He and Rille watched as Sara, damp from the rain, dropped her briefcase on the table by the bedroom door and slowly stripped off her slacks and blouse. The shock of her beauty tugged at Stephen's hips and Rille laughed. She knew that her woman was beyond compare. Sara looked at them, her eyes flickering from where Rille and he were joined, then to Rille's sex-flushed face. She hefted her clothes in one hand as if to toss them, but only walked past the bed to the bathroom where she hung the slacks and blouse over the shower rod to dry.

"No, continue without me," she said to their unasked question, her voice muffled by the cavernous bathroom. "I have to work…"

But she left the bedroom door open on her way to the adjacent office. Sara would hear them and later, Stephen knew, after she was sure that his fingerprints had faded from Rille's skin, she would come back. Then she'd finally let herself enjoy Rille without distractions, without his presence.

Rille grabbed his face, pressing her palms tight against his cheeks. "Me. Now."

She rode him hard, but the rhythm was somehow off. Her body closed tight around him, a hot, bucking weight, but her mind was somewhere else. Stephen could feel it. With Sara perhaps, settling beside her into that gigantic leather chair in front of the desk, wishing that she could be there in body to reassure Sara that nothing was wrong in their complicated relationship. The arrangement that was Rille's idea and that they agreed to because they both wanted her so much.

After, with the sweat still drying on Stephen's skin, Rille left the bed to find Sara. In the office, he heard the rising softness of Sara's voice, a cool blade of reason to the honeyed nonsense leaving Rille's mouth.

"But, baby, I wanted to feel you, too."

Rille closed the door behind her before he could hear anymore. Outside, the rain beat against the roof as if trying to get in. Its drowsy cadence, along with the gray light spilling past the windows, pressed at his eyelids. Stephen turned in the sheets, already half asleep, and pulled his pillow closer.

The First Day of...

Sara/1994

This place was nothing like high school. The people were different. They had sex, they drank, some, Sara heard, even had HIV. She walked around in a daze, soaking it all in, looking, she knew, as naïve as she felt with her big eyes and exclamations of "really?" or "no way." Her roommate, Raven, sat with her in the cafeteria, elbow pressed to Sara's at the long table in the high ceilinged room ripe with the smell of D-grade meatloaf, watery mashed potatoes, and the strangely colored peach cobbler.

Most of the older students walked in then out of the cafeteria, carrying away plastic wrapped sandwiches and small containers of juice, while the newest ones sat captive to their meal plans and limited social opportunities, staring down at the brown and white mess on the chipped canvas of their dinner plates. To Sara's inexperienced eyes, the older students all looked so sophisticated. Never mind that most wore ragged jeans, oversized flannel shirts with their hair long and stringy to their waists or blooming around their heads in intimidating Afros. And that was just the boys. The girls, or women, held Sara in thrall. She couldn't quite look at them; they all seemed too bright, too beautiful, too confident. There was one girl she did look at, though. Raven said that the girl's name was Merille Thompson. She was a fourth year physics major with glass green eyes glowing against her cocoa bean skin and a head full of dark blond curls.

Now, when Merille caught her staring, Sara quickly looked away but not before she saw the smile and quick wink. She blushed, glad that the girl wouldn't see the color through her teak skin, and looked down at her dinner tray. Beyond the glass doors of the cafeteria, the sun slowly sank behind the trees. From the corner of her eye, Sara could see how the falling sun haloed Merille, making her appear ethereal and unattainable.

"Stop being so obvious," Raven said, looking down at her own tray. Today, her chemically straightened hair was braided back over her scalp like tiny fields of grain. Small wooden beads clacked quietly at the end of each braid just above her shoulders.

She was straight, but fancied herself able to give advice because of the nearly six-month gap in their ages. And the fact that she had a boyfriend in Tampa only fifty miles away who made her the happiest first year Sara had ever seen.

"Shut up," Sara said, a helpless whine in her voice. "I'm not being obvious."

"Then why did she just wink at you?"

"She just had something in her eye."

Raven snorted then choked on the toxic meatloaf. A piece of it flew out of her nose and bounced off the tray. With a faint coating of slime on it, the meat actually looked more appetizing than the original version on her plate. Sara said as much and they both looked at the piece of meat.

"Gross."

They looked at each other and laughed. They already loved their new school, but not because of the food.

"We'll have more interesting things to eat at the party this weekend."

Sara looked up at the low, resonant words and almost died. Merille stood quietly next to their table, her long brown hand extended. A piece of paper, bright pink with black ink scrawled across it, dangled from her hand announcing a party later that week. When Sara didn't lift her hand to take the flyer, Merille slid it on the table next to her tray. Sara blinked when the clear gaze caught hers. There was destruction in those eyes, she thought stupidly. And a chance to be reborn.

"Hi, I'm Rille," she said. "Both of you are invited to come."

Her voice was a husky rasp. Somehow, Sara hadn't thought anything else could possibly make the girl more appealing. Obviously, she was wrong. Sara swallowed.

"Thank you," she mumbled.

Rille smiled. "You're welcome. I hope to see you there."

"Are you going?" Raven asked after Rille went back to her table of friends and out of earshot.

Sara swallowed again, still staring at the paper.

"Of course you're going." Raven rolled her eyes, acknowledging she'd just asked the most ridiculous question on earth. "Be careful."

The party was in three days in a part of the campus where Sara hadn't been, Third Court, ruling place of third and fourth years and a few giddy second years. Would she be the only first year at this party? Sara didn't know what she wanted to do first—hyperventilate at her ridiculous luck, or back out, not bothering to show up at that party with Rille and her friends. She wasn't quite sure if she was ready to play with the big girls.

"I don't think there's anything to be careful of," she said, trying to convince herself.

Already she'd heard the fantastical rumors about all sorts of things that the upper class people indulged in on the campus. Vreeland College was what many called a "hippie school," a place of free love, drug experimentation, and a reckless disregard for consequences. Sara, fresh from her parents' house and a high school she gleefully abandoned with her virginity intact, wasn't sure if she was ready for any of this freedom. She folded up the neon invitation and dropped it in her pocket.

The days between the issued invitation and the party crawled slowly past. Sara sat in her philosophy class—the first one she'd ever taken in her life—and thought about the abstraction of Rille, the certainty of her presence at that party on Friday night, and the shiver down her spine at the thought of what would happen there.

All five windows of the room were open to let in the fresh burn of the early morning Florida sunshine. Light reflected off the bald head of Professor DJ Holloran as he perched on the desk in front of the room, looking more like a TV version of an Irish thug than a philosopher.

"If you can't think logically, this isn't the class for you." His mouth twisted into a charming smile that invited the class to share some conspiracy. "I see nineteen people in here. No offense taken if some of you walk out of here right now. I don't mind you wasting my time today. It's the first week of classes, but don't come here next week if you don't want to be challenged." He waited to see if anyone would leave. When the entire class seemed bent on staying put, he hopped off the desk and went to the chalkboard. "Great, now let's take a look at our reading list."

Sara studied the syllabus and the list of unfamiliar names—Voltaire, Kant, De Beauvoir, Fanon—and wondered dimly how they would prepare her for the world here at Vreeland College, for the world beyond its terracotta walls, or even for Rille. But maybe she was asking too much of one class.

❖

"So what are you going to wear?"

Despite her boyfriend's eagerness to see her, Raven stayed in school past her last class on Thursday morning to prep Sara for her first college party.

"I don't know," Sara said. "Jeans. Nothing serious."

"What do you mean? You need to wear something fun and sexy so she can't miss you."

"I thought you wanted her to miss me, pass me altogether in favor of other young virgins to debauch?"

"Don't be a smartass." Raven propped an elbow on her duffle bag—already packed for her weekly booty call to Tampa—and looked Sara over carefully. "You should wear something pretty. Maybe some velvet?"

"What?"

In the end, Sara took Raven's advice and wore red velvet, a quintessential party dress, spaghetti straps, with a bodice fitted over her breasts and belly then flared out in an A-line to make the most of her thick hips and thighs. She arranged her straight permed hair into a French twist, fastening it with red beaded crystal clips and slipped on black high-heeled pumps she'd had for years but never had an occasion to wear.

Her feet felt strange in the shoes, squeezed tight but sexy in a way she'd never known before.

"You look hot. Very fresh meat." Raven's smile slowly faded until she watched Sara with grave eyes. Finally, she turned away and grabbed her bag. "My work here is done. See you Monday. And take care of yourself."

"That's it?" Sara turned to her, hyper conscious of the way the stilettos elongated her legs under the silk-lined velvet while propping her bottom up and out.

"Sure. What else do you want me to say?"

The truth was that Sara wanted company at the party. Raven was the only person she knew on the Vreeland campus, and she often felt out of place among these people who were largely the opposite of chic, but still possessed their own sophisticated mystique.

"Nothing," Sara finally said with the tiniest pout. "Tell Kevin I said hello."

Even though she had never met Raven's boyfriend, they had often ended up talking to each other on the phone while Raven dashed out of the shower or ran up the stairs to their dorm room from a late class.

"Definitely." Raven quickly hugged her and breezed out of their shared room.

It was after ten, too late for anything good to be on TV, but far too early to go to a party that started at nine. Or at least that's what Raven said. Sara waited until eleven o'clock on the dot to leave her room and walk to the other set of dorms across the courtyard. A cool Florida breeze off the nearby ocean brushed against her cheeks and stirred tendrils of her hair.

Was she really going to do this?

Sara slowed her footsteps, but she didn't stop.

Her parents wouldn't approve. Definitely not her homophobic friends from high school whom she'd abandoned after making the decision to go to Vreeland. Yes, the school was a place to indulge in all the excesses she'd heard about but felt too afraid to try—mushrooms, weed, alcohol, sex, skinny-dipping in the ocean under indifferent stars. But the campus also had one of the largest percentages of gay students of all the schools she'd been interested in. When Vreeland had said yes to her application, Sara dismissed all the other universities and their acceptance letters, even Columbia, where her father had hoped she would enroll.

She wanted to be in a place where she could be herself.

She wanted to be in a place where it was okay to have crushes on other girls.

Sara drew a deep breath. Finally, she had arrived at that place.

Third Court was one big party. Loud voices raised in laughter, philosophical disagreement, and general raucousness, immediately greeted Sara as she crossed its invisible threshold. Bright blue Christmas lights decorated the trees in their small courtyard and twined around the cement work balconies. Large Japanese lanterns decorated with flittering dragonflies and cherry blossoms bobbed gracefully in the breeze while marijuana smoke wove its way through the air, coming from all sides and slipping into Sara's hair, dress, and nose.

Boys—and girls—watched her walk by, sliding their inquisitive gazes over her body, up her newly long legs and the shifting heat of her bottom under the dress. She smiled nervously but kept going. With the neon invitation clutched in her hand, Sara walked past each glass door on the bottom floor until she realized that 318 meant the top floor, not just the court number.

Before she could knock on the door, it opened, releasing the scent of more marijuana, and something else, something sweeter than she'd ever smelled before. The person at the door—it was hard to tell if she was a he or vice versa—smiled gently at Sara and tugged her into the room.

If the atmosphere outside was a party, this was a dream. D'Angelo's "Brown Sugar" wove its smooth, jazzy funk through the room, rocking into the bodies gathered there, the sleepy-eyed women in flowing skirts, the liquid-limbed boys lying across the queen-sized bed, passing a pipe back and forth between them, the girls who stood talking around a table filled to overflowing with food. They all seemed to rock gently to the song's beat, mellow and loose.

"Come on in." The stranger's voice was warm and feminine.

"Hey," Sara murmured, shyness suddenly overwhelming her.

Short spiked hair. Dark eyes under slashing brows. Nutmeg skin. The woman gently rubbed her palms up and down Sara's arms, smiling. "Where did you come from?"

"Um…First Court. I got an invitation." She nervously waved the pink flyer.

"You must be a first year. Are you?"

"Yes." Sara cleared her throat of its squeak. "Yes, I am."

"I thought you were leaving, Devi." An unmistakable, throaty murmur emerged from deep inside the room.

Devi, who still had her hands lightly grasping Sara's arms, didn't look toward the voice.

"I was, and now I'm not," she said.

Looking past Devi, Sara saw Rille in the bed. She wondered how she'd missed her presence before. She sat at the head of the bed, leaning back against a wall draped with a plum purple Om tapestry. A woman smoking her own pipe, a bone colored antique with silver accents gleaming in the low light, lay across Rille's lap. Thick white smoke hovered over them, growing thinner as it swam toward the rest of the room. The fourth year caught Sara's eye and winked again just like she'd done in the cafeteria that Monday afternoon.

Rille nudged away her girl to slide across the bed and emerge from the slow moving wave of bodies in the room, a compelling vision in low rider jeans and a tiny tank top advertising shucked and raw oysters. "I was the one who invited her, not you," she said to Devi.

Sara shifted in Devi's arms, suddenly uncomfortable. Everyone at the party, at least those she could see, was casually dressed in jeans, shorts, or vintage frocks. Nothing approaching the formality of Sara's dress.

"I like your outfit," Rille said. "Red velvet. How appropriate."

"Does that mean we'll get the chance to eat you up, too?" Devi asked.

"If we're lucky," Rille answered for Sara.

Sara blinked at them, watching the game between them like the spectator she was.

"You have to learn to share," Devi said.

"I always share with you. All of a sudden you're complaining?"

Rille linked her fingers with Sara's, while on the other side of her, Devi gently held her hand. "You're just in time for spin the bottle," Rille said.

The two women guided Sara to the food table with everything sweet her heart could desire—red velvet cake, chocolate covered strawberries, baklava, and sparkling plum wine. Devi briefly relinquished her hold on Sara to cut herself a slice of cake. Looking at Sara suggestively, she sank her finger deep into the cake then, after it emerged coated in red velvet crumbs and sticky white frosting, sucked it clean. Rille watched her antics with a cool smile.

"Don't try so hard, baby. It makes you look the opposite of fuckable."

Soft color washed beneath Devi's cheeks and Sara reached out to squeeze her hand. She glanced at Rille, surprised by her casual cruelty.

"What?" Rille asked as if she'd done nothing more innocuous than blow her nose. "It's true." She turned back toward the other partygoers.

Everyone seemed to be doing their own thing. Smoking, talking, lingering over the table of edibles. That was until Rille made an announcement, tapping a spoon that had traces of sugar on it against a gigantic glass bong.

"Gather round, one and all. It's time for more festivities to begin." Her gaze swept the room. "Those who want to watch, can. Those who prefer to play, let's play."

A few of the two dozen or so people gathered in the room and arranged themselves in a circle on the floor. At least five chose to stay out of the game, including the girl who had been lying in Rille's lap. She sat back in the bed, still puffing on the pipe with its sticky-sweet smoke, making herself comfortable against the pillows to get a good view of the show. A girl on the floor nearest Sara, with her hair cut close to her head and a wealth of dark skin exposed in very short shorts, sucked her teeth.

"I wish Thalia would take her damn opium pipe somewhere else. She can be such a poser."

But the words tumbled past her lips without any real heat. A few people laughed, but the girl on the bed paid them no attention. As Devi drifted away from them, Rille tugged Sara down on the floor next to her.

"I'm not sure if I'm ready to play this game." Sara had heard of this on television and even whispered about in middle school, but she thought that people in college, especially those at the party, were way past such childish games. Apparently not.

"You have to play." Rille's eyes were heavy-lidded. "I promise you'll have fun."

Devi dropped an empty beer bottle in the center of the circle and dropped herself between a soft looking boy with pretty, full lips and another butch girl directly opposite Rille and Sara. A boy with a thick Afro leaned over to start the game.

"By the way," Rille said, leaning close. "Gender doesn't matter. Whoever the bottle lands on, that's who you have to kiss." Sara had already figured that part out on her own. "You can decide to kiss here in the circle, or in the semi privacy of another space in the room, balcony included." Rille grinned, the perfect picture of a charming fourth year lecher.

Sara sat at Rille's side watching the game, mesmerized. This was what college people did? They spun and kissed, leaning toward each other in the circle, bottoms high in the air, wriggling with pleasure if their kisser was doing it right. No one took the activities away from the circle. When it was Devi's turn to kiss, the boy with long dreads down to the middle of his back and the scent of sandalwood on his skin, neatly cupped Devi's head, sliding his fingers through her short hair and down to the back of her neck. She shuddered when he touched her and they drew back, finally, to catcalls and whistles.

"Very nice."

The D'Angelo CD segued to Johnny Hartman, sinking the room deeper into sensuality with his strong, rich voice and words of yearning. When someone lit a joint and passed it around, the game got even slower with couples taking up the circle to form their own make-out area. The girl next to Rille passed the joint and she took it, holding it between her index finger and thumb like it was something surprising she'd just found. Sara watched her take a hit, drag the smoke slowly into her lungs, her eyes squinting against the sting of smoke. Rille leaned close to Sara, to tell her a secret maybe, and pressed her lips to hers, probed with the quick flick of her tongue, until Sara, caught off guard and still amazed that people did such things in public, opened her mouth.

She coughed and sputtered, the smoke burning behind her face and in her lungs.

"Open. Suck it deep inside," the gravelly voice licked at her ear.

Sara blushed, still coughing, still reeling from the sound of those words so close, and at the feeling they sparked in her body, the electric shock under velvet, the startling zing in her lap.

The people who saw what happened laughed. But the couple in the circle, and now those off to the side, bored with waiting for their turn at the spinning bottle, earnestly made out, reaching tongues and hands in places where Sara could not see. She blushed again. And this time, Rille laughed. She put the joint to her lips again, inhaled deeply before holding it to Sara's mouth.

"Just one," Rille said, smoke trailing from her nostrils.

Sara inhaled, coughed, and pushed the joint away.

"Good girl." Rille kissed her quickly as a reward then passed the weed down the line. "Come on," she said and stood to lead Sara away from the circle toward something Sara wasn't sure she was ready for but wanted to taste anyway.

"Are you a virgin?" Rille asked with her lips a whisper from hers.

They were out on the balcony now, squeezed in next to another couple already half dressed and moaning into the warm Florida night. The lanterns dipped in the air near them, providing a pseudo light, light to seduce and smoke by, to say and believe anything by. Sara closed her eyes, convinced of the magic in the night and in this girl by her side.

"Yes." She felt rather than saw Rille's smile.

"We can take care of that for you tonight, if you like." Rille's breath teased her lips and Sara felt herself leaning closer to initiate contact.

"I'd like," she murmured.

Sex was a surprise for Sara, but no miracle. Even with the hazy high blown into her by Rille's careless mouth, the promise of fulfillment turned out to be just that. Rille tried everything on her—tongue, fingers, the firm pressure of her thigh, until finally, she found an old dildo with a condom already on it from previous use. Rille stripped it off, looking only half apologetically at Sara as she went quickly inside the room to rinse off the dildo and put a fresh rubber on it.

"This will be better," Rille said when she came back out to the balcony.

With her jeans discarded and wearing only her skin and a dildo harness, she pulled Sara down on top of her on the couch. Hot delirium, her mouth. Hair exhaling the scent of marijuana smoke as she nuzzled Sara's throat, encouraged her to touch, whispered sweet filth in her ear. Rille seized the new territory of Sara's flesh. Opened her for intrusion.

She bled and called out in pain, straddling the green-eyed dream in the semi privacy of the balcony sofa. The couple next to them came and went. Rille soothed her until she almost forgot that pain, until she found some sort of rhythm with the red velvet shoved up around her waist and down below her breasts and Rille sighing how beautiful she was. On the inside, Sara felt battered.

"That was really nice," Rille said when they were finished.

Sara's thighs quivered from the ache between them. "Nice" wasn't quite the word. Her cheeks warmed with embarrassment as she moved against the sofa to pull down her dress. She bit her lip. But Rille's eyes glowed in the dark as if she still wanted to devour her. Sara blushed then, feeling somehow special.

"You can stay with me tonight, if you want."

But Sara heard the token offer for what it was. Smoke. She shook her head and adjusted her legs next to Rille on the sofa, trying to take up less space. Rille patted Sara's still smoothly French twisted hair and peered around the balcony door to see what was going on inside.

"Go inside," Sara said. "I'll be fine out here."

Rille smiled, gratefully, Sara thought, and left her outside with the lanterns and the faint strains of music and the laughter floating up from the courtyard. Sara didn't know how long she stayed, but the sky was lightening and the party was at its lowest with almost everyone on the bed or on the floor or in the bathroom. She didn't see Rille's bright head anywhere.

So this was college, Sara thought, looking around. The beginning of everything. More laughter rose up and died from people in the courtyard below. No one noticed when she left the party, passing slowly out the door in her crushed red velvet dress.

Sara's room was silent and dim. After the abundance of the party, it seemed especially lovely. The display on the answering machine flashed. A message waited. She sat on her bed, carefully arranging the soreness between her legs. Her thighs felt sticky. She was sure there would be blood. That was what all the books said.

Sara ran a hot bath and sat in the water with her head resting against the tiled wall. Rille's shadow rose up, kneeling again between her thighs, her mouth on Sara's, her body vibrating with want. Sara closed her eyes.

When she opened them again it was fully light and Raven was shaking her shoulder. A shiver raced through her as she shifted in the water. It was cold.

"You need to get out of there."

Raven brought a towel and spread it wide for her to step into. Disoriented, Sara stood and stepped out of the tub. Raven dried her unresisting body.

"What time is it?" Her mouth felt sticky, as if something old had finally died in it. She shivered again.

"After nine, I think. I called, but you didn't answer the phone."

"I didn't get back from the party until late." Sara registered, dimly, that Raven should've still been in Tampa over fifty miles away with her boyfriend, not crouched over the tub, worry carved into her forehead.

Raven's touch through the towel was clinical but concerned. She only lightly skimmed over Sara's thighs with the cotton, not drying between them. Sara looked down at her body. The glaring red towel looked too familiar against her skin. She wanted to rip it away from her body. But that wasn't a normal thing to do.

"I think I stayed in the water too long." She cleared her throat to get rid of its croak.

"Yeah, a little."

They both looked at Sara's skin, wrinkled and gray from the soak.

"At least you weren't under it."

"The party wasn't that traumatic," she said, stirring finally. Sara gently pulled away from Raven and from the towel, reaching over the toilet to her small stack of clean towels to get another, a green one this time, and securing it like a sarong around her body.

Raven looked away from Sara to the discarded velvet dress on the floor, the balled up panties. "What did she do to you?"

"Nothing I didn't want."

"Is that really true?"

Was it true? Had she wanted Rille to feast on her like a snack, to peel away her wrapping, gorge herself, and leave Sara vulnerable and empty, on the balcony?

"I swear. Yes."

Raven sighed, but said nothing else. Sara looked away from the concern in her face. She was all right. And even if that wasn't completely true, she would be soon. Sara left the bathroom and Raven followed.

"Are you going to see her again?"

The question echoed in Sara's head as, "After tonight, do you think she's interested in you anymore?"

"Yeah, why not?" she murmured. "I think we had a connection. Something."

Raven opened her mouth, dark eyes flashing a familiar fire, but whatever she saw in Sara's face made her sigh instead. Then: "Okay."

HER WORLDLY GOODS

STEPHEN/ATLANTA

The light from the restaurant, amber and sharp, found the hints of red in Sara's hair, blended with the gold in Rille's eyes, and made them easily the most beautiful women in the room. Preening a little under the envious glances, Stephen pulled out a chair for Rille. But when he moved to help Sara with hers, Sara gently shook her head and pulled out her own chair. He smoothed down his tie and sat.

"You look very nice, darling." Rille said, her playful look sliding over the charcoal gray suit and green paisley tie she'd picked out for him weeks earlier. She had a good eye for tasteful things so he'd only nodded at the woman behind the counter at the Burberry in Lenox Mall, not looking at the price tag before she ran his credit card.

At their intimate table for three, Rille reached out, weaving her fingers through Sara's, a reward for the smile and relaxation of the stern look Sara often wore these days. Maybe something at work was bothering her, or at home. Whatever the problem, she wasn't talking. And although Rille had not mentioned it, Stephen knew she worried. She couldn't be that unconcerned, or blind.

The waitress, when she came to their table, was homely in the ubiquitous black slacks and gray Polo shirt the restaurant staff wore. But she had a lovely body that the three of them immediately sat up to appreciate. She smiled at Sara first.

"What can I get you to drink, miss?" the waitress asked.

With her hip a delicate incline in Sara's direction, her smile danced on the edges of flirtation. Rille immediately took notice, watching for

Sara's response with dissecting eyes. Stephen hid his smile. After all these years, she should know better than that. Sara had always been faithful, loyal to their relationship when it would've been in her best interest not to.

"Just water, please, but for my entrée I'll have the wild salmon with the roasted vegetables and potatoes." Sara didn't attempt the Italian pronunciation of the dishes on the menu.

"Salmoni selvaggi," the waitress said, her voice lightly teasing. "I'll put that in for you right away."

Rille's eyes went stormy with jealousy. She tapped an index finger against the table. When the waitress finally arrived at her side, she gave her order in clipped Italian, not once looking up.

"Thank you," Stephen said to make up for her rudeness, surprised that Rille would let her jealousy show.

As the waitress left to put in their orders, Sara turned to Rille with a slightly raised brow. "Are you feeling your oats tonight, Rille?" she asked. "I thought Stephen already soothed all your ruffled feathers."

"You know it takes more than that to calm me." Her hand squeezed Stephen's. "I have a lot on my mind."

"Including terrorizing sweet little waitresses?"

"So you think she's sweet."

"Of course. I know you think so too. If you'd been the one she wanted," Sara murmured.

So Sara *had* noticed the waitress flirting with her. Then again, the girl hadn't been very subtle. Rille smiled, pleased again to be the center of their attention.

Sara shook her head. "I think I will have a drink after all." She pushed back from the table. "Excuse me. I'll be right back."

Sara stood, graceful in the black pencil skirt and white blouse that flattered her hourglass shape. She moved easily through the crowded restaurant to the bar. Male and female alike watched her, helpless to her allure.

"She'll never leave you," Stephen said to Rille, and she startled.

"Of course not." But her eyes were uncertain. They flickered over the cutlery; her hand briefly flirted with the knife's edge even as she looked at Sara again.

At the bar, predators surrounded her. A man leaned close and she turned to him without leaning away, said something, and he withdrew.

She paid for her drink and, with the iced cranberry liquid held aloft, made her way back to the table. Knowing Stephen watched her, Rille's face was carefully blank as she in turn watched Sara.

In the last few days, there had been some tension in the house. It had started with Rille's moodiness and odd disappearances from home for hours at a time, then things went back to normal but not before Sara grew concerned, then fed up, freezing Rille out until she reacted out of desperation, coming as close to begging Sara for affection without actually begging. Stephen had merely weathered the emotional storm, waiting for both women to settle back into place. He had a feeling his wait was just about over.

Sara walked up to the table, set down her drink, and reached for her chair to settle back in its depths.

With the three of them once again seated in the configuration that worked best—Sara and Stephen glowing points in Rille's star—their dinner continued as before. Rille smiled and preened. Sara and Stephen appreciated. But when dinner arrived, they picked at their meals, in separate galaxies, isolated and adrift in their own thoughts.

The restaurant, Stephen noticed, was as much a place to be seen as it was to eat. The mirrored surfaces, ultra modern décor, and extensive drink and food menus were all designed to make the patrons glow a little brighter, their laughter sparkle just that much more. Rille had brought them there for herself.

"Is everything to your liking?" The waitress made another flirtatious appearance at Sara's elbow.

"The meal and service are both wonderful." Sara's playful look brought out the girl's laughter.

"Then I consider my job well done tonight."

To her credit, Rille didn't snap at the waitress and make herself look like a jealous bitch. That would be telling. Instead, she was all charm again.

"Thank you for taking particular care of us, my dear."

Her sugary tone caught the waitress off guard and the little thing looked Rille in the face for the first time. Stephen could almost see her getting ensnared by those sparkling eyes, the saturnine curve of mouth.

"Anytime," the waitress said.

Another Rille captive. When Stephen laughed, the women looked at him in surprise. But awareness slowly settled into Sara's features.

"Can you tell me where your restroom is?" she asked the girl, and the enterprising young thing pointed toward a dark hallway across the restaurant, then, after a telling pause, offered to walk her there.

"Thank you." Sara's manners were impeccable.

As they walked away, Rille's brow wrinkled with irritation.

Stephen leaned toward her. "It's not like they're going to fuck in the bathroom, you know."

She made a noise with her teeth and tongue. "That's what I would do in that little slut's position."

Stephen chuckled, knowing she wasn't joking. From the corner of his eye, he noticed the pushy guy from the bar head for that same darkened hallway that Sara disappeared into. The man smoothed down the front of his gray suit and adjusted his tie as he walked through the restaurant.

"Have you ever even been a waitress?" Stephen turned his attention back to Rille.

"One summer in Provincetown."

"And I'm sure you specialized in providing services that weren't on the menu."

A look of mock surprise took over her face. "How did you know?" Smiling, she plucked a silver pillbox from her purse, shook out Friday evening's dose of meds, and quickly downed the two pills with water.

"A wild guess." Stephen stood. "Be right back."

In the narrow hallway, there was no sign for the men's room, but the man stood there anyway with his broad football player's shoulders and back nearly blocking the passageway. He leaned against the wood-paneled wall talking with someone. As Stephen approached, the man straightened, showing a flash of black and white—Sara's eye-catching outfit. The football player shoved his hands in his pockets, still blocking her in as he talked, still hopeful. Stephen knew that calm look on her face, the one that said her patience was being tested. A movement from the man had her shaking her head and her face changed. Her look of scorn shoved him back one foot, then two. But in a moment, he recovered, asserting his masculinity with a hard grasp of Sara's arm. She winced and tried to pull away.

"That's not really necessary," Stephen said, walking up to them.

The man sized him up then, immediately dismissive, turned back to Sara. He didn't let go of her arm. "My friend and I are having a private conversation," he said without looking away from her. "Go find your own."

Stephen stepped closer.

"I don't need your help." Sara's eyes were venomous. The scornful look turned on Stephen and he understood the urge to violence that drove the bull-necked man, the need to assert that he was not that loathsome thing her look made him into.

"I'm not doing this for you. Rille wants you." Stephen spoke quietly, focusing on her and not the squirming humiliation in his belly at the other man's self-satisfied smirk.

With an abrupt jerk of her arm, Sara freed herself. Her pursuer's grin disappeared; instead, he looked a bit ashamed now with his inflated muscles and model's face dismissed by someone who couldn't care less about his reaction. Stephen knew how he felt. With a brief nod at the poor bastard, he turned and walked away.

The Smile

Sara/1994

The sun flooded through the large window, warming Sara's side as she sat in her bed studying. The rights of man, Hobbes, social Darwinism. The words ran through her head, skating through that place she knew would retain them and give them life when she took the test tomorrow. But even as she studied, a face surfaced, smiling and beautiful. She reached up and touched her ear and the face laughed soundlessly. Sara smiled.

"What are you grinning at?"

Raven walked out of the bathroom, drying her thick hair with a towel. Sara's eyes fluttered toward Raven then looked away.

"I think you forgot to dry yourself," she said.

"No big," Raven said with her gap-toothed smile. "You can look if you want to. I don't mind it."

Sara turned back to her, an uncertain smile on her lips. Raven had washed her hair and showered, but just as the hair she vigorously rubbed the towel through was wet, so was the body with its thin cotton dress. The colorful patterns on the pale cotton didn't hide the press of apple round breasts and hard nipples, softly rounded belly, the cradle of her hips and the dark smear of pubic hair. Raven looked like she'd walked out into the beginning of rain and come back wet.

"Now I'm smiling about something totally different," she said.

Raven snorted. "I know what that second thing is." She sat on her bed with her hair oil and conditioner, the towel draped across her lap.

"The first is nothing. Just homework. Can you imagine being a philosophy major? What would that really prepare you for except arguing?" She gestured to the book in her lap and shook her head.

"I can't talk," Raven said. "My major is women's studies and anthropology so I don't know what good that will do me either except get me ready for grad school."

"That could be interesting, though. Digging up lost things. Finding explanations for the things that we think we know now."

"That's a good way of putting it."

Sara glanced at her with a quick smile. "Life is all about perspective."

Raven nodded. She dried her hair again for a few minutes with the towel then rubbed the hair oil into her scalp and the strands of her short hair. With a slight twist of her body on the bed, she turned to face the mirror she had nailed on the wall, just over her bed against dorm regulations. Looking in the mirror, she started to braid her hair.

"That guy is hot," she said after only a few minutes of silence. "Who is he?"

What?" Sara looked where Raven pointed with her comb. "Oh, that's my brother."

"He's a cutie. If I didn't have a man already, I'd definitely be tempted to ask for his number."

"He would have been a good time," she said, smiling up from her book.

"I bet." Raven grinned with her arms lifted as she pulled her hair together into a long, two-inch wide braid running from the front of her head to the back.

Sara didn't have to look back at the picture to know what Raven had seen. Raven's reaction wasn't unusual. Other girls had sighed over her brother, taken with his flashing white smile, beautiful face, and effortless charm. In the picture, he was wearing one of his typical outfits, thrift store jeans, gray Jimi Hendrix T-shirt that showed off muscled arms. It had been gusty that day, and the wind blew fiercely against him, pressing the cotton against his skin and showing off his flat belly. His head was a tangled disorder of mushrooming hair, thick, wild, and blowing back in the breeze.

"Yeah. I'm sure he never had any complaints."

Although she liked her new roommate, Sara pointedly looked down at her philosophy notebook. She had a test tomorrow and didn't feel like talking about Syrus.

But that didn't prevent her mind from dwelling on him.

The day before Syrus left for the last time, he came by Sara's room.

"Sarita." His light voice woke her from a dream of sand and dolphins. "I'm going to Nicaragua in the morning."

She rubbed her eyes. "What time is it?"

"It doesn't matter."

But Sara could see the shades of gray beyond her curtain. It was already morning.

"I thought you were going to stay for a little bit and at least come with me down to school." It was still early in the summer break, and she would be moving into her new dorm in less than two months.

"I was going to," he shook his head. "But the guy who's supposed to rent the house to Keisha, Max, and me is leaving earlier than planned. He wants somebody to be there before he takes off."

In the dark, Syrus was like a ghost, an already disappearing specter of pale shirt and dark pants and slow smile. The necklace that Sara had given him for his twenty-first birthday shone a dull silver.

"Okay." She didn't try to hide her disappointment. "When are you coming back?"

"Christmas."

"Promise?"

"Promise."

She lay back in bed, content at least about that. Syrus had come back for her high school graduation, leaving behind some pretty girl in Granada he said, just to rush back and give her his congratulations and a bag full of presents.

"Okay," she said again. "Be careful. Call us."

Their parents were already up. She could hear them in the kitchen making early morning noises. Papa getting ready for a day at the seafood plant. Mama making breakfast and talking about their latest phone call from Jamaica. Comforting, familiar sounds. Sara pulled the sheets up to her chin.

"You be careful at school, Sarita. Watch out for those boys, and don't do anything I wouldn't do." His teeth flashed in the dark.

The door closed behind him and, after a time, she drifted back to sleep.

In her dorm room, Sara's eyelashes flickered over her book. Tears blinded her, but she blinked them away before any could fall.

GORGEOUS

STEPHEN/2004

The sidewalk outside the glass was awash in light and color. Chalk graffiti and well-intentioned obscenities passed under designer stilettos and worn Converse alike. Sunday afternoon. Everyone's playground—the rich, the homeless, the clueless. Beyond the wide windows of Different Spokes, the mostly transient world of the Little Five Points neighborhood wandered by. Stephen imagined the day smelled like freedom, while in the store, air-conditioning trapped the scent of rubber and bikes and the incense clinging to Manny from his mid afternoon smoke.

"Fuck!" Manny almost dropped the bike he was trying to hang on the display with the others. "The damn pedal almost took off my dick."

Stephen didn't have to look across the brightly lit store to know that Manny's round face was almost comical in its anger, brow furrowed, gelled black hair frozen in place, meaty hands clenched around the frame of the Iron Horse mountain bike he knew better than to drop.

"You should pay attention to what you're doing then," Stephen said, ringing up a customer.

But it was hypocritical of him. Wasn't he the one staring out the window between customers at the passing beauties, wishing he could be outside instead of caught in the prison he'd made for himself? Not that he didn't like the bike shop. He did. It was his business, after all, and a place where he'd rather work than at some corporate sweatshop pouring out his ideas to thieving peers and unappreciative bosses.

The people he met at Different Spokes were a mixed enough variety to keep him interested. Environmentally conscious vegans, poor students, professional cyclists, terminally hip progressives who just wanted a little bit more padding between their current mode of transport and their flat asses, even lesbian moms with the child seats attached like mini bunkers to the backs of their bikes. Was carrying a baby on a bike even safe in this town of kamikaze motorists and SUV-driving speed junkies?

"Thanks. Have a great day."

The slender teenager in front of Stephen's register barely paid him any attention. Instead, he nodded spastically along to whatever was playing on his iPod, mumbling what sounded like "same to you" after Stephen handed him his change. The boy walked out the door, his bag of bike pedals swinging at his side.

The next customer in a line three deep clutched her air pump in one hand and slid the money across the counter, eying Stephen with a familiar, covetous stare. He rang up her purchase, feeling like she was burning the image of him—Skunk Anansie T-shirt, baggy cargo shorts, and all—onto her retina. His body warmed with equal parts flattery and discomfort.

"Thank you," the frizzy-haired blonde sighed with her change in hand and moved down the counter so the next person in line could get a turn.

Two pairs of bike shorts and a helmet later, she was still there. Stephen closed the register with a quick movement of his hand. "Can I help you with anything else?"

"No, um...well, yes." She fiddled with the handle of the pump poking out from her hemp woven shopping bag. "Can you recommend a good coffee shop around here?"

He knew what she wanted. Even Manny looked over from arranging the bike finally on its display, snickering.

"Yeah. There's one right across the street. On the corner next to the pizza place. The ladies in there make a great mango smoothie too."

She smiled at him, eyes blinking. "Do you want to check it out with me sometime? I'm kinda new in town."

She'd been "new in town" and stalking his shop now for at least eight months. When the girl came in, Stephen usually went out of his way to make her feel welcome, no matter what she bought or how long she stayed. But this was getting a little sad.

"Sorry, Shelly." He knew her name from the credit card she'd given in payment minutes before. "But, no. I'm working here all day. Thanks for the offer. That's nice of you to ask."

From the corner of his eye, a flash of white and gold caught his attention. Stephen looked briefly out the window. Her. He looked back at his customer, at her nervous and blinking softness.

She smiled again, a blush climbing in her freckled cheeks. "Maybe another time." And she left the store with the light tinkle of the bell over the door.

"Steve, don't blame her for stalking when you're the one who comes into work looking so pretty," Manny called out, paying no attention to the half dozen customers still browsing around the shop. "But she'll see in about five minutes just how many other skinny guys with big nappy hair and bright teeth live in Atlanta. After that, you won't even see her in here again." Manny laughed. "Do you think she even owns a bike?"

Stephen didn't respond. Instead, he watched the floating vision beyond the glass in white slacks and a coffee-colored blouse that matched her skin. She'd been coming to their neighborhood for months now, each week with a different person by her side. Today it was a boy, pretty and obviously too young to know better than to put himself in the path of a woman like this. The boy wore a worshipful look, his hands gesturing nervously as he spoke. The woman was attentive, not taking her eyes from him even when the wind whipped her wild curls forward, obscuring her vision.

"She's just a little lonely," Stephen said absently in response to Manny's rude shout. "Nothing wrong with trying to make friends."

The woman walked past the window, her smile a fierce flash of teeth as she gazed at the boy by her side. Stephen watched them until they disappeared over the rise and past the traffic light leading to the other side of the neighborhood.

"If you had to hang up a bike right now," Manny said easily from Stephen's side, looking out to see what he was staring at, "your dick *and* nuts would be gone."

Stephen ignored him and turned back to the register.

Their day passed by in a pleasant blur of customers, idle conversation, and a hefty deposit at the end of the evening. Manny walked with Stephen to the bank's night drop then they said their good-byes among the shifting threads of early evening partiers. It was barely nine thirty. Time for the last of the shop owners to go home. Now, the music in the streets pulsed louder and The Patio, the busiest pub on the strip, rumbled with its cornucopia of customers. Cars drove by slowly, their passengers taking in the short skirts and low-cut blouses giving well-toned bodies some air.

"Hey, Stephen," someone called out.

He waved back to the dark haired boy slouched in the doorway of the punk bar with a cigarette dangling from his lips.

"What's up, D?"

Normally, Stephen would have taken that as an invitation to linger in the neighborhood over a beer and conversation. But he'd been working all day and just wanted to chill. He waved at him and continued on his way.

"Hey, hot stuff."

The high voice and cigarette breath hit him at the same time. A shoulder bumped him as he turned his head and looked down.

"I'm doing a set tonight at the Ten," Poppy said. "You should come see me."

He shook his head, but her long arms held him captive and her breasts pressed against his side, then his chest.

Poppy was tiny and beautiful with her rich earth skin and hair done in tiny braids that brushed her shoulders and back. And if it hadn't been for the mistake he'd made by sleeping with her near the end of a particularly lonely day, Stephen would have still thought she was a nice girl. Her cigarette smell blended with the herb scent wrapped up in her braids, a scent that reminded him of their night together and why he wanted to avoid a repeat performance. Bondage games were usually fine with him, but when his bound partner also asked to be rammed with his fist, pissed on, then called his bitch, Stephen wanted to back out of the deal. Her needs repulsed him. They were too much like his.

"I'm heading home," he said, shaking his head again.

But her long arms were also strong, and he soon found himself at the bar of the Ten-Spot ordering a veggie burger and water. Poppy asked for a vodka cranberry and told the bartender to put it on Stephen's tab. As usual, he didn't say no.

The smell of incense, cigarettes, and spilled liquor that had sunk over time into the bar's wooden floors, powerfully reminded Stephen why he didn't come to the Ten anymore. Lately, either his house or a bar with an outdoor patio and uncomplicated scents suited him better. A tickle in the back of his throat reminded him of his doctor's warning about developing an allergy to cigarette smoke.

"So what's going on with you?" she asked, leaning in, her pixie's face even more arresting under the cool blue lights. On the stage behind them, a band played washed-out Bob Marley accompanied by a mystifying steel drum.

"Not much. The usual." He shrugged.

Stephen didn't tell her that since the last time they talked his parents had died and he got a settlement—blood money—from their car accident. Now he owned his condo outright and had no problems making the rent for Different Spokes even when things were slow. "Business is good. I think half of Atlanta is taking up riding as a hobby."

"Hm. Yeah, I took up riding too when I walked past that big glass window and saw you in there. I'd ride every day if you let me."

Unease surged in his belly, but he didn't look away. She chuckled and sucked on the straw, inhaling most of the drink at one go. Poppy sat on the bar stool with her legs sprawled, the white skirt pulled up to show her long brown thighs. Before they'd ended up together in her bed sweating against each other under its winged canopy, he wondered how come a little thing like her had such a long body. He wondered what it would feel like to climb up its soft length and sink between her thighs. Now he knew. Stephen bit into his burger and began to chew.

"So you don't have a new girl or anything?"

As far as she knew, there had been no *old* girl. "No. No new girl."

Her smile grew wider and she sank even more into her sprawl. Her cheeks hollowed as she sucked the last drop from the clear glass. "Buy me another?"

"No. That's it for this free ride," he said, only half meaning it.

She shook her head and waved at the bartender for a refill.

"I'm not doing anything after my set," she said. "You feel like company tonight?"

Cigarettes and cranberry flavored vodka blew at his lips as her thighs clasped one of his.

"No. I'm good. Work tomorrow and all."

"Oh, please. Your damn shop doesn't even open until eleven." The fact that she knew that should have worried him.

Stephen shook his head. "Maybe some other time."

Behind him, the reggae band was winding down. The last notes of "Buffalo Soldier" tapered off in a flurry of steel drum notes.

"I'm on stage next," Poppy said. "Stay so we can talk after."

As soon as she disappeared through the narrow door leading backstage, Stephen dropped cash on the bar for the food and drinks then left. The three zigzag blocks between him and home passed quickly. With night pressing coolly at his back, he slid his key into the main door of his building and slipped inside. He didn't quite breathe a sigh of relief as he stepped into the vestibule that was neither warm nor cold, but it was a close thing. The dark hardwoods slid under his sneakered feet.

Some days, he had really bad judgment. Tonight, he was actually making sense. He needed to sleep with Poppy like he needed a jellyfish to give him a blowjob. Stephen wrestled his mail from its tiny cage before jogging up the four flights of stairs to his top floor condo. Without turning on a light, he dropped his messenger bag and keys on the bookshelf by the door.

"I thought you'd be home earlier."

He didn't flinch at the voice that came at him from the dark. "I didn't know I had a curfew." Stephen pulled off his jacket, his shoulders loosening in automatic relaxation. *No more pretense.*

"You don't, but I thought…" A sigh. "I don't even know what I thought."

"Let's not go through anything now, okay?" Stephen murmured, pitching his voice low to match Lucas's.

"Okay."

Lucas's reluctant agreement pulled Stephen deeper into the room. Closer, Lucas smelled like soap and toothpaste, like he'd had a recent shower after work, then come right over. His clean scent was the ideal antidote to the stale, smoky heat of the bar and Stephen found himself relaxing even more. After their breakup, Stephen had made it clear that he didn't want Lucas to come over unannounced anymore. Didn't even want him to shower here. But some habits were apparently hard to break. Now it was Stephen's turn to sigh.

His parents' money had paid for this condo when he graduated from Georgia Tech four years ago. He'd been paying them back in small installments from the money earned at the shop. Now he didn't have to repay them. Now, he would be alone. In the dark, he felt Lucas watching him.

"I came by to see how you were doing."

Although he couldn't see him, Stephen imagined Lucas's bulk in the darkness, thighs sprawled wide in the sofa, taking up the space like he owned it while his deceptively drowsy eyes missed nothing.

"I'm good."

"No, you're not." Lucas paused. "Did you see your therapist today?"

"Didn't have time."

"Right." Lucas sniffed the air as Stephen came closer. "You went to a bar? The Ten?"

Stephen nodded although Lucas couldn't see.

"Ran into one of your fuck friends, huh?"

Stephen sat on the burgundy sofa. Its suede fabric rubbed against the backs of his legs, touched him gently through his shirt and shorts. "Yeah."

"Poor Stephen." There was no mockery in Lucas's voice.

He reached out, because Stephen wouldn't, lightly touching a tense shoulder. Stephen shifted, dropped his head in Lucas's lap and closed his eyes.

The warmth of Lucas under him was like a balm, radiating into his head, wrapping him in the familiar space of being desired but with an absence of pressure, no necessity, on his part, to act.

"You didn't have to come over here. I don't need saving."

"But you need something."

He couldn't argue with that. The thing was he didn't know what he needed. A friend? A lover? Space to feel again where the guilt wouldn't crush him like deep water?

"I'm not ready to be with you again."

"I know that."

Still, Lucas hoped. They both knew that. It wasn't as if their breakup had been bad. Though the question still lingered about whether they'd had a proper breakup.

"I can't do this anymore," Stephen said eight weeks ago.

"Okay."

That had been the conversation. Lucas had walked out and found himself an apartment that same day. He called Stephen with his new address and phone number and that was that.

Lucas's inability to give Stephen what he wanted—emotional strength, the freedom to be weak, and the delicate balance between the two—had led to their breakdown. The theory of their breakup. There had been no fights, no calls to the police station. No fag drama. Just a quiet "okay" and a withdrawal. Sometimes Stephen longed for confrontation. For a fight where there was a clear winner and loser. A fight that left bruises and a fleshly ache. Lucas couldn't give him that.

"We all need something, Lucas. Just because I don't know what makes my teeth ache doesn't make me more of an emotional cripple than the next guy."

Lucas chuckled. "If you say so."

But the pain was naked behind the wry laugh. And Stephen just didn't want to take responsibility for it anymore.

"You should go." He sat up.

Lucas shifted on the sofa, waiting. But Stephen didn't want to wait with him. He pushed himself off the sofa and stood. "Let yourself out."

Stephen pulled off his shirt as he walked out of the living room and toward his bedroom. Behind him, Lucas released a small breath. Stephen turned. Faint light, he knew, illuminated his bare chest, rode over the firm hillocks of muscle that made up his pecs, the hairless expanse of belly, solid abs, and the smooth skin that disappeared into the loosely hanging shorts. "I'll call you tomorrow."

He dropped his hand to loosen the top button of his shorts then turned away, releasing the zipper as he went. It was time for him to take a shower. Poppy's smell on his skin was beginning to make him queasy.

In the shower, his mind turned to nothing. The water rushed over his skin, hot and near scalding, making him feel something besides the pain of nothing while everything familiar to him disappeared. Lucas was…the past. He didn't want to go back to him just because he was lost and fumbling in his own indecision, in his own emptiness. Lucas would always be there for him, would always come back to him if Stephen beckoned. He didn't want that. Sometimes he didn't know what to ask for. Stephen closed his eyes and let the nothingness claim him again.

❖

"We need some change," Manny said as soon as Stephen walked into the store.

At almost three in the afternoon on a Saturday, the store was nicely packed with customers who looked like they were buying not just browsing. But Manny apparently had no change to give them. Stephen frowned. He could have sworn that he'd got enough from the bank yesterday evening before he left. If he wasn't losing his mind, business had been really good this morning.

"I'll get some," he said.

Stephen dropped his bag behind the register and grabbed the two hundred-dollar bills from Manny's outstretched hand.

"Back in a sec."

He jogged to the bank, dodging skateboarders and girls in high heels to make it to the credit union before it closed at three.

"You almost missed us," the Mohawked man behind the counter said as Stephen slid inside the door.

There were five other people in the bank. Three at the counter being tended to while the others sat on the hard benches scattered throughout the small room and waited their turn.

Stephen grinned. "Almost."

Walking into the credit union was like stepping back in time. Except for the computers sitting in front of each teller, and the teletype-looking sign that asked customers to turn off their cell phones while in the bank, they could have been out in the Wild West somewhere (or at least Stephen's version of it). Low wooden chairs sat in front of each teller's station, inviting the customers to take a load off while the friendly face on the other side of the counter—no glass partition—counted out their money and handed them carbon receipts of each transaction. Brian's shock value hair was the only disconnect in this holdout from the past.

Brian shook his head and the ferociously gelled hair, colored blue this week, waved like a stiff fan in the air. As long as Stephen had owned his store and been coming to Little Five Points, Brian had worked at the credit union. He hadn't always been the bank manager; instead, he worked his way up through the ranks with the same single-mindedness with which he pursued women. They hadn't hung out in a while. But that was purely Stephen's fault. He knew that Brian was always up for a beer and a dance, even a half hearted make-out session behind the bar when they both felt like something harder than their usual.

When it was his turn, Stephen sat on the chair and slid over the bills.

"Long time," Brian said.

"You're right about that." No apologies. Neither of them wanted that. "We should get together sometime."

"Yeah." Brian counted out the small bills and handed them over. "I'll call you. Or you call me."

"Later." Stephen pocketed the money and, with a tip of his imaginary hat, ambled out of the credit union.

He slipped on his sunglasses against the sun's glare and left the safety of the bank's doorway for the crowded sidewalk. Immediately, he was swallowed by the swimming crowd, ladies in designer thrift as well as Buckhead-bought couture, smelling like sunshine and perfume. Some days, walking in the neighborhood was like torture. So many beautiful sights and smells, so much to take in, only to slip inside the door of his shop and stay cooped up for way too long.

Cars streamed past him on the busiest part of Moreland Avenue and he walked down to the stoplight to wait for his chance to cross. A cream-colored Cadillac truck with its windows down shook to the beat of an old Outkast song. The driver and its passengers—one in the front and three in the back—watched the crowd with lazy interest as the red light brought the cars to a halt. One of the guys in the back, a bright skinned pretty with a bald head, acknowledged Stephen with an upward nod, and Stephen smiled—a quirk of lips—as the man's eyes subtly checked out his body under loose fitting jeans and T-shirt. It felt good to be wanted by a stranger.

He crossed the road without incident and was about to open the door to his shop when he caught a familiar flash of light hair. If he were being honest with himself, Stephen would admit that he had been looking for her. Since his last sighting nearly three weeks ago, he'd searched the features of every blond, cocoa-skinned woman he saw. But none of them had been her.

His hand fell back to his side as he watched the woman amble up the sidewalk, alone this time, wearing a long white skirt that flew around her legs in the wind and a tank top skimming her slim torso like a lover's caress. Corkscrew curls of various shades of blond bounced around her shoulders. Unlike nearly everyone else on the street, she wasn't wearing shades, so for the first time he saw that her eyes were a vicious shade of green, pale and sharp, against her skin.

"Hey," he said when she was close enough to touch.

She kept walking. Her ass was slight, but it moved with a hypnotic rhythm against the material of the see-through skirt. Mesmerized by the shifting presence of her in air so close to him, Stephen nearly let her go.

"Excuse me," he said, jogging up after her.

She looked up but kept walking, eyes floating over his body before coming to rest on his face. "Yes?"

A girl bumped his shoulder as she went past with her group of friends. They eyed him with irritation. But he paid them little mind, keeping his focus on what he suddenly wanted.

"I've seen you around here before."

As soon as he said it, Stephen realized what a weak pick-up that was. He could have cartoonishly slapped his own forehead over the stupidity. Women like this didn't respond to asinine remarks like that. Still walking, she shook her head to prove him right. But she smiled.

"I'm in the neighborhood quite a bit."

He tried again. "You're very beautiful. I think you deserve a man to tend to your needs instead of those boys I usually see you with."

She stopped walking, turned, and adjusted her bag across her chest. Her mouth twitched. The wind whipped up, blowing her hair into her face and toward Stephen.

"I guess you *have* seen me around."

She opened her mouth to say something else, but he shook his head, laughing ruefully. "I'm not a stalker, no matter how that just sounded. I'd like to get to know you better. Can I?"

"I have a girlfriend," she said in a low voice that reminded him of something deep, dark, and moist. She was so earthy that he could almost taste her on his lips.

"That's okay. I have a boyfriend," Stephen said.

And she stopped. Fingers caught at the strands of hair flailing before her eyes. "Really?"

"Well, sort of. Lucas and I aren't really together anymore. We just hang out when neither one of us is doing anything special."

The intrigued curve of her mouth and the hand she lifted to hold her hair out of her eyes kept his attention focused on her face. "That sounds potentially complicated," she said. "But I'll call you."

The dark blond hair flew into her face as she released it. Her eyes glimmered through the strands, pale and piercing and she turned to go. Straight back. Ass shimmying. Ankles flashing dark and slender beneath the hem of her long skirt.

Only after the woman disappeared up the street and out of his field of vision did he realize she didn't have his phone number. And he didn't even know her name.

❖

When Stephen walked back into Different Spokes, Manny gave him a dirty look. "If this was my store, I'd fire you."

"Thank God for small mercies." Stephen handed over the change, grabbed his bag from behind the counter, and disappeared into the office at the back of the store.

Barely an hour later, Manny poked his dark head into the office. "I'm heading out."

"All right. Gimme a sec."

Stephen finalized an order for parts, printed the invoice, and dropped it in the "orders to be received" box before standing up. He was a little behind with the orders, but it was nothing that couldn't be fixed by staying late one night. Or maybe coming in early. Stephen was finding it harder and harder to get a good night's rest. On nights when he crawled into bed at three, he felt lucky to get even five hours sleep. By seven or eight o'clock, he already lay awake, restless and ready to do anything but stare at the ceiling and think about his life.

"I'm ready to take over," he said to Manny as he walked to the front of the store shutting the office door behind him.

The unexpected afternoon rush had eased. Now only one person remained in the shop with them. The girl, who looked a lot like his mother when she was younger with her plump, bitter chocolate skin and pressed hair, rummaged almost meditatively through the stack of clearance bike shorts.

"Cool. I'll grab my stuff and you can have all this to yourself."

Stephen's mouth twisted. "Thanks."

Moments later, Manny emerged from the back office with his backpack slung over his shoulder. "See you in the morning," he said. "Oh, and don't forget that I can't come in until one so you have to open for me."

"No problem. I'll be here."

Manny opened the door and caught himself, almost stumbling into a customer walking in. He mumbled his apologies and kept going. "See ya, Steve."

"All right."

The girl from the sale bin stepped up to the register, and up close he realized she didn't look that much like his mother after all. He tossed a smile toward the customer Manny had almost mowed down in his haste to leave.

"Welcome to Different Spokes," he said, seeing only the vague outline of a female form. "Let me know if I can help you with anything."

"Actually, you *can* help me find something."

On the first word, he knew who it was. Stephen almost dropped the girl's change for the twenty-dollar shorts, but she caught the shower of coins before they fell to the floor.

"Sorry about that," Stephen said. But his mind was already elsewhere.

After his customer left, the woman wandered over.

She had changed clothes, changed her hair. The blond curls were pulled back from her face in what might have been meant as a school teacher's bun, but the loose tendrils around her temples and neck softened her, made her seem ripe for bed. Her eyes were coolly appraising. In jeans and a dark blouse that rippled over her bra-less breasts and her belly, she appeared more accessible.

"Is that your boyfriend who just left?" She gestured vaguely toward the door.

Seriously? He laughed before he caught himself. "That's just Manny. He works here."

"Just because he works here doesn't mean you're not fucking."

The profanity from her was almost exotic. Wicked and matter-of-fact at the same time. It made Stephen think about fucking.

"Good point," he said "But no, he's not mine."

A smile softened the starkness of her face. "I'm Rille. And I'm guessing you're Steve."

"Stephen."

"Better." She dropped a piece of paper on the counter. A phone number and her name inked on its surface. "What time do you get off?"

"Late. At nine."

"That's not too bad. Meet me at The Patio for a late dinner."

"All right," he said, although it hadn't been a request.

"Let me know if you're going to be later than nine thirty." She assessed him again, more thoroughly this time. "See you then."

Rille smiled once more and turned away. Stephen watched her walk out the door, his mind already replaying their conversation. No wonder those boys trailed after her like flame-struck moths. Despite her cool eyes, she was incendiary.

TEMPTATION

SARA/2004

"Why can't men be more like lesbians?"

Kendra looked at Sara as if she held the answer to that question and more. Sara shook her head, smiling gently.

"You're asking the wrong one. Maybe your god would know the answer to that, darling, not me."

Sara leaned back in her chair, letting the gentle spring breeze ruffle the skirt around her calves. The honeyed scent of blossoms from the trees surrounding the coffee shop's terrace blended with the creamed coffee smell of their drinks. Kendra sighed and propped her chin in her palm. Her straightened hair swung heavily forward, curving around one rounded cheek.

Sara's affair with Kendra had been a brief indulgence from the previous year, a blatant rebound after she'd walked in on Rille with a student from the university. The second forgiveness, but not the second infidelity, not by any means. Sara glanced down at the clear glass cup of mochaccino steaming near her hand.

"Vic is acting like a total shit," Kendra said. "I tell him about one damn girl on girl relationship and he gets hysterical, getting jealous of every girlfriend I see. Boys don't even worry him anymore. And in bed, it's worse. Fucking insecure but acting as if it's my fault. It's too bad; he used to be a great lay."

"Before you told him about us?"

"Right." She smiled over at Sara. "You look good though."

Sara laughed. "I know. Martyrdom must really suit me."

"What?"

"Nothing."

She hadn't come here to cry on Kendra's shoulder about the madness with Rille. It wasn't a coincidence that she'd finally agreed to meet up with her after weeks of avoiding Kendra's company. Sara needed the distraction.

Last night, Rille had come to bed with kisses and revelations. After the tremors of satisfaction eased, leaving Sara's body liquid and soft, Rille leaned over her with a different kind of attentiveness. There was a boy she'd recently met. She wanted Sara to meet him. He was beautiful. Special. Sara jumped out of the bed in shock, the air cool on her naked skin, denial of Rille's desire for someone else rising up in her throat like bile.

"No, baby. No. Don't be like that. This is not like last time," Rille said.

No. This wasn't like the last time. Then she hadn't told Sara about wanting someone else. When Sara found them together in Rille's office, the girl's face awash in worship as she knelt before a cool-faced Rille whose legs were spread as wide as the chair would allow. That was different. This was honesty.

Sara grasped her cup and sipped the hot drink, absently licking her lips to rid them of the foam she knew had gathered there. Across from her, Kendra followed the motion with a hungry look then blushed when she noticed Sara's eyes on her.

There were good reasons Sara had chosen her after the short-lived breakup with Rille last year: Kendra's commonplace good looks that were nearly opposite to Rille's peacock-on-a-chicken-farm flamboyance. And her ability to be completely and absolutely immersed in whatever thing she was doing at the time.

Sara lightly tapped the tabletop with a long finger. "Honesty is overrated anyway. Maybe you shouldn't have told him. I've heard that men can only handle bisexual girlfriends in theory."

"You should have told me that before." Her red mouth glistened in the sun as she pouted. "I figure since he asked me to marry him that he deserved to know."

"I don't know why you think that. Have you ever thought that he hasn't told you about everyone that he slept with?"

Kendra sighed again, this time wrinkling her nose. "I don't want to talk about this anymore." The hot coffee she'd ordered sat on the table untouched. She leaned back in her chair, flickering her eyelashes up to look at Sara. "Distract me."

It would be easy. She could just reach across the table and touch her hand, slide her fingers between Kendra's and suggest a quieter place, something wetter, saltier on her palate. But she didn't. She never did. Still, her thoughts continued on the same route. Teasing. Familiar.

Life was simpler with Kendra: days of laughter and food and sex, the nights with more of the same. But even with the sweat drying on her skin and Kendra tugging on her body for another round, her mind was with Rille, steeped in its misery, remembering her smell and their own after-sex rituals. No, she hadn't been happy with Kendra; she had been waiting. Sara released thoughts of Kendra's hand and smiled.

"Come on. Let's go to the park. We can sit in the swings and eat ice cream."

Sara thought she saw a droop of disappointment to Kendra's mouth, but was too busy gathering up her things to pay attention.

Expectations

Stephen/2004

Stephen had to ask a group of students which classroom was hers. Once they told him where to go, he found it with no problem, jogging up the stairs and to the first room on the right. Stephen stuck his head through the open door.

She sat at her desk in front of the class, carefully putting papers and books in a slim briefcase. Equations in a crooked but clear handwriting marched across the board behind her in pink chalk. The room smelled of chalk dust and chewing gum.

A week ago, he'd asked about her schedule, deciding to one day soon go up to the university and see her during one of his lunch breaks. Manny could handle the store by himself for an afternoon while he went courting this mysterious woman who insisted on slipping into his dreams with frightening ease and frequency. He wouldn't be surprised if she'd planned it that way. Everything about her seemed intentional. Purposeful. Intense.

Stephen stepped inside the room.

"I'm glad you're still here," he said, tucking his hands in his pocket as he walked toward her desk.

"For a good reason, I assume." She leaned back in her chair, looking up at him with her face ambivalently blank.

Behind the desk, she was all professor. Hair pulled tightly away from her face in some sort of bun that showed off her jaw and strong throat. Wire-rimmed glasses amplified the piercing quality of her stare.

"Lunch?"

She smiled, finally. "Definitely a good reason." Rille stood and picked up her briefcase, smoothing the dark blue suit jacket over her hip. "Let me grab some things from my office and we can go. Where are you taking me?"

When they walked through the doorway with the orange lettering and owl eyes, Rille looked briefly at him and laughed. "Really?"

"The wings here are really good," he said.

A waitress immediately came up to them, her beautiful smile and C-cups on display in the trademark tank top. "Two for lunch this afternoon?"

"Yes," Rille said. "A table with a view of the street, please."

The girl left them with menus and the promise that someone would be right back to get their drink orders.

Rille had left her briefcase in his car, but she still carried herself like she was in the classroom. The pale blue ruffled blouse she wore spilled lace under her throat before tucking into a darker blue skirt just a breath from being tight. Once at the table, she shrugged off the jacket that had seemed more appropriate for the chilly building they'd just left, not the pungent heat of an early May afternoon. Her arms were bare.

A half smile played at her mouth as she looked at the menu. "The wings, huh?"

"Yep," Stephen smiled. "The parmesan garlic is worth the price."

When the waitress came back, Stephen ordered the parmesan garlic chicken wings. Rille got the steamed clams with extra butter. Sipping her water, she watched the waitress walk away.

She jerked her chin at the girl's barely covered backside in the orange shorts. "Are these the kind of girls you like? Because if that's the case, I don't know what you're doing with me."

Stephen shook his head. "Not really. I thought *you* might be into this."

Rille coughed on her water, laughing again. "This is definitely not my scene. I prefer subtlety in my women. Or something more in-your-face."

He couldn't imagine anything more "in-your-face" than these Hooters girls with their tits and ass on display with more promised to the highest tipper.

Rille sipped her water again. She made a show of looking around the restaurant, deliberately staring at the girls in their tiny shorts, the customers—mostly men in suits or khakis—chatting them up with hungry eyes, devouring their tight young bodies as eagerly as they did the fries and chicken wings on their plates.

"Oh, what you must think of me," she said. Her eyes glittered behind the glasses.

Stephen didn't answer. He played with his glass of iced tea, turning it in slow, wet circles on the coaster. Although he wanted to know her, to understand how she lived, to *see* how she lived, Rille wouldn't let him. Over the past few weeks, she only let him get so far with her before pulling back.

The things he wanted to know were simple: Was Rille the name she was born with? How did she like her eggs? Did she want him as much as he wanted her? But she denied him the truth of all that.

It had barely been two weeks since he talked to her for the first time, running after her like a lust-struck teenager in the middle of Little Five Points. This was their third date.

The first two times, they'd met up and talked about nothings. Nothings that circled nothings but took up so much time that before he'd even formed a real question to get to the truth of her, it was time for them to part ways. Each time, he was tempted to say "fuck it" to his responsibilities elsewhere just so he could lie under her steady gaze. But she had her own responsibilities, too. Including a girlfriend she'd told him almost nothing about.

He was in the strange position of wanting everything from her. Usually, it was the other way around. Lovers wanted. He withheld. His mind flinched from the threat of Lucas. New guilt made him back away from the thought of his ex.

"I think about you a lot," he finally said.

"Do you?" She squeezed a lemon wedge into her water and stirred it with a lazy finger. The ice cubes tinkled against the glass.

"Yes. I want to know you. Will you let me?"

Rille took off her glasses and put them carefully on the table. "Do you know what you're asking for?"

"Yes."

Stephen didn't bother to be embarrassed at his vehement tone. He'd long ago grown past the stage of being embarrassed by his own emotions. If he wanted something and another person was able to give it to him, he asked. At times, he thought all his emotions had died with his parents, so when a feeling came to him with such strength and certainty as his desire for her, he grasped at it with everything he had. In this moment, she was what he wanted.

"Yes," he said. "I'm asking for you."

"In that case, be very careful," Rille said. "And be very sure."

The waitress came with their food and saved him from himself. While they ate, the nothings circled between them again—in what part of town did he live? Where did she go to school? When did she have her first girlfriend?—until lunch was over. Water glasses drained, bill paid, they stood and headed out to his car.

Rille walked beside Stephen with her jacket draped over one arm, her pace slow and thoughtful as she glanced between his face and the shops they passed in the Underground shopping district. He felt her eyes like a physical touch. It was early afternoon with the last of the lunch crowd passing through the once busy shopping and entertainment area to go up the escalators and back to their offices in the buildings looming overhead.

Hip-hop blared from the speakers of stores selling "urban" clothes. Young boys walked by with their pants sagging around their butts, their knowing swagger and the flash of eyes under the brim of their ball caps at once a come-on and a dare.

"I like you," Rille said.

They approached a kiosk selling key chains and belts, some of them personalized, some advertising the city of Atlanta, all of them small and tacky and aimed at luring tourists. Rille stepped closer to peer at a row of belts with different names spelled out on the buckles.

"I wonder if they have my name on any of these," she said with her familiar half-smile.

Stephen peered over her shoulder at the display. A silhouette of the city of Atlanta made out of neon-colored rubber had his name spelled out underneath it. A fridge magnet. "Rille is not an everyday American name," he said. "I doubt they do."

In a fit of curiosity about her, he had looked up her name and found out that it meant "groove" in German and was used mostly to describe long, narrow channels on the surface of distant planets and moons. Rille was a groove. She had marked him.

"Maybe they'll have Merille. I think that's more common."

He felt surprise and pleasure at this unexpected revelation. So Merille was her real name. Something new to add to the small packet of information he knew about her.

"They can make anything you want," he said.

"Yes, miss." The vender, a thin, brown-skinned girl with thick thighs and a respectable ass, came around the other side of the kiosk to smile at them. A gold tooth winked from between her dark red lips. "We can put any name on any item we carry."

"I was just looking," Rille said.

Strangely enough, she did seem interested in the tourist trinkets. Her fascination certainly wasn't for the girl. She barely glanced her way at all.

Rille smiled unexpectedly. "I know these things are stupid, but I love them." She picked up a key chain with "Michelle" stitched into the leather. "When I was younger, I used to pretend my name was Michelle. It was such a simple name. You could find it on a mug or T-shirt anywhere, especially at Disney World. I wanted that." With a twist of her mouth, she dropped the brown leather in a pile of other Michelles. "Now I can't even imagine being that ordinary. I'd rather be Merille than anyone else."

"But you still want a key chain with your name on it."

She laughed and turned away from the kiosk. "Yeah, but I'll get over it." Rille smiled her thanks at the young girl and walked toward the escalator, clearly expecting Stephen to follow. He did.

Walking a few steps behind her, he allowed himself the pleasure of her small ass and thighs pulling tight under the dark blue skirt. She looked back at him, caught him staring, and stopped a few feet from the escalator.

"Enjoying the view?"

"You know I am."

On the escalator slowly moving up toward the crisp blue sky and balmy Tuesday afternoon, they stood hip to hip. Stephen inhaled the light scent of her perfume mixed with sweat and the faintest traces of melted butter from her lunch. At the top, he moved in the direction of the parking garage where they'd left his car, but she touched his arm.

"Walk with me."

Stephen looked at his watch. The hour and a half lunch break he asked Manny to cover was almost over. He only had enough time to drop Rille off at the university before making his way back to the shop.

"Okay," he said.

He grabbed his cell phone from his back pocket and called Manny to let him know he'd be at least an hour later than planned.

"What a surprise," Manny grumbled before agreeing to stay later.

"I'll be there as soon as I can," Stephen told him.

Manny only grunted. "See you when I see you."

Rille looked at him from beneath her lashes. "That guy doesn't have any respect for you, does he?"

"He's a friend," Stephen said. "Our respect is mutual. He just tells it like it is. I like that."

Rille shrugged. "Potato-Potatoe," she said.

"Superficial signs of respect aren't things I worry about." He shrugged.

"Really?" She glanced at him sideways, lashes nearly shielding her eyes. "Then what do you worry about? What makes you lay awake in bed at night?"

He chuckled. "I don't have any trouble falling asleep. My life is not one of *those*. I'm not crippled by modern angst about the state of my life and its mysterious direction. Life is good. I have everything I need."

After his parents, after Lucas, it felt good to say these things and mean it.

"You don't need a boyfriend, yet you have one. You want me, but that's not something you have. That's something you may not get. What about those dissatisfactions?"

"I'm not dissatisfied. Everything I have, I want." He glanced at her. "If you want to ask me about my boyfriend or any potential or actual lovers lurking around my life, all you have to do is ask. There's no need to go through China just to get to Decatur."

Rille smiled. "You'll learn that when I want to know something, I ask it. I'm no shrinking violet."

Stephen nodded. At least he knew that already. And with each step they took together through downtown Atlanta, he felt closer to some further knowledge of her. Rille didn't do phone calls so there were no giddy hours spent on the phone dissecting their lives for each other's pleasure. She had a woman at home. If she didn't, Stephen would be more than willing to regress to high school again. To linger on the phone until early in the morning when he should have been sleeping. To undress his life for her. To press into the bed with the phone tucked against his ear, pretending that she lay beneath him. All those things he would do if she let him. But it was not only the two of them in this.

"What does your woman think of you seeing me?" he asked.

"She doesn't like it, but she won't stop me."

Stephen looked around. "Good. Then I won't expect Joey Greco to jump out of a white van any second now with a full camera crew. I'm too old for that shit."

Rille laughed. And Stephen grinned back at her, pleased that the *Cheaters* reference wasn't lost on her. Another thing he was wrong about. He was sure she wasn't the kind to watch that ridiculous but voyeuristically entertaining show.

"What?" she asked, an eyebrow raised.

"You know what."

"Ah. More assumptions about who I am." She leaned closer. "I'll have to let you know me better now, if only to shatter some of those illusions."

"That's a good enough reason to me." Stephen grinned.

They ambled down the sidewalk through the busy downtown, past the train station, the stores selling incense, hats, and fake designer handbags. All the while, her slow footsteps kept up with his longer tread. A cloud passed overhead, hiding the sun and taking away some of the afternoon's warmth. Rille put her jacket back on.

"I love this city." She slipped her arm around his. "It took leaving here to go to college in Florida for me to appreciate everything about Atlanta. There's so much beauty and diversity here." She squeezed his arm. "So much to love."

They crossed the street together, caught up in the stream of pedestrian traffic flowing from one side of Peachtree Street to the next. The smell of Chinese food from one of the nearby restaurants came to Stephen on the breeze, triggering hunger even though he'd just eaten.

"Yeah, it's a great place to be," he said. "I can't imagine being anywhere else. I was born here and even though I traveled while I was in college, I never wanted to live anyplace else."

"Home is home," Rille said, nodding. "When I first got back from Florida, I was a mess. I wouldn't leave the house, then once I got over myself, I just got in my car at night and drove through Decatur where my parents lived, into the city to watch the lights and hear the sounds of the people and their music." She smiled, looking around.

Why were you a mess? He looked at her but didn't ask the question. *Soon*, he thought. *Soon*.

They strolled past Woodruff Park, the kiosks on the sidewalk, pigeons pecking at scraps of food people dropped on their way. Although he'd never felt a need to be anywhere else, Stephen didn't think he loved Atlanta like Rille seemed to. There just had been nowhere else that resonated with him, no place that made him want to give up this sense of home and safety and of life proceeding as it should.

Up ahead, a couple walked with a stroller. In the scattering of early afternoon foot traffic around the park, they were able to stroll slowly side by side without disrupting the pedestrian flow. A woman with a big handbag and piles of brown hair tumbling around her shoulders moved quickly past them, turning back to give a cold glance to Stephen and Rille. But Stephen caught her eye. Her face thawed and she kept walking but at a slower pace, her shoulders more relaxed. As she passed the couple ahead of them with the baby stroller, she looked back over her shoulder and smiled. Stephen smiled back at her.

Rille chuckled. "I thought she was pissed at us."

"She was. I think we were walking too slowly for her schedule."

"And then she took one look at your face and that was that."

"Sometimes all a stranger needs is a smile or a look from another stranger to let them know that the day isn't that bad. Life isn't that bad."

"It also helps if the stranger is cute." Rille laughed.

Stephen shook his head. "The world isn't ruled by the superficial, you know."

Rille squeezed his arm, smiling. "It's sweet that you don't think so."

"Oops!"

She grabbed his arm as a floppy-eared gray mouse fell out of the stroller rolling placidly in front of them. The couple walked on, oblivious. Rille slipped her hand from his and scooped up the stuffed toy before anyone could step on it. She hurried ahead to catch up with the couple.

"Excuse me." She got the woman's attention with a light tap on the shoulder.

Startled from conversion with her lover, the woman glanced back at Rille.

"This fell out of your stroller." Rille held up the stuffed mouse with the bright red bowtie. "Nobody stepped on it, but there's a little dirt."

"Oh, thank you," the woman said. "I didn't even realize it."

She was pretty, in a Buckhead sort of way. Gucci handbag, matching heels. Perfect makeup and salon-straightened hair. A tasteful hint of cleavage decorated the unbuttoned neckline of her beige dress. She took the toy and wiped it with a napkin from her purse before tucking it into the recesses of the large bag. In the stroller, the baby—apple-cheeked with powdery brown skin and a string of drool running down her chin—slept on.

"Thank you very much," her man said.

Stephen felt the man's dismissive gaze on him before it settled on Rille, casually drinking her up. In his flip-flops, jeans, and Bob Marley shirt, he knew he was hardly a match for Rille, who looked both professional and sophisticated in her body-skimming skirt suit and high heels.

Oh, great. Another asshole who measures his dick by the size of his bank account.

Stephen's mouth twitched in amusement. He shoved his hands in his pockets and did a quick inventory of his own. Designer jeans and a long sleeved shirt with the first two buttons undone. Pointy-toed alligator shoes. A man who wore his money and probably liked using it to get women other than his wife into bed. Stephen knew the type well. This man's confidence was an expensive suit that the right person could easily tear from his body at any moment.

"I'm Trevor." The man extended his hand to Rille then Stephen. "And this is my wife, Mariah. We really appreciate you stopping to return Mister Mouse to us." He directed his smile at Rille. "Our baby girl would've been screaming the instant she realized he was gone. No one needs that."

His wife glanced sharply at him, the smile frozen on her face. From her look, she was used to this type of thing from him, the warming of his voice, his body inclined flirtatiously toward another woman.

"It's no trouble," Rille murmured, taking a small but definite step back.

She aimed her words and a non-threatening smile at Mariah whose knuckles stretched tight from her grip on the stroller. "I'd want someone to do the same thing for me. So in the end I'm just being selfish." Rille laughed softly, inviting her to do the same. But Mariah couldn't.

"Thanks again for stopping," Mariah said coldly, turning her freezing smile and frustrations to Rille. Trevor kept his overly friendly look on Rille, oblivious to his wife's anger.

Stephen stepped forward. "Enjoy the rest of your walk," he said. "It's a beautiful day for it." He touched Rille's waist. "Ready, honey?"

"Yes, baby." She said this with an ironic twist to her mouth. "We have to get you back to work."

Rille inclined her head at the couple. "Take care of your girl." She didn't look down at the child in the stroller. Instead, she stared at Trevor whose leering smile still hadn't left his face. "She's beautiful and deserves to be happy."

But he didn't hear the message. As Rille turned, he looked down at her ass, ignoring his wife's furious expression and the savage way she pushed the stroller down the sidewalk. Stephen and Rille moved away from the couple, footsteps taking them back to the parking garage and Stephen's car. She moved stiffly at his side, obviously bothered by the encounter.

"That was so disrespectful," she finally said, eyes flinty behind her glasses. "How could he treat her like that? They have a fucking kid together."

She stalked beside Stephen, her heels stabbing into the sidewalk with each step, eyes narrowed as if seeing something other than the sidewalk and buildings rising up around her.

"Asshole," she hissed.

Stephen walked at her side, silent, not knowing what to say.

SAID THE SPIDER

SARA/1994

The concrete cafeteria steps scraped against the backs of Sara's thighs under her pleated skirt, but it was a bearable sort of pain. Something to take her mind off other things. The approaching sunset, its colors a fiery burst that covered everything in sharp contrasts of light and shadow, brought Sara's hand up to shade her eyes. She sat on the steps waiting for Raven to come with the car so they could go shopping for bathing suits.

A car pulled into the roundabout. In the haloing light, it could have been any make of car, any color. Was that Raven in the driver's seat? The figure climbed out of the car, its silhouette obviously male. Maybe the next one. But something tugged her attention back to the driver, back to the boy with the fluttering Afro who stepped into the sun. Sara's belly clutched. Her throat dried. *Syrus?* But the driver came closer and materialized into a freckle-faced boy with a shock of bright red curls, long arms, and an indifferent glance in her direction as he passed. Sara blinked against the wind that blew in her eyes, sparking sudden tears.

"Hey, little Sara."

She swallowed and turned, preparing her face for Rille. Rille stood perched two steps above her with a leather backpack hanging off one shoulder.

"Hey," Sara said, feeling the unease in her belly subside in the wake of Rille's smile.

They hadn't spoken since the night of the party, almost two weeks ago, but Sara had thought about her often. From the corner of her eye, Sara noticed the freckled boy appear and disappear behind the glass windows and steel columns of the cafeteria. His hair waved at her as he vanished for the last time.

"How have you been?" Rille asked in her smoky voice.

"Pretty good. You?"

"Not bad. I heard from Devi you're in the study group they have at the café on Wednesday nights. I didn't know you were in that philosophy class."

The study group? So far, the get-togethers seemed more like a reason for her classmates to gather over coffee and have arguments about abstract things that had nothing to do with real life. Sara enjoyed it.

Getting out had felt good, especially when she found out that Devi was in her class. Devi flirted with Sara, even after what had happened at Rille's party, and insisted on buying her drinks and even walking back with her to the dorms that night. Devi didn't try for a good night kiss at Sara's door, but her breath teased Sara's lips during the smiling farewell. "I'll see you in class."

"I *am* in that class," Sara said to Rille. "It's one of the new things I'm trying."

"Sounds fun." Rille moved lower on the stairs, squinting against the glare. Was it vanity that prevented her from wearing sunglasses and hiding the alluring glow of her eyes against the blazing Florida sun? "Do you want to do something after class tonight?" she asked.

Sara blinked, not sure if she'd heard correctly. She opened her mouth.

"I hope I didn't keep you waiting for too long!"

Raven's shout came from the open window of her green Honda Civic as the car stood idling the wrong way in the roundabout. One sandaled foot stood flat on the ground outside the car. Her head and an arm hung out the window.

"Um. No." Sara picked up her purse and stood to face Rille. "I already have plans. But maybe later." Before Rille could respond, she hopped off the steps toward a scowling Raven.

"What did that bitch want?" Raven asked, as soon as Sara got near the car. She didn't appear concerned that Rille was still standing there, watching them.

"Not much. She wanted to do something later."

"Like what, fuck you over again? No way." Raven slammed her door and put the car in gear. "She is such bad news. The last thing you need to do is hang around her again."

But Sara was barely listening. Instead, she watched Rille, still standing on the steps, grow smaller in the rearview mirror.

Wanted

Sara/1994

And don't forget, your papers are due in my office mailbox no later than three thirty p.m. next Thursday."

Professor Holloran dropped his chalk in the long tray that ran the length of the blackboard. As he brushed off his hands, chalk dust billowed up around him, dancing in the sunlight flooding the large classroom. He sauntered to the podium.

"Twenty pages. Ten point Courier font. One inch margins. Anything else and your paper will get an automatic F."

Holloran braced himself against the wooden podium and forced his steely gaze on each of the sixteen faces in the classroom. Then, as if satisfied each student knew he was serious, he grinned. His hazel eyes sparkled like holiday lights above his ruddy cheeks. "If you have any questions, see me after class or in my office later today. Class dismissed."

Sara blew out an explosive breath as she stood. "Jeez!"

"You look worried. Don't tell me you haven't started your paper yet?" Devi bumped into Sara's shoulder as she came up from the seat behind, adjusting the strap of her bag across her shoulders.

"Of course I started. I'm just not done. Hopefully, I can find a free machine when I get to the computer lab tonight." Sara walked out with Devi, mentally calculating how many hours it would take to finish her philosophy paper, the first essay over ten pages she'd ever had to write in her life.

"You don't need to do shit tonight. Thursday is, like, eight days away." Devi ran a hand through her short, spiky hair, then abruptly apologized to a passing classmate when her elbow grazed his shoulder. The boy grinned and waved a dismissive hand before continuing past.

"Yeah, but I have other things to work on too. That exam for my international relations class. And that ten-pager to finish for Gender and Sexuality."

"That's what all-nighters are for, gorgeous." Devi grinned. "I'm having a little get-together at my place tonight. You should come over."

Sara shook her head. She was an unrepentant nerd. Not to mention she felt that so many of the other students were smarter than she was. While most of them could party all week long before a test, not study, and still manage to get a hundred percent, she couldn't. Every good grade she ever got, Sara worked hard for. Sometimes she envied her friends because there were days when she just wanted to let loose and have everything sort itself out later.

"Come on," Devi said, slinging an arm around Sara's waist. "It's just one night. You can go back to being a good Vreeland girl tomorrow."

"Easy for you to say. You barely need to study."

Devi was the classic example of the other students Sara was up against. Though Devi was a chemistry major with a more than passing interest in philosophy, Sara rarely saw her in the labs or even in the library. But she heard from Raven that one of Devi's papers had been published in the *International Journal of Biological Chemistry*. This was her last year at Vreeland, and the word on campus was that she was heading straight to MIT for her doctorate.

"I study plenty. But I also make time to have a little fun." Devi grinned, showing her slightly crooked teeth. "Life is much too short not to sample the sweets along the way."

Sara rolled her eyes. Devi was so cheesy. But Sara could also see her point. College was supposed to be the place to have fun before being thrown under the big bus also known as "the real world." Sara adjusted the straps of her backpack that drooped heavily from its load of books. "Okay. If I get enough studying done for my exam, I might stop by later."

Devi lightly bumped Sara with her hip. "Excellent. I'll await your illustrious presence at my humble abode."

Yep. Cheesy. Sara waved at her as they parted ways at the bike rack. Devi hopped on her shiny blue Schwinn and rode toward the bay and the chem lab while Sara climbed the steps leading up the overpass.

She had her last class of the day in a couple of hours and wanted to reread her notes one last time.

❖

At 12:18 a.m., Sara glanced away from the clock and back to the textbook spread out across her desk. The pink highlighter dropped to the desk as she pressed a fist to her mouth and fought back another yawn. Study time was definitely over.

Raven had long since left their room for more fun pursuits. She was off with fellow anthropology geeks on a late-night hiking trek through the dense woods adjoining the college. Sara had teased that in her short white shorts and tank top Raven looked like she was going out to catch something. Raven had confided that she had a "minor crush" on one of the boys in the hiking group, a pale-haired and blue-eyed ex-Jehovah's Witness with a penchant for expensive weed, retro drugs, and wide-eyed first years. But Sara wasn't worried about Raven. The most Raven would let the boy do was look at her ass, dreamy-eyed, across the campfire before she cut anything else short with the news that she had a steady boyfriend.

Sara blinked eyes that were beginning to blur and closed the international relations textbook. Devi's party should still be going strong. She stood and stretched until her back popped with a muffled but satisfying sound.

Fifteen minutes later, dressed in the same jeans and T-shirt she'd been studying in, Sara knocked on Devi's room door. After a muffled, "Just a minute," the opaque glass door opened, releasing the thick sound of bass-heavy Bhangra and Devi's smiling face. She held a glass of something clear and cold in her hands.

"Hey." The word slurred past her lips. "You look hot in those jeans."

The Indian music pulsed around Devi, seemed to flutter the deep green satin of her robe. She reached out a hand, but Sara stepped back, looking over Devi's shoulder. There was no sign of a party happening in the room.

"Where is everybody?" Sara asked.

"Come inside and see for yourself." Devi stepped aside, sweeping her arm wide in invitation. The smell of marijuana kissed Sara as she passed.

Devi's room was nothing like Rille's. The thought came to Sara as she walked past the nearly five-foot-high water pipe by the door, her feet sinking into a thick Turkish rug spread across the otherwise bare floor. Where Rille's room was nearly Spartan in appearance except for a few hedonistic touches like the deep purple Om tapestry on the wall and the thick black velvet draped from the ceiling and enclosing the bed, Devi's room was downright cluttered. It was a beautiful mess: a stack of two antique looking trunks supporting a fringed lamp next to the queen-sized bed, a sofa sitting against the wall and piled high with thick violet cushions, elegant floor lamps, a mini fridge, and a television on top of an old-fashioned armoire. Devi had decorated the room like she intended to stay in it for a long while.

She batted at the air before her face. Smoke curled languorously around her, slipping into Sara's clothes, her hair, her nose. And inside the beautiful mess was no one but her and Devi.

"I thought you said this was a party."

"It is. A private party for me and you." Devi closed the door and leaned back against it. The smile she gave Sara was not at all repentant.

Shit. "Dev, you know that I'm not interested in you like that."

"Not yet, baby. But tonight that's going to change."

What? You're going to transform yourself into Rille? Sara rolled her eyes and stepped deeper into the cluttered but comfortable room. Even though she didn't feel like putting up with Devi's antics, the alternative of going back to her empty dorm had no appeal. If Raven could take a guilt-free night off from the usual, so could she. Since the night of Rille's party nearly two months ago, Sara hadn't gone to any parties, just the study sessions at the campus café and a welcome event for the first year students in her dorm. An odd fear held her back. What if she saw Rille again? What if she didn't?

Sara had seen Rille around campus a few times. They'd even had one brief conversation. But that was it. Sara was never one to chase after what she wanted, no matter how much she wanted. And looking at Rille, it felt like the most ridiculous of things to chase her, this lean lynx of a girl who seemed to relish the chase herself and would never allow anyone to catch up to her.

Without being asked, Devi poured Sara a drink over ice cubes shaped like stars, and she drank it, nearly choking on its intense sweet tartness. She sank into the sofa and moved aside when Devi slid in beside her, the satin robe rubbing cold into her skin.

"It's vodka and peach schnapps," Devi said.

She sat sideways in the sofa, leaning back against its arm, a bare leg curled under her. It was obvious she wasn't wearing anything but the robe. Sara scooted back a bit more away from Devi until her back hit the opposite arm of the sofa. On the second sip, her drink wasn't quite so bad.

"So what do you say, Sara?"

"About what? You didn't ask me anything."

Devi sniggered. "I guess you're right." She swirled the floating ice stars in her glass. "But I think you know the question I want to ask."

Against her will, Sara's mouth quirked in amusement. "I didn't realize that it was a question."

"Question. Statement. Whatever. As long as we're on the same page." Devi put down her glass and leaned into Sara with a shaky leer.

"Come on. It could be fun." Her cold fingers traced down the back of Sara's neck.

Sara shivered. Would anything change if she slept with Devi? Would she stop wanting to erase the memory of Rille's touch from her skin? To get Rille out of her mind? To get the real thing back in her bed? She allowed Devi to come closer. The smell of the alcohol on her breath, the weed in her hair, the subtle gentling of her approach made Sara allow the light touch, the tugging off of her shirt. Then her jeans. Devi's curious hands combed through her loosened hair.

"Nice."

Devi sounded flatteringly pleased. Quickly, she shook off her robe and touched Sara's face and throat. Her eyes touched everything else.

"Oh, you are magic," she sighed. "Your body is so nice." Her fingers wove feather-light patterns on skin. "Except for here…" She palmed the round curve of Sara's belly. "…you're perfect."

Sara drew back, blinking at Devi who stared at her body with amazement, apparently thinking that she'd just paid Sara the best compliment of her life. Sara opened her mouth. Then a knock sounded at the door before it opened. A bright head appeared.

"I didn't know you were busy tonight, Dev." Rille's eyes swept over Sara, seeming to miss nothing.

Sara imagined how Rille must see them. Her. In a pale copy of the night they had shared together. Devi drunk and Sara willing. The embarrassment she felt before was nothing to the heat that scorched over her face, her pride, at the look on Rille's face. She curled up in the sofa, pulling her knees up to shield her breasts. She didn't go as far as dropping her face into the dark comfort of her knees, but she wanted to.

"It's only Rille, baby, relax," Devi said.

But Sara shook her head. Gripped one cold hand with the other at her ankles. Devi looked away from Sara to Rille who was still perched in the doorway, hand on the doorknob, looking as if she already stood inside the suddenly too-warm room gazing at them with naked curiosity. She might as well have stood against the wall with arms crossed, watching the two like a movie she'd like to see play out. But something else moved behind those clear yet opaque eyes.

Sara could feel herself shut down. Whatever it was that she had been willing to do with Devi was over. It couldn't continue beyond what it was now. And Devi sensed that.

"Shit," Devi muttered and sank back in the sofa, making no move to put on her robe. "Come on in, Miss Merille. I was busy, but not anymore." She grabbed her glass and raised it to her lips.

And still, Rille didn't move.

Tired of the standoff, Sara reached for her shirt and pulled it on.

"No need to rush off," Rille finally said.

But Sara shook her head. She was doing a lot of that lately. With cold fingers, she pulled on her jeans and slipped her feet into sandals.

"I'm going," she said.

Sara glanced briefly at Devi before slipping by Rille and her crisp scent of the sea, and out the door.

"Is that what you called me over here to see?" Sara heard Rille ask as she fled down the stairs and back to the boring safety of her room.

DRY

SARA/1994

He wasn't in that box.

The words came swiftly, like pain. Sara heard plates fall, a crash, and the sound of shards flying. The Vreeland catalogue slapped the floor as she ran to the kitchen.

"Mama?"

Her mother stood clutching her belly, staring wordlessly at the television. Her mouth in a silent O of denial. On the screen, breaking news about a downed flight to Nicaragua. Everyone on board suspected dead. Sara knew what she was thinking.

"That's not his flight. It's okay." *He wasn't in that box.*

Her mother had been putting away plates, the clear ones that were Syrus's favorite. Their jagged shards trapped light on the kitchen floor. Footage of the wrecked plane floated inside the tiny screen on top of the fridge, the local news channel's logo lay fixed across the screen, branding the scene of death, of charred lives, and ruined families as theirs. They'd got there first.

Sara winced. "Daddy is at work. Should I call him?"

"No," her mother said. "No." The word repeated, spilling from her lips like blood. She covered her mouth, but the word came still, wrenching itself out of her throat, crowding into the small kitchen.

Sara blinked under the suddenly bright fluorescent lights and turned to the phone, shutting out her mother's voice. The "no" now an animal scream, a wailing cry as her mother sank back against the kitchen counter, sliding toward the floor. Toward the broken glass. Sara pivoted from reaching for the phone and pulled her mother up. Hands under her mama's hot armpits, the sour scent of her fear in her nostrils.

He wasn't in that box. "It's okay."

She lifted her mother into her arms, the body limp except for the corded and veined neck, the word spilling through her fingers. Sara put her mama to bed, under the sheets—apron, slippers, wailing, and all. Then she walked back to the kitchen, called the factory, left a message for her father. Tracking bloody footprints across the linoleum.

Now. Or was it Then. The pallbearers lowered the coffin into the ground, carefully. Slowly. Mama and Daddy clung together, their black clothes fluttering in the breeze. Sara stood at her father's side in jeans and a Jimi Hendrix T-shirt, staring at the lowering coffin strewn with purple irises. Dry-eyed.

He wasn't in that box.

Grief, some said, can be a long process. It could take weeks, months, or even years to work through. Sara didn't want to wait that long.

WET

SARA/1994

I'm glad that I get to see you outside of class," Devi said, peeking at Sara over her tall glass of iced tea. Tiny mint leaves floated in the glass of pale green liquid.

"Yeah. It's good to talk about Fanon and cultural liberation outside the classroom. It makes me feel like what we do in there is actually relevant."

"That's not what I mean. And you know it." Devi smiled, pretty and butch from her slouch in the chair.

Around them, the small campus café released more of its lingering customers. The girl behind the register flicked annoyed looks their way while her co-worker packed up the day's unsold pastries and took them to the back. Above the counter, a clock ticked closer and closer toward eleven. Closing time. But Devi didn't seem to care. If anything, she slouched even deeper into the chair, adjusted her feet in the one across from it. Sara sucked up her guava smoothie through the gigantic yellow straw and tried not to look at her.

"I think you're really hot," Devi said. "From the second you walked into the party the other night, I thought that."

Sara touched her burning cheek to the sleeve of her white blouse. She'd gotten more attention at Vreeland in her first month than her entire four years of high school. It felt good. But strange.

"I'm not…" She paused. "I don't really want to see anyone right now."

"Anyone except Rille. Yeah, I get that." Devi looked only slightly disappointed. She put her glass on the table, gazed at Sara from under her spiky blue-black hair. "Just try me. I'll be gentler than Rille."

The breath left Sara's chest in a rush. Yes, Devi had been there that night. She, along with anyone else at that party who'd cared to look, had seen what Sara let Rille do to her. What she'd enjoyed on that naked balcony. Yet not. Her blush became a brushfire that consumed her face, her pride. She shook her head.

Devi held up her hand. "Sorry, I shouldn't have said that. Rewind. Erase. Start again."

But they couldn't. In some part of her, Sara wanted to think that no one had seen her on that balcony. That no one was interested enough to watch Rille's skilled seduction and Sara's inevitable fall.

"Rille isn't—"

"We're closing." The cashier, a gaunt Goth girl with a silver hoop in each nostril, appeared behind Devi. She carried a limp wet rag in one hand and irritation in her eyes.

"We're not done," Devi said.

Sara pushed to her feet. "Yes, we are. Thanks for being patient with us," she said and grabbed Devi's arm.

Devi slowly stood, kicking the chair away from her legs, then rising to her full height. Goth cashier was still taller.

"Yeah, thanks." Devi gave the girl's body a dismissive leer before allowing herself to be towed away. She didn't leave a tip.

They stepped through the glass double doors and into a moist late night. The hands of Sara's watch pointed to 11:17. Although it was October, the air still throbbed with heat; no sign of a crisp Halloween in sight.

"Let's go down to the bay." Devi reversed their positions until she was the one leading them into the night. "At least I know they won't throw us out down there, and I can get you a real drink."

She pulled Sara underneath a low-hanging bluff oak tree. As they passed, trailing waves of Spanish moss brushed their shoulders. Couples and some threesomes and four, passed and called out to them as they made their way down the stone path, past hulking banyan trees and through the rose garden bright with scent, the flowers bleached of their vibrant color by the jealous moon. Other shadows and veiled whispers reached Sara with each step, but no more greetings came.

Devi didn't stop her friendly tug until they sat, hips pressed together, in a cement womb of a chair—someone's midterm project from years before—nearly hidden in a small wilderness of palm trees. Though they weren't alone on the lulling bay front, with the enclosed chair and the view of the water waving like a dark hand under the moon, their perch felt completely isolated.

Devi burrowed into the tufted grass in the broken corner of the cement chair and came up with an opaque bottle that looked white in the moon's meager light. Liquid sloshed inside as she held it up to Sara's gaze.

"Vodka. The good shit." Devi unscrewed the cap and took a long swallow before passing it to Sara. "Try it."

She wrinkled her nose, but reached for the bottle anyway. *Why not?* The burn made her nearly drop the bottle. Devi caught it, laughing, while Sara sputtered open-mouthed and chuffing air to dampen the fire in her chest.

"This is supposed to be good shit?" Sara felt her eyes go wide and owlish as the heat slowly subsided.

"It tastes better cold, but yeah." Devi laughed again and took another mouthful.

When Devi tried to pass it to her, Sara held out a palm in the universal sign for No Thanks.

"Well, if that doesn't get you going, how about"—Devi reached into her pocket and brought out a baggy half full of weed, a tiny wooden pipe, and a plastic lighter—"this?"

Sara shook her head again.

"Come on. So you do this with Rille and not me?"

Had she done this with Rille? Sure, she remembered Rille blowing the sweet smoke into her mouth again and again until her limbs had loosened and everything seemed possible. But this wasn't quite the same.

"It's not the same."

"Does that mean I can blow smoke into your mouth too?" Devi's teeth flashed in the dim light.

Sara giggled and dropped her hot face into her hands. "No, you can't."

She sighed into the darkness of her palms. Rille. Rille. Rille. So many things came back to Rille. Sara's first time girl lust. Her hopes to be transformed into someone strong and fearless. Her hopes to be someone who didn't flinch from life.

The alcohol already spread searing fingers through her belly. When she looked up again, Devi had already filled the bowl of the pipe, working quickly with little light and, Sara assumed, a lot of practice. She flicked her thumb and a small flame burped from the lighter. Closing her eyes, Devi sucked for a few seconds from the pipe. Like a dragon, she blew the smoke out through her nose and into the air away from Sara.

"Your turn."

Devi pressed even closer, her arm around Sara as she held the pipe to her mouth and the lighter at the ready. Suck. Release. Hold it in. Burn. It burned. The smoke singed her nose, inside her head. She coughed, holding out the pipe to Devi as her eyes watered and her lungs rejected the smoke.

"It's your first time; you're supposed to do that."

"I think you're trying to kill me," Sara croaked, holding her chest.

The second time, smoke slipped into her like breath.

"That's it," Devi said, her hand a warm weight through the back of Sara's blouse. "You're a natural. You sure you haven't done this before?"

"No," Sara giggled.

She relaxed against Devi, not even realizing that she had been tense. A sigh left her mouth. That breath, along with her clarity, disappeared. She blinked at the darkness beyond their chair, the buttons of light higher up. Stars.

"So back to this thing you got going with Rille." Sara turned to watch the words form on Devi's bow and arrow mouth. "I know you like her a lot, and that's cool. But maybe…" Devi leaned closer. "Maybe we could do it together. You know. Rille, me, and you."

She made a strange attempt at waggling her eyebrows. Like Magnum PI, Sara thought. But not as bushy. And no mustache. And straight hair instead of curly. Closing her eyes, she shook her head.

"I don't think I could ever do something like that."

"It's easy," Devi said. "You'd be surprised just how."

Devi's hand made slow circles on her back, and Sara sank into the warm touch, wondering what it would be like if she peeled off her shirt and kissed her. The thought came and went. Devi wasn't what she wanted. Even with her short hair and angular body, she was soft. Sara didn't want soft. She wanted someone who would make her feel. Feel something that would batter against the screaming thing inside her and make it shut up.

"My brother just died."

The words tripped off her tongue and fell into her lap, irretrievable. She covered her mouth. Shook her head.

"That sucks." Devi's words came slowly, and she leaned back into the chair, dropped her hands away from Sara, and reached for the bottle of vodka.

"I know." Before Devi could put the bottle to her own mouth, Sara pulled it from her. "It really, really sucks."

The vodka burned again, but she didn't care. It made her feel like she could blow flames. Sara threw her breath into the night, but no fire shot out. She grabbed the bottle again. Same disappointing air as before. Another drink and Sara was surprised to find it salty. She choked.

"You all right?"

Devi looked at her with droopy-eyed concern. "Why are you crying?"

"Am I? I didn't noti—" A sound cut off the rest of her words. Then she felt like she was vomiting, vomiting sounds that curled up Devi's face and changed her rubs into pats. On her back. Her thigh.

"Don't cry." Devi patted her harder. "Shit. Come on. Everything's going to be all right."

But Sara's sobs didn't stop. The sounds grew louder. Her throat raw.

"Okay, let's just take you home. Okay?"

Sara nodded and Devi helped her lurch to her feet. The tearing flapped loose in her. She couldn't hold it closed anymore. She couldn't. Sara's hands grasped blindly at the back of Devi's shirt and they stumbled from the chair. The cement and bits of wire poking through in sporadic jabs scraped her hands and the backs of her legs. Sara, with Devi at her side, fled through the gauntlet of eyes piercing them in the darkness, then past the rose garden that made Sara gag with its sticky sweetness. She closed her mouth to the smell, and Devi must have felt the same way about the flowers because she dug hard fingers into Sara's side and hurried them past the garden and underneath the intermittent streetlights that led to the other side of campus. Silence amplified their footsteps.

"I'm really sorry that your brother is dead. Real sorry."

Sorry. Everybody is sorry. "It'll be all right," she said, tears dried on her face like glue. *Sometimes it's nice to think that.* "Syrus isn't really dead. He's just away. Nicaragua, I think. Or maybe back to Jamaica. He really had a thing for Jamaican girls." She paused. "Has. He has a thing for—" The words dropped back down her throat.

Devi rubbed her back again, looking helpless. "You gonna be okay?"

Sara didn't answer. She shoved her hands in her pockets and bit her bottom lip.

They walked past the library, its silent doors, the trees swaying like ghosts in the moonlight. Sara's legs felt heavy as she climbed the steps up toward the overpass with its hissing of cars from the local highway down below.

"He's always going somewhere. Mama keeps saying how he should be an ambassador or something."

She stopped, stared hard at the vines clinging to the chain link fence that covered the inverted trough of an overpass. The world blurred before her eyes. In spring, the Vreeland brochure said, purple and white trumpet flowers exploded from the vines, giving the small overpass the look of a wedding arbor. Now, it was far from springtime. And the vines looked more like dark snakes winding through the fence overhead, threatening to sting the heads of passersby.

With one foot still on the stairs, Sara clung to the railing. Beyond her clenched hand was nothingness. A gap between the hip-high barrier—meant to guide the infirm and uncertain along the stairs—and the sheltering arch of the chain link above the walkway. A small gate. The brochure didn't say how easy it was to escape the cage of vines and flowers, to slip through that opening. On the outside of the overpass sat thick concrete planters, like theater seats, filled with dirt and the thick roots for the yet unbloomed trumpet flowers. While Devi leaned against the railing, sulkily staring into the darkness, Sara slipped past the gate and stepped free.

Devi jumped off her perch. "Wait. What are you doing?"

She stumbled as she came toward Sara. But Sara didn't have to do anything she didn't want to. With her face pressed against the fencing, fingers lashed through it, she balanced on the planters. Her feet sank into dirt and tangled in strong brown roots. A wave of dizziness assaulted her and she whimpered, squeezing her eyes shut. The crushed green smell of the vines pressed against her face. Below her, traffic rushed. People in cars hurrying home to their families. To brothers safe in their beds and sisters waiting for them to wake up. Her heart beat faster and faster.

"Sara! Come back down here."

The fence felt cool against her palm. It dug into her hands as she crouched, back to the traffic speeding below her. Under her thin ballet shoes, the cement was hard. Syrus had given the shoes to her when she turned seventeen. She'd always wanted to take ballet, but they were too poor and she was too old. "*For your dreams,*" he said, putting the curling black slippers in her hands.

A noise coughed up from inside her. He wasn't really dead was he? No, he wasn't dead. The world couldn't be that unfair. He was coming back. Her fingers, hooked into the fence started to shake, then her whole body.

"Why couldn't I be the one who died?"

She threw the words out of her for the first time. Knowing as she said them, why. Syrus was the adventurer, not her. He sailed off for the unknown after high school. He made friends with boy soldiers and refugees. He sent presents that smelled of a faraway sea. He'd taken a chance, burned in a steel box rather than live the kind of life he had nothing but contempt for: college, corporate slavery, creeping death.

"No one has to die." Devi's voice came from far away, sounding as shaken as Sara felt. Maybe worse. "Sara, come on! Quit fucking around."

Clinging to the outside of the overpass, crablike and immobile, Sara bit her lip until it bled. Trembled as if gripped in a fever. She heard other voices, but couldn't make them out. Was she afraid? Is that why she was here instead of buried halfway to Jamaica in a pretty coffin only those looking at it from the outside could appreciate? Was it her fear?

Hands grabbed and pulled her away from the fence. She screamed. "I don't want to be afraid! I don't. I don't."

"You *need* to be afraid, you crazy b—"

"What's she on?"

The cement scraped her knees. She swung wildly for a moment over the gallop of cars. Air rushed past her face.

"Grab her!"

She stumbled into someone. Two someones. Cold hands gripped and swung her around to face a tight pale face. No one she knew.

"Are you all right?"

Sara shook her head. Her body trembled. With gummy eyes, she looked around, peering between the white faces and the darkness. "Syrus?" Another tremor came and she hugged herself. "Please help me." Sara swayed from the hands that held her captive. "Please."

With the sun already a dull white ache behind her eyes, she woke up in her own bed. Naked and tucked under the thin covers. From the shelf above, Syrus's photograph smiled down at her. Raven's face hovered next to his. Not smiling.

Raven sat on the bed beside her. "My mama always said you should only do drugs with people you trust."

But that wouldn't be brave.

A smile wavered on Sara's face. "Next time," she said.

But it wasn't drugs that she wanted for her next time. And as soon as she felt well enough to take what she wanted, Sara went after it. With the sun a warm weight on her shoulders, she wove through the courtyard, empty except for a couple sitting under the waving shade of a palm tree. Third court lay sleeping too, sullen in the full glare of a mid-afternoon sun, waiting for night to fall and one of a half dozen parties to begin. The hammocks strung across some lower balconies swayed forlorn in the light breeze, waiting for bodies to fill them. Sara walked underneath the Japanese lanterns connecting many of the third floor balconies. In the light, they looked cheap. Like overpainted knockoffs, some torn and dingy from constant exposure to rain and sun. As she climbed the stairs to room 318, the smell of old beer, piss, and vomit followed her.

She knocked on Rille's door with only a little bit of fear trembling in the pit of her belly. Rille's surprised face appeared at the threshold, and though Sara saw Thalia sprawled on the bed, her naked thighs barely covered with a thin sheet, she took what she wanted.

"I'm not afraid," she said.

Rille watched her, snake-eyed, waiting for more. "Okay."

"I want to see you tonight." Her breath slowed, waiting for the rejection.

But Rille's eyes opened wide with surprised pleasure. "All right. What time?" She didn't turn back to look at the girl lying on her bed.

"After class, six thirty," Sara said.

"Come back to my room. I'll get food from the cafeteria for us."

Class came and went. Night arrived quickly. When Rille answered the door a second time, there was no one in the bed. It lay empty, piled with pillows, plump under a swirling fog of incense. Across the small room, the balcony door was open. Strings of multi-colored holiday lights shyly illuminated two plates of brown rice with pale slices of chicken breast, a saucer of orange crescents, and two small bottles of orange juice. Sara crossed Rille's threshold, breathless and clear-eyed. And it was easy, she thought. Like jumping off a cliff.

Show Me Love

Stephen/Atlanta

Rille's head poked around the bedroom door, curls catching the first rays of the morning sun. "Are you up?" She didn't wait for an answer.

Stephen yawned and stretched the sleep from his body, back cracking in a series of satisfying pops. Beside him, but separated by the usual ocean of space in their king-sized bed, Sara stirred. Rille came fully through the door, holding a tray weighed down with pancakes, maple syrup, scrambled eggs, and sausages. Except for a black apron and a pair of panties, orange with multicolored heart-shaped peace signs, she was naked. The apron made a tease out of her nakedness, allowing small glimpses of hip, breast, and waist as she moved toward the bed.

Stephen was *definitely* up. He dropped Rille's pillow across his bare lap, consciously not meeting Sara's gaze.

"Did someone deliver breakfast?" Sara asked, shoving her thick dreads and traces of suspicion from her face. She sat up against the pillows and tugged down her nightshirt.

"What, you think I didn't cook this?" Rille thrust out her lip, eyes sparkling early morning dew.

She shoved Stephen's book off the bedside table with her elbow—it dropped to the wooden floor with a dull thump—and moved the tray in its place, being careful not to overturn the carafe of water sitting nearby.

With a dramatic flutter, Rille tugged a napkin from the pocket of her apron and draped it over her shoulder. When she knelt on the bed to plump Sara's pillows, a pale brown nipple popped from behind her apron.

"I know it's early, but we have a long day ahead of us," Rille said. She stepped back from the bed to look at them both, smiling. Her narrow shoulders moved like bird wings under the loose straps of the apron.

One after the other, she pulled two empty plates from under the white bowl of eggs and sausages, whipped serving tongs from the pocket of her apron, and shared out breakfast. She brought the plates to the bed, putting one on Sara's bewildered lap and the other on Stephen's.

"I'll be right back." She grabbed the carafe from the nightstand and left the room.

"What's going on?" Sara yawned, looking at the food on her lap as if live snakes lived there.

He shrugged. Whatever it was, he liked it. He bit into a sausage link and moist, meaty flavor exploded in his mouth. Turkey. Sara's favorite.

"It's good," he said. "Try it." Stephen waved the bitten end of his sausage under her nose, grinning, knowing she wouldn't taste it.

Sara pulled back, nose wrinkling. "I'll try my own, thanks."

Stephen laughed. "I think she's doing this, whatever *this* is, for you."

"I doubt that."

"What do you doubt? That I can cook?" Rille tripped back into the room with three glasses and the carafe full of grapefruit juice.

"While you two weren't paying attention, I mastered breakfast. The pancakes I made from scratch, squeezed the grapefruit juice fresh—"

"And the eggs you laid yourself?" Sara plucked at the fluffy yellow eggs with her fingers since Rille seemed to have forgotten to bring forks.

"Very funny, darling." Rille served her own breakfast, poured juice into the three glasses, and brought it all to the bed on the tray. She sat on the bed facing them, the tray just touching her knees.

"I'm taking you both out today. Eat up and shower. Obviously, I'm joining you for both." She grinned. "And wear comfortable clothes and shoes."

This was a side of Rille Stephen hadn't seen in months, the playful lover with the wicked smile he could never resist. And Sara couldn't resist either no matter how much she tried to. Under Rille's warm gaze, she made a burrito out of a pancake, eggs, and sausage, drizzling maple syrup over the creation before taking a cautious bite.

"That's my girl," Rille murmured, leaning in to wipe a smear of syrup from the corner of Sara's mouth.

She sucked the sticky sweetness from her thumb before tucking into her own breakfast with both hands.

"Don't we get forks?" Stephen asked, more for Sara's benefit than his.

"Use your hands," Rille said around a mouthful of eggs. "Everything tastes sweeter when you eat it with your fingers."

Stephen chuckled. "You might be right about that." He swiped his pancake through the syrup on his plate and bit into it. Next to him, Sara laughed, covering her mouth and batting away the fingers Rille danced across her ribs. He swirled the food across his tongue and swallowed. It *did* taste sweeter.

❖

"Oh my God, this is fantastic! I haven't been to one of these in years!" Sara's voice rose above the noise and music and the sound of cheers surging up from the crowd around them. Calypso music blared from the speakers on top of the passing carnival truck.

Peachtree Street swelled with hundreds of vibrant bodies, all throbbing to the beat of calypso, soca, and reggae music that pulsed from the gigantic speakers on the passing parade floats and trucks. It was Caribbean Carnival time. In front of Stephen, a thick woman, dressed in fringed jean shorts rising sharply into the crack of her butt, jumped out from the crowd of spectators to join the parade. She pumped her hips and jiggled her breasts to the beat of the music, inciting a small riot in the group of men standing nearby.

"Jump on the truck!" the men called out. "Jump on the truck!" A man leapt behind the woman, his naked chest gleaming with sweat as he rode her ass, teeth flashing in masculine triumph.

Stephen laughed. "Damn!"

"Woai!" Sara shouted, caught up in the excitement. She clapped her hands and danced to the music, graceful and curvaceous in her tank top and tight jeans.

Dancers, male and female, fluttered like exotic birds from the floats moving past. The women wore elaborate body-baring costumes, peacock tail feathers flaring up high over their thonged and glitter-scattered backsides. Little more than strips of cloth covered their nipples while animal masks decorated their faces, hiding their features except for the brightly painted and smiling lips.

The carnival atmosphere beat against Stephen's skin, insistent and jubilant. Attached to his hand, Sara laughed out loud again, releasing him as one of the male dancers, bare-chested and sweating the glitter from his hard brown body in rivulets, jumped off the float and pulled her up against him, whirling his hips against her backside. Cheers from the crowd rose and fell around them.

Rille tumbled into Stephen, laughing. "Oh my God!"

And Stephen staggered, in shock that Sara was allowing a half naked *man* to grind up on her.

"She looks so happy!" Rille said with a wild laugh, teeth like lightning across her face. "This is perfect."

"Is her happiness what you're on the hunt for today?"

"Yes, absolutely." Her head fell back, throat damp from the May heat.

In the midst of the crowd, Rille danced against him, moving her body to the frantic soca beat. She looked so awkward, jerking without rhythm, her narrow hips incidentally bumping into his. He kissed her, chuckling against her mouth.

"Despite what you might think," Rille said breathlessly. "I want her to be happy."

"She'd be relieved to hear that." *Maybe even surprised.*

Stephen looked down at her knowing that, despite everything, he would stay by her side and do his best to make *her* happy.

Rille shimmied and shook in front of him, grabbing fistfuls of his shirt while she flung the hair back from her face. "My Sara knows—"

"Hey!" Sara's shout cut through the crowd and jerked Stephen's head up.

She pushed her way through the crowd toward them. Her male dancer's tail feathers flashed from up ahead where he ran alongside the slow-moving float, winding his waist and leaping onto other welcoming women.

"Are you two going to stand there looking serious or you comin'?" Sara's usually buried Jamaican accent tripped off her tongue on the uptilted question.

Rille grinned back at her and shoved Stephen forward. "Go ahead. I'm going to get us something to snack on."

He fought his way through the revelers to meet Sara halfway. When they reconnected, she grinned up at him, her face naked with euphoria. A girl with the Jamaican flag draped around her shoulders as a shawl bumped into them, grinned in apology before leaping away, disappearing like laughter into the parade.

"We haven't done this kind of thing in a long time," Sara shouted against the music, the noise.

"I know," Stephen agreed.

Their lives revolved around home and work and Rille, creating something resembling happiness despite the obvious complications. Rille was happy, Stephen knew that. Because of this, his own happiness was assured. Sara's was more of a tricky thing. Uncertain at the best of times, elusive at the worst.

Here, in the middle of the celebrating crowd, her delight was obvious and beautiful to see. He hadn't realized how much he'd missed it.

"Here." Rille emerged from the crowd, laughing and breathless. She shoved a steaming hot beef patty at Stephen and turned to Sara with a half-wrapped circle of bun and cheese. The brown bun, sliced in two, was still warm and smelled sticky sweet, absorbing the melting edges of the cheese pressed inside it.

"Hm." Stephen bit into the patty's flaky crust, eying Sara's food. "That almost looks better than mine." He felt his patty flake, the crumbs falling from his mouth to his shirt.

Sara brushed at the crumbs caught in his goatee, her smile emerging as she chewed a bite of her bun and cheese. "It is better than yours."

"Look! The Jamaica truck is coming!"

A thunderous blast of reggae music obliterated the soca sound of the passing Trinidad and Tobago truck. Cheers erupted and more people jumped the flimsy barrier to join the parade, their shouting laughter ringing out as they ran alongside the float, calling up to the dancers on the floats with their gleaming skin and muscular bodies moving in a frenzy to the music.

"Come on!"

Stephen startled when Sara grabbed his wrist, almost jerking the patty from his hand, and pulled him through the wall of human flesh and police barriers separating the spectators from the passing parade. He barely had the presence of mind to reach back for Rille's hand and pull her along as he was being pulled into the pulsing stream of bodies.

They rode the parade's wave of excitement, dancing, eating, running after the trucks, bumping hips with rambunctious strangers until they were all grasping at the edge of exhaustion.

"That was fantastic!" Sara grinned as she fell into Rille. "We should do this every year."

Answering laughter bubbled up in Stephen's chest. His body tingled with the aftereffects of strenuous and spontaneous dancing. A piece of ginger still burned his tongue from the black spice cake that Sara dared him into trying. Yes, this was definitely fantastic. The sun. The music. Sara's unguarded laughter. Rille seemed to drink it all in, watching Sara with a yearning that surprised him.

They wandered away from the crowd of sweating bodies and relentless music into a quieter alley of vendors, people chatting in the patois of various Caribbean islands. Sara stumbled into Rille's arms and then they spilled into his, giggling and giddy.

"I have to get some of that sorrel to take home with us." Sara pointed to a nearby vendor's stall and the tall glass bottles of ruby liquid, heavily spiced with rum, on display.

The bottle of sorrel they had already drunk from another vendor sang in their veins, giving them a nice buzz that carried them through the parade.

"It won't be as good as the one you make." Rille threaded her fingers through Sara's hair before turning away to approach the bored Rastaman behind the food cart.

"How much?" she asked, eyes crinkling in flirtation. The Rastaman immediately perked up.

"For you, beautiful lady, name your price."

Stephen shook his head, laughing. No one could resist her for long. He toppled into Sara's eyes.

"She's amazing, isn't she?" Sara murmured, not really questioning. A ghost of a smile played at her lips.

"She is." He nodded.

"She can never belong to anyone. I hope you know that. I learned the hard way. Twice."

"I don't want to claim her, just share. Isn't that what we've been doing the last few years?"

"Is it?" Sara's eyes dipped past Stephen's shoulder as if to check on Rille's presence, or absence. "These years have been torture." Sara looked at him again. "I don't know why I've put myself through it."

Rille turned back to them, the sweat of the humid afternoon glowing against her skin. She raised a bottle of sorrel triumphantly in one hand, the other hand reaching out to both of them.

Stephen nodded toward Rille. "You did it for her. I would too."

"But what would she do for us?"

Her tone was low, mocking. Aware. Rille would do what she wanted to do. That was how it was and always would be.

"I would do anything for you, my Sara." Rille came up and kissed Sara's cheek, pressed the glass sorrel bottle just under the hem of Sara's shirt. Sara squeaked and pulled away from the sudden cold, laughing.

"I'm not falling for that one again." Her laughter was liquid in the air, careless.

All too soon, it faded.

HOMECOMING

SARA/1994

Sara wanted to go home. She wanted comfort. Rice and peas steaming from the enormous pot on the stove. Her mother seasoning the chicken and getting it ready to cook. Daddy already chopping the lettuce, grating carrots into long, thin slices for the salad that was his specialty. His *only* specialty, her mother used to joke. She didn't joke anymore.

"Can I come up with you to Tampa this weekend?"

Sara spoke from her side of the room. John Stuart Mill's *On Liberty* lay open in front of her on the bed, but her thoughts had nothing to do with philosophy or school.

Raven glanced up from her desk. "I hope it's not a threesome you're after. Bryan isn't adventurous enough for that."

"You're not funny." She bit the tip of her erasable pen, lightly marking the white eraser with her teeth. "I want to see my parents."

The smile left Raven's face. "Okay. We can leave early Friday after your last class if you want."

"Yes. I would definitely want. Thank you." Sara gave up and closed her textbook, shoving it and her notebook out of the way so she could sprawl on the bed.

"Any time. You know I always worry about you being by yourself on campus every weekend."

"You know that I'm not by myself."

She had made a few friends on campus, even played a regular game of basketball in the fitness center every Saturday afternoon before heading out to dinner with that same group of girls. And then there was Rille.

"Technically, that's true." Raven seemed to consciously ignore Rille, the pink elephant in the room. "Still, I'm glad I was here when you had your little adventure on the bridge."

"I'm glad you were here too, although, it really wasn't that traumatic."

"Nearly jumping off a bridge after smoking some bad weed wasn't traumatic?" Raven pointed her pencil at Sara. "I don't know about you, but after seeing what shape you were in the other night, I was definitely ready for my trip to the trauma ward."

"Drama queen."

"Whatever, bitch."

In the spaces between their shared smile, Sara forced herself to acknowledge that what happened nearly a week ago had been serious. She could have ended up hurt, or worse. Still, she felt no regret. Everything that happened on the bridge made what she had now worth it. All she wanted now, though, was to see her parents and bask in the warmth of home. Touches from people who wanted nothing from her but happiness. Nothing but love.

Sara got to the house in Tampa before her parents returned from the factory where they worked. Silence blanketed the space that had been so alive before; perhaps not with noise but with the possibility of an effervescent presence showing up to lighten the mood, to remind everyone what life was supposed to be like. Now everything sat, heavily. Reminding Sara of what things used to be like.

Raven looked around the house. "Your house is nice."

"Thanks."

Sara knew Raven didn't really mean it. That was just something you said when visiting someone's house to be polite, no matter the hole they lived in. Garbage in the corner? It didn't matter. The visitor was obligated to find something to say on the good side of neutral. "Your decorating style is very natural." Or some such thing.

Looking at her house through Raven's eyes though, what she saw was a revelation in "make do." The small house they'd been lucky to afford after four years of living in a housing project needed tending to. With both of her parents working overtime at the factory, it was hard for them to find the strength to clean up their own house. Exhaustion often ravaged their faces. After a ten-hour shift, Papa collapsed on the couch with his glass of iced water and a copy of the *Jamaican Gleaner*, while on the television a nature show droned quietly until it was time for dinner or bed.

The cream carpet with its blackened trail of scorched nylon leading from the kitchen to the glass doors and backyard was the main eyesore. A few years ago, Mama had accidentally caught a pot of oil on fire, then in a panic, she raced to the sliding glass doors with it, scalding herself and the carpet in the process. Replacing the patch of carpet had never been an affordable option.

The white walls were mostly bare except for a small tapestry of the Jamaican coat of arms and a cascading arrangement of photographs of Syrus, following him from birth to a few months before he died. Furniture straight from the catalogue of a local store sat in the usual arrangement while a thick, leaning shelf full of books (mostly Sara's romance novels) punctuated the wall between the room's only window and a cabinet full of porcelain figurines and souvenirs from every visit the family had ever made to Jamaica since they'd left seven years before.

"I'll stay with you until your parents get home." Raven dropped her shoulder bag on the couch.

Sara turned from investigating the contents of the fridge. "You don't have to. It'll be a while."

A while turned out to be nearly four hours. Sara and Raven were sitting on the back porch near the open screen door, drinking rum punch and slapping off mosquitoes when Sara heard a key in the front door.

"Daddy!"

She dashed through the house to give her father, who was struggling through the door with his small cooler and thick work boots, a tight hug.

"Baby, what you doing here?" her father asked, looking her over with tired concern. Still, he hugged her back. The smell of seafood from the factory clung to him.

"I'm just visiting. I missed you and Mama."

He dropped his work boots by the door. "You sure?"

"Yes, yes."

At the noise behind her, Sara reached back blindly, gesturing for Raven to come closer. "This is my roommate from school. Raven."

"Raven, huh? What a name." He clasped her shoulder then passed them for the kitchen. "Sara says nice things about you."

"It's good to meet you, sir." Raven smiled at him, looking shy for the first time that Sara had ever seen.

"Call me Neville," he said, then at her stricken look, laughed. "Or Mr. Chambers.

"Okay, Mr. Chambers."

"I'm going to bathe," he said, "before I stink up your air anymore. When your mother's shift ends in another hour or so, I have to go back and pick her up."

They worked at the same place but in different departments, so sometimes one of them would come home before the other. Luckily, the factory was less than two miles away. They'd always shared one car and somehow made it work.

As her father disappeared into the bathroom, the sound of another car pulling into the driveway drew Sara toward the front door. Outside, a dark green sedan—an old one that looked like a boat as it bumped into the dip Syrus made years ago during an experiment with antique cannonballs—shuddered before coming to rest. Its lights and engine stayed on.

"Thank you for the lift." Her mother struggled from the front passenger seat, the heaviness of her movements contradicting her too-thin frame.

Sara shoved her feet into flip-flops and went quickly outside. "Mama, let me help with whatever you have."

But her mother carried nothing. Not even a bag for her lunch.

"Sara."

Her mother looked at her then back at the car to wave tiredly at the figure behind the wheel. The car backed slowly out of the drive, lights bobbing as it bounced into the street.

"Good to see you, baby."

The work ID badge dug into Sara's chest as she hugged her mother. Skin, bones, breath. That was all her mother felt like.

"Have you been eating, Mama?"

"Of course. Otherwise I'd be dead."

Sara flinched at the last word, but kept her arm around her mother. They walked into the house together, the smell she'd been used to all her life, of seafood and exhaustion, clinging to Millicent Chambers like too-strong perfume.

"You look like you haven't been eating," she said. "If you were, you'd be fat like me." Sara pinched at the skin on her forearm for her mother to see, and she offered a smile at Sara then quickly withdrew it.

Inside the house, Raven stood at the refrigerator wrestling the jug of rum punch back into its crowded interior.

"Hello, Mrs. Chambers," she called out over her shoulder.

Under Sara's arm, her mother stiffened. "Who's that?"

"That's Raven, Mama. My roommate. You remember, don't you?"

"You two sleep in the same room down at the school?"

"Yes, that's right."

Sara's hand fell to her side as her mother pulled away, moving into the kitchen with that same heavy step Sara never got used to. Her black sneakers squeaked against the vinyl floor. She reached around Raven to open the refrigerator, pulled out a bottle of store brand cranberry juice, and poured herself a small cup.

"What brings you girls up here?"

"Not much. I just…" Sara hesitated. "I just wanted to see you and Daddy. It's been a long time since I've been home."

"Nearly two months."

"Too long, I say." Sara's father came into the living room wearing gray sweatpants and a white T-shirt with a hummingbird on it. He sat on the couch, turned on the television, and switched it to a nature show. "But whenever you come home, we're glad."

There were new lines around his mouth, Sara noticed.

"Yes. Glad." Sara's mother said the word as if she didn't know what it meant anymore. She shoved the bottle of juice back into the fridge and turned, cup clasped between her hands, to face them. Her gaze found Sara. Then Raven.

"So many young girls are wearing pants now," she said. "It's nice to see one of you in something more feminine."

From the corner of Sara's eye, Raven straightened in her frilled baby doll dress. Raven fumbled for the keys in her pocket. And cleared her throat.

"Thanks, Mrs. Chambers." The *I think* hovered loud and clear in the silence. Raven moved toward her bag on the couch. "I'm heading out," she said. "It was really good to meet you both after all the great things Sara's told me about you."

"Don't run off yet," Sara's father said. "Have a bite to eat with us or something."

But Raven shook her head. "My boyfriend is expecting me any minute. Sorry."

"Ah. A boyfriend. I wouldn't have thought." Sara's mother unfroze from her position in the kitchen and came toward Raven. "Well, that's nice to know. It was good meeting you, dear." She put an arm under Raven's elbow and walked her, smiling stiffly toward the door. "It's too bad that you have to go. But it's good to know that Sara has a friend like you down there at the college. You seem very nice."

"She *is* very nice, Mama." Sara met Raven's eye. "With or without a boyfriend."

Her mother's mouth tightened as she stood in the doorway. An uncomfortable looking Raven gripped the straps of her shoulder bag. Raven's eyes darted between Sara and her mother. "Still," her mother went on, "it is nice that she has a boyfriend. That way I don't have to worry."

"Worry about what?" Sara asked.

"I *really* do have to go." Raven threw the words between Sara and her mother. With an awkward smile, she pulled away from her mother's light grasp and stepped through the open door. "See you Sunday afternoon, Sara." Then as an afterthought. "It was good to meet you, Mr. and Mrs. Chambers." Her heels clicked down the driveway as she walked quickly to her car.

Sara's mother closed the door with a sigh. "Such a nice girl."

"Mama, you practically ran her out of here."

"But she'll be back Sunday, right?"

"Yes. To pick me up for school."

"Sara's right, Millie. You almost shoved the girl out the front door."

"Calm down, both of you. I didn't do anything to the child. She'll be back. They always come back, right?" She sat on the couch, put her feet up in Sara's father's lap.

Sara watched her parents settling into the rhythms their lives had fallen into without her (or Syrus) in the house. Her mother rubbed at her forehead with a thin hand. Her father grasped her mother's bare feet and began a gentle massage, keeping a concerned eye on her face.

"You're tired," he said. "Maybe it's time for bed."

She nodded and lay her head back on the armrest, relaxing more fully into his gentling movements on her feet. Sara felt, suddenly, as if she were intruding.

"It's late." She manufactured a wide yawn. "I'm going to my room, okay?"

Her father patted her shoulder when she leaned down to kiss him good night while her mother, with closed eyes, allowed Sara's dry kiss on her cheek.

"Sleep good," her mother said.

Sara's bedroom smelled like the last time she lay in it. The faint scent of baby powder from the talc her mother scattered under the fitted sheet each time it was changed. And from outside the open window, perfume from the overgrown rosebush, thick and cloying. Deep orange blossoms with pale, nearly yellow hearts hid the view of the neighbor's house and the street. The original intention of planting the roses at the window was to maintain Sara's privacy; instead, the roses blocked most of the natural light and choked her with too-sweet scent. She knelt on the bed and pulled the window shut.

Under the covers, she couldn't sleep. Instead, memories from the last time she lay in the bed tumbled behind her closed eyes. Nightmares of falling. Her body in flames as the earth rushed up. The screams that jerked her awake and kicking in tangled sheets.

She turned over, bed squeaking in protest and nightshirt twisting around her hips, to stare out the window. Thick green leaves and sunset petals muted gray by darkness crowded against the glass as if anxious to get in. They rustled, shifting silent shadows, in the fall breeze while beyond them slivers of moonlight fought to peek through.

Tomorrow, Sara thought. She pressed her fingers to the cool glass. *Tomorrow.*

❖

Hours later, the smell of simmering mackerel woke her from an uneasy sleep. Cobwebs from her restless night clouded her mind before she blinked them away. She sat up in the bed. Syrus's face, leftover from her dream, drifted briefly before her eyes. She shook her head and threw off the covers. After a quick shower and brushed teeth, she made her appearance in the kitchen. At the stove, her mother peeked into a deep pot that drifted steam up toward her face, while her father set their small table. The air felt less tense than it had last night.

"Good morning."

Her father smiled at her greeting, and her mother waved the fork dripping with oil from stirring the mackerel. "Wash up. Food is almost ready."

"I'm ready too." Sara held up clean hands.

"Good. You can get the tea," her father said. "The kettle is already on the stove. Just bring it to the table when it's hot."

Just then, the kettle shrieked. Sara lifted it from the bright orange circle of heat on the stove, clicked off the burner, and brought the water to the table, setting it on a warmer in the center. A box of assorted tea bags already sat next to it. Her mother quickly served each of their three plates a portion of breakfast—boiled dumplings, yam, and bananas with a heaping spoonful of mackerel sautéed in onions, tomatoes, and swimming in its own juices. She sat at the table, looking tired even though the day had just begun.

"Did you sleep well, Mama?"

"As well as can be." Her mother poured hot water over the teabag in her cup, added two spoonfuls of sugar, stirred.

"She doesn't sleep too well these days, you know," her father said. Her mother looked at him with a hiss on her lips. "What? You know it's true. Why hide it from the girl?"

Sara hadn't slept well either for the first few weeks after her brother's death. Only after being at Vreeland and away from the house where she'd spent too short of a life with Syrus had she been able to rest. At least most nights. She'd locked everything up and left it here in this house. Her sadness. Her pain. No wonder her mother couldn't sleep.

"I sleep fine," her mother said. "Just a little restlessness some nights. Anyway—" She dismissed the subject with a wave of her hand. "Enough about that. How are things for you at school?"

"They're okay." Sara slowly chewed a small bite of mackerel.

"Just okay? I remember when you couldn't wait to get down there." Her father's look was determinedly cheerful.

That was before, Sara thought, looking at him. And he knew. "I'm really enjoying my time at Vreeland. It's actually good to be—to be away from the house."

"Yes. It would be nice not to be here." Her mother put down her fork.

Sara put hers down too. "Mama. Daddy. There's something that I wanted to talk with you about—" Her mother looked sharply at her and Sara lost her words. Under the table, her fingers dug into her thigh through the jeans, nails scraping against the rough denim material. She felt lightheaded.

"There are certain things you shouldn't say, Sara." Her mother's eyes cut at her from across the table.

Her father opened his mouth. "Sweetheart—"

"I'm gay. That's what I came here to tell you." The words tumbled from Sara's mouth in a rush. She felt breathless. Stunned. As if she'd just run a marathon at full speed.

Her mother's fists slammed into the tabletop. Their plates jumped. "Don't you ever say that again."

When would she ever have the need to say those precise words again? The question buzzed through Sara's mind, an annoying fly newly dropped into the ointment. *Fuck. Why did I say it like that? Fuck. Fuck.* Sara bit her lip.

Her mother's hand darted across the table, grabbed hers, and squeezed. Hard. "Do you understand me?" The bones in Sara's hand groaned in protest. She tried to pull away, but the unexpected strength in her mother's thin frame held her immobile. "My son is dead and you come into my house to kill my daughter, too—don't you dare!"

"Millicent!" Her father's chair fell backward as he jumped to his feet and to her mother on the other side of the table.

Shock slammed into Sara's chest. "Mama?" The hurt in her hand spread through the rest of her body like a stain.

"That's enough, Millicent. Let her go." Her father's tired face hovered over them, as if he'd expected this moment to come and was helpless to stop it. He touched her mother's shoulder.

Her mother abruptly released Sara's hand as if it were unclean. "Go back to your school, Sara. Only come back when you have something different to tell me."

"Mama, this isn't—"

"Don't say anything else."

"Milly, this is our child. Stop acting as if Sara is a stranger. We've always known who she is."

Her mother jerked in her chair, as if from an electric shock. "She needs to be a different Sara before she can come back into this house."

Bone. Her mama's face was like bone. Sunken and hard.

"Daddy?" Sara's neck popped as she swung around to plead with her father.

He held up his hands. "Give her some time. She just needs time to adjust to your news. Don't—"

"I don't need time." Her mother started to put away the food, although none of them had finished eating. She slammed full plate on top of full plate, splashing oil and bits of fish on the front of her dress. Sara sat frozen in her seat, staring, wanting to see some sign of regret on her mother's tight face. Tears. Eyelashes flickering in distress. Something more than this absence that was worse than—than anything.

Her father tried to pull her aside. He pressed quiet words against her ear. But nothing. Her mother dropped the plates in the sink, ignoring the sound of them shattering. The sounds, a muted echo of one Sara had heard in this kitchen only months before.

The sound unlatched her from the chair's prison. It propelled Sara to her feet, down the hallway, and into her room with its rose-sick smell. Breath churned at the back of her throat. She shoved clothes into her backpack, sniffling at the annoying wetness dripping onto her hands and shirt. Barely glancing back at the kitchen where her parents argued in a tense quiet, she opened the front door and blinked in the sun's glare. She ran.

My son is dead. Her mother's words hurried her feet down the house-bracketed street, onto the sidewalk off the main road. *Kill my daughter, too.* The bag thumped against her back as she ran. Stones poking through her thin shoes. Sun scorching against her face.

Before her brother left on the first of his many trips, she had gone to a backyard party. An expatriate celebration of Jamaica's independence with jerk chicken and pork smoking from the spout of the big drum transformed into a homemade grill. Women sat in a circle of plastic and rattan lawn chairs, some with babies leaning into their breasts, sharing their laughter and their stories. Around them were small cousins, children laughing as they ran playing tag in the abbreviated backyard, the smell of meat catching in clothes, masculine laughter, the slam of dominoes. Beres Hammond crooned love songs from the speakers, also homemade, that were set up just outside the screen door. Syrus was inside the house somewhere.

Sara, fourteen, stood with her prettiest cousin, Nyasha, their backs to the chain link fence dividing the neighbor's house from the two-story wonder that Nyasha's parents had bought with their combined government workers' income. Talk of school sputtered from Sara's lips as she stood next to her cousin, watching the children but feeling intently aware of the slightly older girl at her side. The word "faggot" penetrated her consciousness and stole her attention from where it wanted to be.

The men. The men were talking.

"—and queers should get stoned dead," an uncle said, slamming down a double deuce and making the domino table jump.

"Yes, man," another one agreed, dark green mesh marina shifting over his beefy shoulders as he leaned in to match the two. The table jumped again.

"Then burn them up and shoot the stinking carcasses to the moon."

Prickles of unease stung Sara's armpits. A woman walked out of the house holding a large plate of festivals, still hot from the frying pan, in her arms. "Stop talking foolishness, Clyde," she said, reaching back to pull the sliding mesh closed. "Vivian's boy may be funny that way, but he's still her child. Don't talk about stoning anybody especially with the children right here."

"Mind you business, Clarice. You can't take a little joke?" He shifted the dominoes in his hands, not looking up. "This is man talk."

Clarice sucked her teeth and kept on walking toward the white tent where the rest of the food rested, meshed and safe from flies and darting children.

But Sara was paralyzed by fear. Nyasha looked unconcerned, only kept talking about skipping two grades and entering high school in the fall. She didn't notice. She didn't care. Sara searched for her mother among the women. She sat near Clarice, smiling at something Clarice said. Something inside her relaxed then. If she was friends with this woman, then surely she didn't think the same thing her uncles did.

But that *something* inside her had also held on to that four-year-old incident as validation for withholding the truth about herself. The truth that in the end made her run from her parents.

At the Chinese take-out place down the street, she called Raven from the sticky payphone. "Raven." Her hands gripped the black receiver. "Can you pick me up before Sunday?"

The answering machine in Bryan's room dutifully took the rest of her message, before Sara, spotting a bus lumbering down the road toward her, hung up the phone and got on it, jerking her way down the aisle, past other passengers staring dully ahead, past intimate smells of incontinence, leaking mother's milk, and into an empty seat in the back.

On the bus, she ended up at the library. Through the automatic doors releasing the blast of cool air and the musty comfort of old books against her face. That was where Raven found her nearly six hours later. Curled in her favorite corner, the well-thumbed pages of *No Telephone to Heaven* flat under her dry and unseeing eyes.

THREE

STEPHEN/2004

The other woman looked nothing like Stephen imagined. He had anticipated another Rille, all charm and captivating looks, drawing people in by their basic need to be near such brilliant light. He imagined the two women drawing men into their intimate sphere, breaking them down into nerves, gasps, and orgasm then turning away afterward, with lips and eyes only for each other. This Sara, the real one, was a revelation. She stood underneath the amber lights at the restaurant's front door, pants-suited with her long dreadlocks twisted in a bun. She wasn't smiling.

He got out of Rille's Mercedes and handed the key fob with her name stitched in the brown leather to the waiting valet. He felt a burst of something—pride? possession?—every time he saw that key chain, pleased that she actually used it. Grinning, Stephen helped Rille from the passenger seat.

In a pretty summer dress, high waisted with spaghetti straps and billowing skirts like a 1950s TV siren, Rille stood in sharp contrast to the woman who waited. Sara looked like she'd just left work, had only left the requisite leather briefcase in the car but still was every inch the lawyer in a cool green suit that skimmed her figure enough to let him know that she had one. There was no makeup on her smooth face. No jewelry winked from her fingers or throat.

"It's good to finally meet you," he said, holding out his hand.

She looked at it, considering, glanced sideways at Rille, before taking it. "I've heard a lot about you," she said, then gestured toward the restaurant. "Shall we go in?"

The question was rhetorical because she immediately stepped away and reached for the heavy looking industrial door that took them into the recesses of the restaurant. Fire-lit yet draped with intimate shadows, the place looked nothing like the warehouse it once was. With high ceilings, lushly colored murals on the walls, towering fireplaces in each corner of the room, Red and White was one of trendiest places to eat in Atlanta. On a Wednesday night, it was far from crowded and, Rille had said, the perfect place for her two lovers to meet.

They were quickly seated at a quiet table near one of the fireplaces. The table, a semi-circle with padded seats and a view of the cool darkness outside, allowed Rille to sit between them and gently squeeze both their hands before settling against the cushions with a look of the cat who'd gotten all the cream. And the mouse too. After drinks were ordered and the whole idea of eating dispensed with altogether, Rille put her hands on the table.

"Well," she said, smiling from one to the other.

Sara raised an eyebrow but said nothing. Close up, she was beautiful. Supple, unlined skin, brows carefully shaped over eyes that missed nothing and a firm mouth that could not mask the vulnerability underneath her lawyer's disguise. Stephen immediately felt sorry for her.

"I'm not here to take your place," he said, beginning to relax for the first time all evening.

She looked at him. "You *can't* take my place."

Just then, the waiter came by with her martini, Stephen's beer, and Rille's glass of red wine. Sara took her drink with a tight smile, then sipped it once before setting it on the table.

"Look, Rille wants you here, and because of that, I won't make a fuss. And that's why you're here. No other reason. I don't want someone else in my bed, especially not a man, but because I love Rille, you're here. Because she loves you, you've made it here with us."

Stephen wanted to ask her what she wanted. In her coolly controlled face, he could see hints of himself, someone hopelessly carried along on the tide of someone else's desires, while her own was diluted to the point of being nonexistent.

"If you say you don't want me here, I'll go," he said.

"It's not that simple." Her lashes flickered, but she did not look away.

He could see the war being fought behind the otherwise opaque brown of her eyes. The urge to rip him—the trespasser—apart and pitch his entrails to wild dogs. But Stephen wanted. He wanted very much. The strength of his attraction for Rille overwhelmed both him and his common sense. He wanted her, and even though Sara's "yes" was filled to bursting with "no," he would take her and ignore the pain of the other lover. In time, Sara would get used to his presence. Or learn to bury her own misery.

For him, it was easy to bury his pain. Especially in other people. That kind of sublimation had come so naturally for him, especially in the last few months. Wake up, turn to the empty space in bed (certainly not the gaping hole of his grief), if there had been someone there, it would have been another kind of hole, another kind of burial, but it was still just as empty, as meaningless. With Rille, it wasn't like that. She filled him. She freed him from himself. That firm, sure hand. The flint in her gaze that directed him without hesitation. That was what he needed. And that was what he would have.

Between him and Sara, Rille stirred.

"Sara, if you don't want this—"

Sara's gaze lashed Rille's and to Stephen's surprise, Rille fell silent.

"We'll do this," Sara said. "Because this is what you want. No other reason. I'd rather you do it this way than sneak behind my back. I've had enough of that. Enough."

Rille's thigh tensed beside his, other than that, her only reaction to Sara's words was a smile with a glint of triumph beneath her lowered lashes. She didn't seem like the type to cheat. From the beginning, she was adamant that their relationship remain honest, and that all parties involved know it was happening. On that first night, they'd met for dinner, despite the sparks that flew over his skin at her touch, despite her nipples tightening under the thin shirt for him, she insisted that her girlfriend know everything before they went any further.

Then later, after four months of tease and retreat, when his skin craved her beyond reason, Rille told him something that nearly made him call the whole thing off. But of course he hadn't, and they'd continued. Carefully, then passionately, greedy like animals who'd just discovered the magic of flesh.

Looking at Sara across the table's semi-circle, he felt again that pinch of remorse. The knowledge that he was going to continue with Rille even though this one did not want him to. Her look, he realized now, reminded him of Lucas. Stephen brought the beer to his lips and willed himself not to flinch from it.

Three Point One

Sara/2004

Stephen was pretty. Sara could see why Rille liked him. His skin glowed an impossible shade of dark that Sara could imagine Rille touching with awe. White teeth burned the eyes each time he spoke, and his hair grew strong and wild around his face. He was beautiful. Because Rille was vain, she liked that.

With dinner finished, they walked the darkened streets of the neighborhood, meeting each other's pasts for the first time in words. But between these words, Sara sensed Rille's eagerness for bed. In the way her gaze flitted between them, her two lovers, as if in the midst of a decision. In how she squeezed Stephen's arm, touched the small of Sara's back before allowing her hand to drift down. Rille's body was liquid with desire for them. Sara could smell it.

Later, Rille got what she wanted. Them both, panting and eager for her. Unfamiliar drama in the queen-sized bed that Rille and Sara used to share alone. Afterward, the darkness was kind. Sara lay in it beside them, knowing that only Rille slept. Steven's skin was sweat-soaked, drying. The muscles beneath his skin rippled lightly in the dark. She touched them, his belly, the sharp hip bone and that ridge of flesh, that V that some boys coveted. His warmth was the poison. It was what made Rille want him. Sara laid her hand flat against his skin, washed it down the hard plain of his belly. She dipped a finger into his belly button. Moisture. His hard penis nudged her hand.

Sara looked up and met his eyes. She blinked and slowly withdrew, pulling her hand away from him, pulling her body, its drape across the sleeping Rille, to lay back on her side of the bed.

THE VISIT
SARA/1995

Sara walked in on Rille searching. Outside, the sun burned brightly through the faint trailing clouds, showing off another beautiful Florida day. In Rille's room, though, it was still night. The vertical blinds were pulled shut in front of the doors leading out to the balcony. Suspended from the ceiling, black velvet drapery hung down around the bed but gapped open, revealing rumpled sheets.

"I'm so fucking broke," Rille said, looking inside a jewelry box, under books, in drawers, apparently compartments for a secret stash of cash that was all dried up. "I need money for dinner. Sushi. That's what I feel like tonight."

Sushi money? That's what all this fuss was for? From the bits of rumor, gossip, and truth floating around campus, Rille came from a family of doctors—a plastic surgeon mother and a father who was a pediatrician—so she had no reason to search so desperately for cash.

Sara sat on the edge of the bed, pushing a pillow out of her way. "Why don't you just eat at the cafeteria tonight? Your meal card is practically full."

Rille ignored her and kept searching. Sara had a full scholarship to Vreeland plus an extra grant that paid for her non-academic expenses. She saved most of her money because she had to. If she ran through it, there was no money coming from anywhere else. Her parents' factory jobs paid for their own household expenses and barely little else since Syrus's funeral wiped out most of the savings they'd had.

"There has to be some money around here someplace." Rille looked at Sara. Was she really going to—"Hey, can you spot me a fifty for food? I'll pay you back later."

Sara looked at her, not sure if she was joking. Then she shook her head. "No. I don't have it like that."

"Like what? All I'm asking is to borrow some money until next weekend." She straightened to glare at Sara. "Don't look at me like that. Just put it on your credit card."

"I don't have a credit card," Sara said.

"Don't your parents have a credit card they let you use?"

"No. Why would they? If they have one, it's for them to use." She rolled her eyes. "Not everybody has the kind of life you do."

"What kind of life are you talking about? This is just regular shit."

Of course. She *would* think that it was normal for everyone to have two rich parents with extra cash lying around for their kids to use.

"My parents aren't rich, Rille. That's not the kind of stuff I'm used to."

"My folks aren't rich, either. What are you talking about?" Rille dropped heavily into the bed next to Sara. "Do you even know what you're talking about?"

Her look was teasing, an abrupt change from her frantic search for sushi money. She grabbed a pillow and threw it at Sara. Caught by surprise, Sara flung her hands up to shield her face then Rille was on her, shoving her, squealing down into the bed. Rille straddled her in the bed, pounding on her with the pillow.

"Stop it!" Sara giggled, hands over her face.

She twisted in the bed until Rille was trapped under her and at the mercy of her tickling fingers. Rille erupted into giggles and screams.

"Sara! That's not fair! Sara!"

They rolled around on the bed, laughing, with Sara's skin getting hot under her clothes. The mattress bounced with their weight. Rille twisted her thin, agile body, slipping under Sara's arm to pin her to the bed.

"Ha ha!" Rille gloated. She pressed Sara under her, laughing. "Let's see who's tickling now." She flicked her fingers under Sara's shirt, up under her bare sides.

Laughing, they squirmed together. The smell of Nag Champa incense rolled in the room around them, exhaling its heavy plumeria and sandalwood scent from the velvet drapery surrounding the bed.

The smell reminded Sara of sex, of the eighteen nights and days they'd twisted together under the canopy while incense sticks smoked from the long ceramic burner on Rille's desk.

Sara's body became liquid under Rille's fingers. She wrapped her legs around her, drawing her closer between her thighs. Their laughter trickled away.

"Kiss me," Sara demanded.

"What if I don—"

Sara rose abruptly in the bed to kiss her, pressing her open palms against Rille's cheeks. Rille laughed into her mouth, kissing her back, pushing her into the bed. Her hands caressed Sara's skin under the shirt, trailing up in minute increments toward her breasts, a slow torture of sensation that tightened Sara's legs around Rille. She gripped her shoulders and kissed her harder.

"What's that noise?" Rille asked, pulling back and panting above Sara.

It's nothing, Sara wanted to say. But she heard the noise too. Insistently repeating in the room outside the haven created by the velvet drapes.

"The phone." Sara licked her lips. She squirmed against Rille again, but she pulled away and slipped out of the bed.

"Hello?"

Sara sighed and rolled over, clutching the pillow to her chest. She breathed deeply into the scented cloth.

"You're in town?" Rille asked whoever was on the phone. She paused. "Oh, that sounds nice. I don't have any plans tonight." Rille's voice came closer to the bed. And she sank down into the mattress.

"Can my girlfriend come too?" Rille looked at her. *My parents*, she mouthed. "That's great. What time?" She laid a hand on Sara's shirt, her fingers a light pressure on the cotton. "We'll be ready. Just come to the roundabout." Her hand slid under Sara's shirt. "Okay. See you then." Rille hung up the phone.

Her grin was pure triumph. "We're having sushi tonight. For free!" Rille squeezed Sara's belly. "My parents are coming to take us to dinner." She blinked down at Sara. "Oh wait, can you come? Do you have other plans?"

"No. I—uh, I don't think so." She and Raven had talked about eating dinner in the cafeteria together but hadn't confirmed it.

"Good. They'll be here in about two hours." Rille leaned down into the bed, nibbling on Sara's chin. She licked a hot line down Sara's throat, hands sliding slowly up Sara's belly under the shirt. "That gives us plenty of time to finish what you started."

They barely had time to shower and get dressed before stumbling through Palm Court, giggling and falling over each other with kisses and hot touches, to meet up with Rille's parents. Just before they walked out of the room, Rille had stopped to stare at herself in the mirror.

"Do you think I look all right?" she asked.

All Sara could do was stare. Who was this person and what happened to the hyper-confident Rille?

"You look great," she finally said.

But she was still infatuated. Anything Rille wore looked good on her. And this familiar outfit of jeans and the violet blouse that brought out the streaks of light in her hair was no different. After Rille had dressed, Sara clasped her waist between her palms, breathed the fresh scent of her skin after the shower. She could have stood there next to Rille's warm skin under the purple shirt forever.

"There they are." Rille pointed to a dark sedan parked in the last parallel spot in the roundabout.

Two shadows sat in the front seats of the idling car. Rille waved, hurrying down the steps with Sara. At the car, she opened the door and the interior lights came on, revealing the luxurious beige leather upholstery. It smelled new and of a floral perfume. Rille scooted across the backseat and motioned for Sara to come into the car with her.

"Hey, Dad. Momma." Rille leaned into the partition between the passenger and driver's seat to kiss her parents.

"Merille." Her mother greeted her with a penetrating look, touching Rille's chin. "You need a haircut."

Mr. Thompson sighed. "She looks fine, Beverly."

He pulled the car out of the parking space and drove slowly toward the exit, mindful of students crossing the street, most of them paying no attention to the big car.

"This is her last year of college. She'll be interviewing at graduate schools soon. Merille can't afford to look like a drugged out hippie when she goes before those admissions boards."

"As you're always saying, dear, the women in your family know how to dress for every occasion. Our daughter is no exception."

Rille flushed. But she fumbled for Sara's hand, saying nothing to her mother about her hair or graduate school admission. "This is my girlfriend, Sara." Her tone was belligerent. Challenging.

Mrs. Thompson stiffened, but Rille only pulled Sara closer to the middle of the backseat so her parents could have a good look.

"Hello, dear," Mrs. Thompson said, barely glancing back at Sara.

Mr. Thompson nodded his bald head once in her direction. "Pleased to meet you, young lady."

"How do you do?" Sara murmured, uncertain of how to act with this rigid family.

Rille squeezed her hand. In the car's illumination, her parents looked very ordinary. Nothing like she thought the people who created this electric girl would be. Fletcher and Beverly Thompson didn't even look like doctors. They looked like people. Average. Quiet. Cold.

Mr. Thompson was conservatively dressed in khakis and a pale blue Polo shirt. Her mother wore a white, sleeveless linen dress with a jade beaded necklace and matching bracelet that jingled as she turned down the music on the car's radio. Music from the seventies.

On the surface, her mother looked just like her. The same lean figure. Curly pale hair and green eyes. But where Rille was darker, skin like cocoa powder, her mother was almost beige. Rille had obviously gotten her color from her father and her personality from somewhere else altogether.

"We read a great review about this place down in Saint Armand's Circle. The sushi, they say, is phenomenal and so is the view of the water." Mrs. Thompson glanced back at Rille. "I think you'll like this place, Merille."

"It's not far from the conference hotel," her father said.

With the sun setting on the palm tree-dotted landscape, they drove through the early evening. The air-conditioning and closed windows shut them off from the salty sweetness outside the car.

When I get a car, I'm never going to turn on the AC.

Beside her, Rille sat perfectly still against the leather seat, eyes straight ahead, watching either the road or her parents. Sara couldn't tell which. Her hand rested lightly on Sara's jean covered thigh, like an afterthought. Or no thought at all. Sara glanced out the window. Even though there were three other people in the car with her, she felt alone.

"The restaurant parking is right there, Fletcher." Mrs. Thompson pointed at an upcoming driveway.

The big black car smoothly turned, pulling into a large parking lot with dozens of other cars. They parked beside a silver Jaguar and everyone got out. Sara looked around. The restaurant was small but pretty, like something out of a book; a Japanese-style pagoda with an archway flanked by full-sized bonsai trees. Dark red bricks lined the walkway to the entrance.

Mr. Thompson opened the door with a restrained smile. "After you, ladies," he said.

In the restaurant, Sara didn't know what to do with her hands. They flopped in her lap while the Thompsons looked over the menu, discussing what roll they wanted to try or what they didn't prefer to eat.

"The mackerel is disgusting," Rille said in response to something her father suggested. "I'll never get it again."

"It's not for everyone," he agreed.

Beverly Thompson touched his hand. "Honey, do you want to share the chef's choice with me?"

Mr. Thompson turned back to his wife. "That sounds perfect. A good decision." He closed his menu and glanced at Sara. "What about you, dear? What do you think about the selections here?"

Her face burned when all three sets of eyes turned to her. Was that scorn on Beverly Thompson's face?

"I'm not sure about this sushi stuff," Sara said.

She looked down at the menu, the safer choice of vegetable tempura and udon noodle soup more appealing to her inexperienced palette. Although she had been in America since middle school, Sara had never tried the different kinds of food available in her new country. Jamaican food was comfort. It was home. Only at school, where the menu items were completely American, was she forced to try something else. She had never been ashamed of her choices until now.

"Try the smoked salmon roll, then," Rille suggested. "You might like that. And maybe the California roll. Most newbies like that."

"Uh, thanks." Sara clasped her hands together in her lap, head bent to stare at the menu.

She glanced at Rille, surprised she made time to help her with the sushi. Under no illusions about her new lover, Sara knew that Rille often looked out for herself in most things. And in this moment, Rille wanted nothing more than to slide some expensive raw fish in her mouth, glutting herself on what she'd wanted for hours, even happier because her parents were picking up the check. Why in the pursuit of her pleasure would she even care about Sara's inexperience with this type of food?

The answer sat in front of her face in the form of Beverly and Fletcher Thompson, the most elegant couple that Sara had ever seen. It was weird how they perfectly complemented each other. His dark to her light. The way she picked at Rille while he assured his daughter she was already perfect.

Mrs. Thompson used her thumb to brush something from her husband's cheek. He held still while she ministered to him, his eyes filled with her. In that moment it seemed like there was no one at the table with them.

When the waiter came back, Rille ordered for Sara, both appetizers and entrees, while Beverly Thompson ordered for her and her husband. Edamame. Basil rolls. Vegetable tempura. Bowls of miso soup. A squid salad. For skinny people, they sure could eat.

The food arrived and Sara stared at them with eyes rounded with amazement as they sampled plate after plate of appetizers. This wasn't even the main course.

"You want to try some of this tuna tataki, Sara?" Rille gestured to the mostly raw slices of tuna on her plate. The fish, arranged like the petals of a sunflower around a mound of shredded carrots and purple cabbage.

"I don't think so." Sara shook her head. "I don't eat raw meat."

"It's just fish. And it's not raw." Rille pointed to the edges of the deep pink meat that were a pretty golden brown and dotted with white and black sesame seeds. "See, that part is cooked."

Sara shook her head again. "Sorry, no." But she wasn't sorry. Usually, she'd take a bite just so she wouldn't offend, but her parents taught her to only eat cooked food.

"I'll just eat my fried rice." The safe choice.

She felt Mrs. Thompson's eyes on her again. "You can try anything you want, dear," the woman said. *We're paying for it*. Her unsaid words lingered contemptuously in the air.

"Thank you." Sara forced a smile.

When the entrees came, the Thompsons dove in, also diving into the conversation, as if that was the signal they all had been waiting for to talk about things that mattered. Mrs. Thompson asked Rille about her prospects for graduate school and where she wanted to go. Her father nodded with approval when she mentioned Yale and Johns Hopkins as strong candidates. The discussion seemed like a familiar one to all three of them.

"But what about Emory back home in Atlanta?" her mother asked, swirling her chopsticks into a mixture of soy sauce and wasabi. "Or even Georgia State? There are plenty of good schools up there." She sucked at the tips of the chopsticks.

But Rille looked like she'd rather press her face into the hibachi grill than go to any of the schools her mother mentioned.

"Momma, I told you I'm not going back to Georgia."

Her father patted her hand. "Whatever you decide, Merille. As long as you go somewhere you like. You'll excel at any school." His smile was fond and proud, touching Rille a moment before going back to his wife.

"You're absolutely right, darling," Mrs. Thompson said. She turned to Sara. "What about you, dear? What are your plans after Vreeland?"

Surprised by the woman's apparent interest, Sara glanced in panic at Rille before looking at Rille's mother. She shrugged. "I don't know. I haven't thought much about after college. I just got here a few months ago."

"But surely you have *some* idea of what you want to do with your life. You've been here for a few months and have been influenced somewhat by your studies. You have to know something about your desires."

All I know is I want Rille.

Desire for Rille was the only thing that had become real for her since being at Vreeland. This desire was all that had flowered out of the pain of losing her brother, pushing her to experience life like she thought he would live it, with gritted teeth and fingers clinging hard to someone who pushed her beyond herself. But she didn't think Beverly Thompson would like that answer.

"I want to enjoy my life, Mrs. Thompson. I don't have to map it out to get the most out of it. Vreeland is fun." Sara shrugged. "I'm enjoying learning new things about myself and about the world. I'm not in a rush to commit to one profession or school or whatever."

Mrs. Thompson pursed her lips. "You don't have much of a personality, do you?" She didn't wait for Sara's response. "That sounds like just the kind of crap that hippie school has in their brochure. Did you just read all about Vreeland from the brochure and absorb all their ideas and ideology as your own?"

"Beverly!" Mr. Thompson stared hard at his wife. His chopsticks, heavy with a slice of raw whitefish, pink ginger, and green wasabi, hovered inches from his mouth. "That's uncalled for."

"You don't know me," Sara said, feeling the tremors of impotent anger through her. An uncomfortable heat burned under her cheeks.

"I know enough." Mrs. Thompson's tone effectively dismissed her.

Sara clenched her hands in her lap. "Excuse me," she said, getting up abruptly from the table without waiting for a response from any of them.

She stumbled blindly toward where she assumed the bathrooms were. But she blundered into the kitchen and into an annoyed waiter carrying a platter nearly overflowing with steaming bowls of rice and clear soup floating with white noodles. The black and white image of the waiter wavered in the steam from the bowls.

"The restroom is there." He jerked his chin toward a door hidden in a dark corner of the restaurant.

In the bathroom, Sara locked herself in a stall and leaned back against the door, breathing deeply, trying to control tears of anger. *That bitch!* She gritted her teeth, while some part of her realized that Rille made her just as angry at times. Rille said things to her that were ridiculous and often made her want to throw something and walk away.

But she wasn't fucking Beverly Thompson. The bathroom door opened with a faint squeak.

"Sara, are you in here?" Rille's voice found her over the stall.

She swallowed. And swallowed again. "Yes, I'm peeing." She flushed the toilet, took another quick breath, and pushed open the bathroom stall.

Sara washed her hands in the sink and splashed water on her face, all without looking at Rille. She sensed Rille's impatient presence, her need to be acknowledged. But for the first time, she didn't give Rille something she wanted, something Sara had in her power to provide. Only after she rinsed and wiped her hands did she glance at Rille.

Rille stood by the bathroom door, pouting in the flower-purple blouse and jeans they had picked together for her to wear. Her arms crossed her chest and she watched Sara for a moment before moving closer.

"I'm sorry about Momma," Rille murmured, running her hands down Sara's arms. Soy sauce and something spicy sat on her breath. "She can be a real hard-ass. I'm used to it."

"I'm okay," Sara said, shrugging to loosen the tightness in her chest. "It was no big deal. I've seen worse." But she hadn't. She'd never met someone who completely disdained her and had no reservations about letting her know it.

You're not worth my daughter's time. That's what Beverly Thompson had said under all those words.

"I just had to pee," Sara said, meeting Rille's eyes in the mirror.

Sara stared at Rille in the mirror, at herself. How their bodies were an illusion of complement. Rille's wild, pale curls. Her wispy but neat bob. Rille's blouse and jeans. Her yellow dress with the small white flowers. Dark and darker. Lovers. Together but not.

From behind, Rille pressed her cheek against Sara's, her body held in an attitude of concern. Why? Were her parents outside in the restaurant ignoring her again?

The bathroom door opened. Three women came in, each giving them a brief glance before rushing for the empty stalls. Their heels clicked against the tiled floor.

"Come on," Rille said. "The parents are waiting."

At their table, the parents weren't waiting. They had pushed their chairs even closer and were having a very intimate conversation.

"Fletcher, that's ridiculous!" Beverly Thompson bent her head into her husband's throat, giggling like a teenager.

He laughed with her, his teeth like smooth white stones. In that moment, his hand moved to his wife's shoulder, two fingers slipping under the thin linen to rest against her skin. A prelude to undressing.

Sara and Rille sat at the table and waited for Beverly and Fletcher Thompson to notice them.

THE FIRST TIME
SARA/1994

Like clockwork, Shayna, the girl downstairs began her porn star wails to the dim rhythm of the bed knocking against their shared outer wall. Sara and Raven looked at each other and rolled their eyes.

"Do you think he's really that good?" Raven asked. "Or is she giving him a really good show?"

"It could be a 'her,'" Sara murmured. "We should ask next time we see Shayna."

The first time they heard their neighbor, it was the second month into school, a Friday night that Raven had decided to stay at Vreeland instead of driving up to see her boyfriend. This weekend was his turn to come down. Her brow furrowed over Franz Fanon, Sara blinked when a faint but insistent knocking broke her concentration. Her highlighter stopped moving over the page. Across the room, Raven sat at an identical desk, her chin propped up on one fist while light from the desk lamp illuminated the round cheeks and lower lip caught between her teeth.

"Do you hear that?" Sara asked.

And after a moment, listening in silence, Raven grinned. "Yup. That damn Shayna."

When the wails began, startling and loud, they burst out laughing. Long minutes passed before they could get back to their homework without an attack of the giggles. Over the past few weeks, the downstairs performance had lost much of its humor, but Sara and Raven learned to adapt themselves, get all their homework done before Friday, or make the late night trip to the library or the student center across the quad to study.

"Good thing we're done being nerds for the week." Raven dropped a packet of M&M's into the wicker picnic basket and closed it.

"Yeah." Sara looked at her. "Thanks for coming with Rille and me. I know it's a weird idea."

"No, it should be fun. A late night picnic on the bay. Besides, maybe this is my chance to get to know Rille as more than just a parasite and heartless scab." Raven flashed her teeth.

"Stop it. She's not that bad." Sara lightly poked her side. "In fact, she's very, very good."

"Oh gawd! Please, no more. If you say another word I'm going to shove a pen into my ears."

"Ugh! Dramatic much?"

Raven glanced at her with a teasing smile. They hadn't really talked about Sara's visit with her parents. The little she revealed to Raven had broken her down into useless little pieces in the front seat of Raven's car. Even now, almost a month later, Sara couldn't believe what had happened. But she handled the pain like she did everything else: she tucked it away in a box, locked it, and lost the key.

"Come on, girl." Raven grabbed the picnic basket. "Let's not keep your chyk waiting."

They left their room, locking the door behind them and, with Sara in front, headed to Rille's dorm room.

"What are you and Bryan going to do down here anyway?"

"What else? Go to the beach, eat ice cream, and fuck like bunnies when you'll let me have the room." Raven stuck out her tongue.

"Oh, shut up." Sara laughed in spite of herself, glad to have Raven with her for once on the weekend even if she would spend most of it with her boyfriend. She reached for Rille's door, knocked once before pushing it open.

No. She reeled back across the threshold. Raven cursed as Sara stumbled back into her. The image of Rille on her knees, Dev with her gloved hand and wrist buried in Rille from behind. Rille's face buried between Thalia's thighs. All this, spread on the floor on blankets. On the blanket that Sara had brought over for their night-time picnic. She didn't see any of that. She didn't.

"What's wrong?" Raven's voice reached her from far away. Raven put a hand out to touch, then she poked her head past the half open door. "Oh, fuck!"

Sara knew then that her eyes had been right the first time.

"Um, let's go back to our room and study," she said, her face hot with anger. With humiliation. "Maybe we won't do that picnic thing after all."

"Yeah...." With the picnic basket in one hand, Raven grabbed Sara's arm with the other and steered her away from the door. Sara tripped down the stairs behind Raven, half expecting Rille to rush from behind the door to chase her down and apologize, try to give her some kind of explanation. But she made it all the way down the stairs with no trace of Rille. No sign of the repentance she was sure to come after... after *that*.

In their room, Raven banged on the window, yelling "Shut up!" to the oblivious Shayna downstairs, then twisted on the radio to drown out her braying cries.

"That fucking girl is no good for you," Raven said.

She kicked at the picnic basket by the door, as if it were the source of all Sara's worries. But Sara sat on her bed, staring at the closed door to their room, the scene on Rille's floor still playing like an amateur porn video behind her eyelids. That was her girlfriend.

Syrus was gone. Her parents had abandoned her. And now this. Now she really had no one. She was empty and alone.

Nausea abruptly swamped Sara's senses. She slapped both hands over her mouth and ran for the bathroom, barely making it in time to clutch at the sides of the toilet as sour hunks of her breakfast gushed out of her mouth, splashing up in the toilet until the water turned a swimming, thick yellow. Her stomach heaved and she retched, jerking over the toilet. Her knees scraped against the cold tile. She clutched at her raw throat.

Raven's hand came into her line of vision, holding a damp paper towel. Sara reached out gratefully for it, wiped off her mouth, and pushed up. Raven stood nearby, holding a wet rag against her face, deliberately looking away from the contents of the toilet. More than anything else, Raven hated the smell of vomit and had often told Sara that was one of the things she'd never help her with. But Raven stood in the bathroom, the dark blue washcloth held against her nose and mouth to keep out the smell, brown eyes soft with concern. Sara reached over and flushed away her embarrassment then leaned over the sink to rinse the taste of sickness from her mouth. *This is pathetic.*

"I'm okay," she said stumbling back to the bedroom and to her bed.

Raven sat beside her. The washcloth lay twisted between them on the bed.

"Actually, you look like shit." Raven folded her arms tight across her lap. "You deserve so much better than that slut."

"She's not—"

But Raven's hard stare shut her up.

Rille was that and so much more. There was nothing that Raven was about to say that Sara hadn't thought of herself. Or worse. A shudder quaked her insides. Then she realized it was a hard bang at the door.

"It's me, Sara. Open the door, please."

Raven looked at her, then back to the door. Whatever she saw on Sara's face, forced a sigh, harsh as a slap, past her lips. Before Sara could say anything, Raven grabbed her backpack, flung the door open, and pushed past Rille without saying a word.

"You weren't supposed to see that," Rille said.

She closed the door. Sara imagined that she smelled the sex on Rille, the weed scent Devi wore like perfume, and Thalia's sticky cum tangled in Rille's hair.

Sara crumpled the damp paper towel in her fist. "But I did."

"I won't apologize." Rille shoved her hands deep in the pockets of her jeans and walked further into the room. "I was like this before you met me. If you think a change is going to happen then you're with the wrong girl."

Had she thought that things would change? Rille hadn't pretended to be more or less than she was. A seducer. A taker of things. A cold, selfish bitch who wanted what she wanted when she wanted it.

"Do you ever think about someone else's feelings other than your own?" Sara asked the question as if it had no importance. But she held her breath.

"Do you want me to lie?"

Disappointment leaked from Sara's lips. "No. I don't want you to lie."

Rille knelt in front of her, curved her hands around the solid weight of Sara's thighs. "I like you," she said. "I like you in my bed. I like you in my life. Don't spoil this."

Sara felt herself trembling and couldn't stop. Was this what she wanted for herself? A relationship like this? She couldn't focus on anything. Especially, not on her needs. Her head swam from Rille's nearness. She closed her eyes.

"Can you at least promise me that you won't…" She paused, thinking about what she was going to ask. "That you won't sleep with any men?"

Rille nodded. "I can do that for you." She curved her palm around Sara's neck and drew close. "Absolutely." Her promise, the kiss, pushed away the last of Sara's senses. She didn't resist when Rille rose up and pressed her into the bed.

What would Syrus have said? The question plagued Sara through her reconciliation with Rille, through facing Devi in class without imagining her behind Rille, through the times in Rille's bed when she hardly remembered her name and sweat was the only language she knew. *What would Syrus have done?*

Raven's look was unforgiving and stayed that way long past the time when Sara thought Raven should get over it.

"I can't get over that girl treating you like garbage, especially when everyone on campus knows what she's doing." Raven's cold face stared at Sara across the room every evening for days. She gradually melted, but never wanted to see Rille in their shared room. Never even wanted to hear Sara say her name, if possible. It wasn't, but they moved beyond that. Eventually.

Would Syrus have supported her choice?

Sara had wanted to tell him. Too many days, the words had hovered on her tongue. Words she eventually swallowed. With her mother reacting like this to the news that Sara was just a little different than she thought—some days Sara was glad she'd never told Syrus. But she still wondered. Still longed for her brother's advice. She missed him. The dart games they played in the converted garage that was his bedroom. How he took her to get a fake ID then talked with her over beers—that he drank—about problems with the male gender that Sara should watch out for. "We all have tricks to make you believe every word we say," he remarked once over a microbrew with a milkmaid on the bottle. "Don't fall for them."

Was that the advice to take now?

She wondered this as, in Rille's room, the long vertical blinds rustled in the night breeze. Nothing else moved. And that was when it came to her, past the brush of Rille's hair against her throat on their shared pillow. Through the quiet contentment of their post-coital spooning. Syrus *would* have had something to say about her enslavement. He was gone, but at that moment in Rille's bed, she thought she could feel him lean down, hear him whisper urgently at her ear: "Run."

MISSING PIECES

STEPHEN/ATLANTA

The headstones stood in formation like soldiers. From afar they seemed alike, but up close were disconcertingly different. Some sat above grandmothers who'd seen full and long lives. Others guarded babies who'd barely taken a day's breath. There were names that Stephen knew, and those, thankfully, he did not.

The grass shrank under his feet, releasing pungent green into the dew spattered morning air, as his steps brought him closer to the reason he was here. And not at work. Not at home. Doing something he was helpless to stop himself from doing year after year.

Clayton Osbourne. Aisha Barrett-Osbourne. Beloved parents and friends.

"Mom."

He greeted his mother first because she was his favorite. Beautiful and patient even when she teased him and despaired about his decision to "throw his degree away" at the bike shop instead of becoming an engineer like so many of his classmates. He in turn would tease about her chemically straightened hair and the other signifiers of her oppression by white society, because other than that, she'd made all the right decisions in life. *My son, the bike seat radical*, she always said.

"Dad."

Crouched low in the grass before the headstones, he could, like on so many other occasions, imagine himself lying next to them. His body grown delicate in a satin lined coffin. Over time, grass growing up and through him, wriggling and alive through his sockets that once held the warm jelly of his eyes. Enfolding his arms, pressing around his heart that had long since turned stiff and dry. That was how he imagined it.

The sun, though newly risen, pressed down on the back of his neck and through his thin T-shirt. If Stephen closed his eyes, he could pretend it was his mother's hand, warm and constant. He sat in the grass. By the time he stood and brushed off the damp seat of his shorts, the sun had moved across the sky to sit in its middle, hotter than before, telling him it was time to leave.

Stephen's sadness about his parents' death had never left him. Like mist, it clung, slipping into his nose at unexpected moments, choking him and blinding his eyes. His last words to his father, "Hurry up, I have reservations for eight," had been so mundane. Forgettable. He *wished* he could forget them. And had been the cause of his accident. The car, slamming through a red light. Twisted metal. The wailing chorus of his parents' screams. In his mind's eye, he could see his father reaching out to grab his mother tight, pressing her face against his chest so she wouldn't see the worst of it. Their love had always amazed him.

Later, at home, he moved in that same mist, prodded by the reminder on the fridge to call the doctor and make appointments for him and Sara to get their bi-annual HIV tests. He'd forgotten to do it the week before. Then he made lunch—reheated butternut squash ravioli in cream sauce—and took it out to the front porch along with a glass of iced tea. He ate mechanically, feeding his body to get through this day and make it to the next. Halfway through his last bite of ravioli, a silver Volvo pulled into the drive, past him and down the slope toward the garage. He heard the electronic whine of the doors rising. The slam of a car door.

"What are you doing home?" Sara asked, coming up the walk. The pale blue suit stretched taut over her thighs as she strode, briefcase in hand, up the steps leading from the driveway.

"I didn't know you were leaving work early to spy on me."

She shrugged, not responding to his sarcasm. "I just thought I'd come by for lunch and work from here for the rest of the day. A change." But the already slim line of her neck was taut with stress.

Stephen briefly wondered why she didn't come into the house from the garage as she usually did instead of walking all the way back up front and through the low garden gate.

"Make yourself something to eat and come on out here," he said instead of commenting on her out of character behavior. "The view is nice. You can let this breeze blow your troubles away."

"You mean this same view we've had for the past two years?" Her mouth twisted with scorn, but her heart didn't seem quite in it.

He noticed the fine lines radiating from the corners of her eyes and a certain tightness around her mouth. Her gaze narrowed as if aware of his close scrutiny. Stephen picked up his iced tea.

The slap of feet against pavement, a rush of sound, pulled Stephen's attention away from Sara. Over a dozen pairs of sneakers attached to long legs chuffed against the pavement lining their street. The women's track team from the university. Sara too watched them jog past, keys hanging from her hand. She pursed her lips. Then disappeared into the house.

Nearly a half an hour later, Stephen looked up in surprise as Sara returned to the front porch, dressed now in black yoga pants and a white tank top. Balanced on a small tray, she held her lunch of a grilled cheese sandwich, carrot sticks, a glass of water and a pack of cigarettes enclosed in a secretive little black box.

"Move over."

Stephen stood and took the chair farther to the left, bringing his iced tea with him.

Sara sat, stared at the empty street with its myrtle trees whispering to each other like children in the wind. "Did they come back yet?"

"No." Stephen laughed softly. "Probably in another few minutes."

They sat together in silence, Sara eating her small lunch until it was all gone while Stephen sipped his drink and watched the street for a sign of the jogging women.

Too long ago to remember, Sara had taken up smoking to annoy Rille. At least that's what Stephen thought. She took a luxurious drag of the black clove cigarette, lashes falling nearly closed in pleasure, and blew the smoke away from him. Her eyes barely flickered when they caught him looking.

"It's a boring habit," she said. "Don't pick it up."

"I'll try to hold back."

Then they fell silent again as a different set of women, this time basketball players from the looks of their tattooed arms and leanly muscled thighs, ran past. Sara leaned back in her chair, her tongue peeking past her lips, the cigarette forgotten in the Waterford crystal ashtray Rille had bought her as a joke.

"Nice," Sara breathed after the last shifting rear end, solid with muscle, had disappeared. She reached for the smoking clove. "Must be the reason we bought the house."

"Why else?"

Other than the fact that Rille liked it. The two-story Tudor house was just down the street from the university where she taught, barely a fifteen minute walk. And because she wanted it, all three had chipped in to make the purchase despite the fact that it only had a two-car garage and was miles away from Stephen's bike shop in Little Five Points. The first time he had to drive to work, Stephen nearly passed the store, unfamiliar with the route. After that, he left his tiny yellow Smart car in the driveway and rode his bike. It was much easier to park anyway.

Sara lightly tapped his arm and brought Stephen out of himself. "Showtime."

The passing girls were gorgeous. Incredibly fit. More fit than he had ever been, even in college when he played baseball and ran every day to keep his mind off sex. Blond, Indian, and everything in between. They ran past, brown-skinned girls with big breasts held captive in less than effective sports bras, tiny girls with tails of hair waving at him as they cut through the mild afternoon. Beautiful and energizing young bodies. He was sure Rille loved being among them on the campus.

"I wasn't too much older than them when my parents died," Stephen said. "Then, I was living so much in my body. All I thought about was how the world felt through my skin and how the next pleasure would come." Stephen put the glass of iced tea to his mouth.

He felt more than saw Sara turn to him, scented smoke still streaming between her lips. "And you're not that way now?"

But her attention had drifted from their conversation. Instead, she watched his face for something she just now thought to look for. Before he could answer, she opened her mouth again.

"You normally disappear to that conference of yours for a week at this time of year. Why aren't you gone now?"

There was no conference. But he always told Rille and Sara that was his destination because he couldn't stand to be with anyone during the anniversary of his parents' death. In the room he usually booked for five days after visiting the cemetery, he spent the week in a stupor looking down at the busy streets of Savannah and wishing there was some other way to get through the pain.

He took another sip of his drink. “It was too much trouble to go this year. Staying here seemed easier.”

She nodded, looked out at the street as if seeing something else besides the murmuring myrtles and the two-story, stone façade house across the street that was nearly a mirror to theirs.

“Maybe you don’t need the conference as much as you think you do,” she finally said.

“Nice thought,” he murmured.

She crushed out the cigarette and brought the glass of water to her lips. “I’m just full of those today.”

THE SECOND TIME

SARA/1994

The rainbow flag unfurled from the pole, like a stripper taking her brief turn in the spotlight. It waved and curled in the late afternoon sun.

"You know this is my first gay pride?" Raven said.

"No, really? I can't tell." Sara rolled her eyes at her. "I don't even know any particular reason you'd be at pride. You're the straightest person I know, apart from my mom." Her face froze at the mention of her mother, but Raven grabbed her arm, gave it a little shake, and pulled her toward the student center.

"Come. Let's get your T-shirt before they sell out."

Sara allowed herself to be pulled along until they were in the cool air-conditioned student center, a late Thursday afternoon that was like a weekend with rainbow posters and flyers splashed all over the walls. Laughter broke in waves around them, high-pitched shrieks of the gayest of gay boys strolling together in groups past tables selling beads, books, rainbow thongs, all things gay and fabulous for the weekend festivities.

"Oh, Jesus," Raven muttered under her breath.

"What?" Sara looked at her then glanced around the student center.

"Nothing. Let's go get dinner first then come back and get your shirt."

But Sara had already seen. Rille, of course. Sitting in a group of about half a dozen fourth-years who had taken over two of the large sofas at the back of the room. Portishead murmured mournfully from the boom box at their feet. Rille sat on the sofa's arm, one foot curled under her. The other, bare and tapping silently against the red tile floor to the music, was perched near her abandoned sandal.

"Come on, Raven. You're going to have to get over hating her sometime."

"Sometime, but not today."

"Come." Sara found herself bouncing over to the girl who'd snatched her heart out of her chest. That empty space hurt every time she looked at Rille. She barely noticed that Raven drifted away from her.

"Hey, babe."

A smile flowered on Rille's mouth just for her. "Hey, beautiful." She leaned her head back and drew Sara down for a leisurely kiss. One of her friends whistled. Someone else clapped.

Sara pulled away. "Oh, hey, Devi." She smiled tightly at Devi who was sitting in the sofa across from Rille. "How are you?"

"Same as ever." Devi winked and continued to watch them.

An image flashed in Sara's head and she felt her face grow hot. She turned away from Devi's gaze.

"Anyway, I just came by to say hi. Raven and I are just going to buy a pride shirt."

"You should come to my room later on so I can take it off you." Rille squeezed her hip through the jeans.

The few who weren't immersed in their own conversations giggled.

"Can I come too?" Devi pursed her lips at Sara.

Rille answered for her. "Maybe, if you're good."

"Come on, Sara. Let's grab some food before the good stuff disappears." Raven called from all the way across the room.

"What's wrong with that bitch anyway? It's not like—"

"Shut up." The words shot out of Sara's mouth at Devi. She smiled to cover their fierceness but didn't stop the ones that followed. "She's my friend and the best person I know here. You don't deserve to have her name in your mouth."

Devi and Rille exchanged looks, but Sara ignored them. "Anyway, I gotta go. See you later." She kissed Rille again, quickly this time and walked away to join Raven.

"I'm starving," she said. "Ready to buy a shirt then dinner?"

But Raven was looking past her shoulder. "I know that guy from somewhere."

Sara turned to look. "No shit. He goes to school here."

Vreeland was home to only four hundred or so students. Chances were if you didn't know someone personally, you were sure to know their face. There were no strangers on the campus.

"No. From somewhere else. What is he to Rille, anyway?"

"Her friend, I guess."

The boy in question sat two bodies away from Rille. With milk-white skin, a hair full of thick black curls, and a slim but muscular body that curled comfortably around the giggling girl in his lap, he was nearly the exact opposite of Rille in coloring. As Sara watched, he laughed at something one of his friends said, then nudged a girl sitting on the floor with his foot. The girl grabbed it and pretended to bite his ankle. Smiling, he gently shook her off.

"Hm. Okay." Raven shrugged.

Sara bought the T-shirt, and with it tucked safely in her backpack, she and Raven went to the cafeteria for dinner.

"Isn't it cool how the English language is made up of all kinds of non-English words like cafeteria and booze?"

Raven paused. "Booze?"

"Yes, from Dutch *busen* that means to drink in excess."

"Uh huh." Raven seemed to doubt her sanity, then decided to play along. "What about fellatio?"

"God! You are so disgusting." The pale woman in a hairnet across the food counter gave her an impatient look from washed out blue eyes. Sara laughed. "Sorry. Tater tots, please."

Raven smiled, but her expression was strained.

"You okay?"

"Yeah." Raven looked at the hamburger and salad on her tray before turning to Sara. "Maybe."

They found a table in the crowded cafeteria and sat down.

"What's up, roomie?" She ripped open six packets of ketchup in quick succession and squeezed the red mess over her mound of tater tots. Sara bit into one and nearly groaned as the crisp potato pieces sank between her teeth and floated across her tongue. "You want some? This is really good."

Again, that strained smile. "No, thanks. I'm not a starch-aholic like you."

"Now you're really starting to freak me out." Sara pushed away her tray. "Tell me what's going on. Please."

Raven's eyes fluttered away again, this time to look around them.

"Let's go sit outside. If I'm going to be an asshole, I don't want there to be witnesses."

Sara frowned, trying to ignore the sudden heavy feeling in her belly. She and Raven picked up their trays and headed outside to sit at one of the stone picnic benches under the blossoming kumquat tree. The smell of the white blossoms, sweet like those of oranges, lightly perfumed the air over their heads. Instead of calming Sara, like aromatherapy, she thought dimly, it only made her more nervous.

Raven took a breath. "You know I work in the clinic, right?"

"Yeah."

Sara could feel her brow wrinkling again in a frown at this piece of seeming randomness. Of course she knew that Raven worked Tuesday and Wednesday afternoons in the campus health clinic. It was the newest reason they didn't get to spend nearly enough time together this semester.

"Because of clinic confidentiality I know I shouldn't tell you this." Raven searched Sara's face as if something in it would stop her from saying whatever *this* was. "That guy has HIV."

Sara felt her jaw drop open. Of all the things she could have imagined Raven telling her, that was definitely not one of them. A breath of relief blew past her lips.

She reached for a soggy bite of potato. "I feel bad for him and all. But what does that have to do with me?"

It was Raven's turn to nearly unhinge her jaw. "Are you joking?

"No. What?"

"Rille is fucking him."

Sara recoiled as if Raven had slapped her. "Why are you saying that?"

"It was obvious. Did you see her playing in his hair?"

Honestly, Sara hadn't seen anything. Just Rille and her friends being loud as usual. The guy was handsome, true. But…

"That wouldn't happen. She promised me." Sara opened her hand to the half-eaten tater tot smashed in her palm. "No guys. That was our agreement."

"I'm sure it was *your* agreement, but are you sure it was hers too?"

Sara shook her head. She shoved the tray away. It scraped loudly over the harsh cement surface of the table. Sickness bubbled in the hollow of her stomach. Up and around the tater tot she had eaten until the small bit of potato roiled in her throat thickly flavored with bile. She swallowed it.

"I'm going back to the room."

Sara picked up her tray and emptied it in the nearby trash can then left it on top with a few others. She didn't look at Raven. She couldn't.

Alexander Student Center was a large, single-story building that housed the student government offices, cafeteria, several meeting rooms, student mailboxes, campus convenience store, game room, and an old-fashioned jukebox. The building was surrounded entirely by glass. There were many nights when Sara had wandered through its endless corridors, lulled by its silence and its smells, or when she ran into someone she knew, played a leisurely game of late night foosball until she was tired enough to attempt sleep again.

These days Sara slept much better. More often than not, night found her curled inside the warming cradle of Rille's body, Rille's legs tangled with hers, the balcony blinds drawn and the sliding door left open to let in the breeze that they both preferred to the artificial and too-cold air-conditioning. On those nights when they slept naked, she wondered if Rille felt exposed to anyone who might care to see them. Did Rille feel naked now with Sara's eyes on her as she leaned over to whisper something in the boy's ear then pulled back and, like Raven had said, left her fingers tangled in his hair? Did she *ever* feel naked?

Sara pulled herself from around the corner where she peeked like a thief and walked instead, in the open, toward her. A few feet from the sofa that nearly overflowed with bodies, she stopped.

She called Rille's name. "Can I talk with you for a second?"

Rille turned, brow wrinkled as if in annoyance, but she came, unfolded her lean shape from the sofa, slipped her feet back in her sandals. In her white peasant skirt and pale green tank top, with her hair a flyaway mess around her smiling face, Rille seemed too innocent to ask the question Sara needed to ask.

"What's up?"

"A lot. Or nothing." Sara's hand tightened spasmodically on Rille's arm. She hoped it was nothing. Prayed. "Can you come up to your room with me?"

"Um…sure. Just let me tell them I'm going." Rille's frown deepened the lines in her forehead.

She went to her friends, and in moments, she was back and walking with Sara toward her dorm. Once in the warm silence of the room, Rille closed the door behind them. Sara sat on the bed.

"That guy you were sitting next to in Alexander Center, do you have something going on with him?"

Rille came close to the bed in front of Sara but did not sit down. She crossed her arms and looked down into Sara's face. "What do you mean?"

Everything revealed itself then in Rille's body. Sara felt surprise that she was able to read it all so clearly. In the tightened jaw, Rille's outrage that Sara would question her actions. A subtle toss of the wild curls, eyes hardening with impatience that Sara had called her up here for nothing more interesting than this. Could this girl ever feel shame?

"Did you sleep with him?" Sara asked quietly again, feeling hysteria climb in her throat despite her resolve to be as calm and passionless as Rille was now. But how could she? How could Rille have broken her promise so easily?

Rille's face spoke of an urge to lie, to misdirect Sara to look elsewhere for answers, but she seemed to surprise them both. "Yes."

"Did you—" Her voice broke. "Did you use a condom?" *Please say yes. Please.*

"Of course. I'm not stupid." Then Rille's face changed again, a movement of muscle and bone under skin.

"You used a condom the first time," Sara said, interpreting the look, seeing with her knowledge of Rille the play-by-play of what must have happened. Her voracious appetite, her impatience, the boy not caring as long as he got more of what she had to give. A frantic tremor began in her spine.

She clenched her cold hands together in her lap. Fingernails dug into the backs of her hands. "I think he has HIV."

Rille froze. Then she laughed. "Don't fuck with me. That's not funny." But the truth of it must have shone in Sara's face. Her laughter quickly dried up. She backed away from the bed and from Sara, shaking her head. "This doesn't even make sense."

"Yes, it does." The words burst from Sara in thin-voiced panic. "Did you give it to me? Am I going to die too?"

"Stop it!" Rille jerked close to Sara, her face only inches away. "I don't know what you're talking about. I don't think you do either."

"He went to the clinic!" Sara hissed. "It's in his file."

Realization dawned in Rille's face. She knew that Raven worked at the clinic. "Did that cunt roommate—"

"No!" Sara jumped to her feet. "No. Don't blame her. *You* did this."

The look Rille flashed Sara was almost like hate. Eyes slitted and her neck like plucked strings. In a blur of white cotton and pale curls, she flew from the room, the door slamming open so hard that it banged against the wall and the opaque glass rattled. For shocked seconds, Sara could only stare after her, blinking in the aftermath of Rille's poisonous anger. Then she followed quickly out of the room. Sara gripped the banister as she scrambled down the stairs then across the courtyard, her sandaled feet slapping against the tiles. Palm Court flew past. Stares, curious and surprised, peppered her skin.

"You nosy, jealous bitch! Open this fucking door. I know you're in there!"

Rille banged on the door to Sara and Raven's room, first the doorframe then on glass. "Coward!" She banged again and set the glass trembling.

"Rille!"

As Sara ran up the steps toward the room, she saw a few doors open. Heads peeked out. A few whispers and stifled laughter. Her closest neighbor, Ling, stood in her doorway wearing an oversized T-shirt and bare feet. Her short hair stood up in spikes around her face. When she noticed Sara, her face retreated into embarrassment. For Sara. With a brief flickering glance at Rille, she closed her dorm room door.

"Dyke drama," a voice said just as the door down the open corridor clicked shut.

"No." With bared teeth, Rille shoved Sara away. "Get away from me. I want your bitch ass roommate to come out here so I can teach her a fucking lesson about messing in other people's business!" Her fist banged even harder on the door, punctuating the last three words.

"She's not in there! Let's talk reasonably about this." Sara reached out for Rille, but caught herself in time, gripping her own arms before Rille could shove her again.

"There's nothing to talk about. You've said enough. There's nothing else that I want to hear from you. Not a damn thing."

"Let's go in the room and talk. People are looking," Sara said, her cheeks heating with embarrassment. She twisted around Rille to shove her key in the door, or try to, but another key blocked it from the inside.

Sara put her mouth close to the door. "Raven?"

"Take that slag somewhere else, Sara." Raven's voice was muffled from the other side of the door but unmistakable. "I don't want her in here."

Rille flew against the door again, fists flailing, spit flying from her mouth. "I knew she was in there. Coward! Come out here, you fucking cunt! Ass chomping little parasite!" Her face glowed damp with sweat and the breath whistled harshly through her teeth.

Sara gasped as Rille's fist crashed into her cheek. "Shit!" She fell back, pain exploding in her face.

Urgent footsteps sounded against the stairs behind her. "What's up with all this noise?"

Jason, their RA, jogged up to Sara. His hair, thick and flowing to his waist in a jet-black fall, kept moving even after he stopped.

Sara breathed a quiet sigh of relief at his presence. She couldn't control Rille. Someone else had to help deal with her.

"I thought this weekend was supposed to be about love and all that shit." Jason spoke in his calm, almost sing-song voice. "Rille, why are you disturbing the first-years?"

Rille pounded on the door again. "Back off, Jason. Just back off. I'm handling personal business." Her eyes were vivid circles of desperation.

"No. You're acting like a psycho. And if you keep that up"—he gestured to the door, his mouth smiling faintly—"your hand is going straight through that glass and this will become another situation altogether."

Sara hugged herself, pressed her cold hands against her sides, gaze swinging between Rille and the RA.

"No, *this* is a situation, Jason. Something really fucked up." She still banged on the door, but more slowly, as if signaling someone far away for help. Her mouth began to tremble. "You don't understand."

"Then come make me understand." He held out his hand to her.

She shook her head, and the hair floated across her face, sticking to the sweat and sudden tears. "I don't understand this." She sank to her knees in front of the door. *Bang.* "I don't understand." *Bang.*

Jason pulled her to her feet and against his chest. "We can go talk about this more privately." He turned to Sara. "Do you want to come with us?"

"No! Not her." Rille turned her face from Sara and into Jason's T-shirt.

Pain hitched in Sara's throat, but she stepped back and let Jason take Rille away, cradling her to him while she muttered over and over again, "Not her. Not her."

Rivalry

Stephen/2004

"I met your girl today."

Stephen looked up from the bike catalogue. He'd heard the store's front door open a few minutes ago when he was busy checking out a customer, but aside from greeting the man with a perfunctory "Hi, welcome to Different Spokes," he barely paid any attention.

Now, Lucas's tall figure in work drag—charcoal suit, muted silk tie, heavy-lidded gaze—stood in front of the register. At nearly closing time, the store was empty. Manny had long gone home, and the audible hum of the air-conditioner only amplified the silence.

"Who's my girl?" Stephen asked.

Lucas dropped his arm against the counter in front of Stephen, fingers in a loose fist. "I guess you're right. She's not really a girl but a grown woman who should know better than to do half the things she does." His mouth tightened.

"Who are you talking about?"

"Merille," Lucas said. "Merille Thompson. The campus succubus."

Lucas had recently started taking a theology class at Emory. To help him understand life better, he said.

Stephen closed the catalogue and gave Lucas his full attention.

"You didn't think I knew you were seeing someone else?"

"I didn't think it was any of your business if I was seeing *someone*," Stephen said, deliberately not adding the "else."

Lucas's eyebrow twitched, an indication of pain that lanced across his face before he could mask it.

Fuck. "What I mean is, you and I aren't together. It shouldn't matter if I'm seeing someone or not. We didn't work out because there were things you couldn't give me."

"And she gives these things to you." The tone in Lucas's voice made it clear exactly what he thought Rille was giving that he couldn't.

Stephen tried to hold back the heat from his face. But he knew he couldn't hide the other less obvious signs of his embarrassment. The minute flicker of his lashes. His body tightening with a faint squeak against the leather stool. As much as anyone alive, Lucas knew him.

"Yes," Stephen said.

In the next moment, Lucas's composure left him. His strong face crumbled under its skin. His fist tightened against the counter.

"Does she soothe you back to sleep when you wake up screaming for your parents?" Lucas asked. "Does she give you half the things that I did?"

Rille gave him none of those things. She forced nothing on him but the strength of her presence and the certainty that she knew where he was going and how he would get there.

"Have dinner with me tonight," Stephen said, not quite sure where the impulse came from. "I close the store in a few minutes. We can go to The Patio for beers and burgers."

Lucas watched Stephen from beneath heavy brows before finally shrugging. "Okay."

Of course it was okay. That cruel and honest part of him acknowledged that Lucas would still do anything to be in his life. Stephen wanted to relieve Lucas's agony, not prolong it. And dodging Lucas, pretending that he hadn't chosen someone else wasn't going to do either of them any good.

Stephen put the catalogue away and began the closing up process for the night. He had just counted the money and dropped it in the deposit envelope when the bell above the door jangled and someone walked into the store.

Standing in front of the magazine rack across the room, Lucas looked up from a fitness magazine. A look of grim amusement flashed across his face. The days when Stephen wanted to close the shop on time were the ones most likely for someone to step in at the last minute. This same thing had happened too many times during his and Lucas's relationship when he'd wanted to close at nine on the dot, whether to go meet friends or grab a quick fuck in the back room.

Stephen put on his most charming smile. "Welcome to Different Spokes. Can I help you with anything tonight?"

"No, thanks. I'm just looking." The man, goateed and balding, glanced distractedly at him before moving deeper into the store.

After nearly a half hour of searching, the customer confessed to looking for vegan cycling shoes in a size eleven. While Stephen put in a special order for the shoes and took the man's deposit, Lucas turned off the store's neon "OPEN" sign then went back to his magazine.

"God! Was that like old times or what?" Stephen laughed as he and Lucas crossed the lamplight-yellowed street.

They passed a group of teenagers sitting on the edge of the sidewalk in tattered sneakers and designer jeans, smoking cigarettes and arguing about the feasibility of reparations.

"Yes. Old times. Gone times." A bittersweet smile ghosted Lucas's mouth.

Stephen sobered. "Whether or not Rille came along, you and I were over. You have to admit that."

"I hadn't given up on us yet."

"You should have. I would have given up on me a long time ago."

"You mean too much to me for that."

"No. No." Stephen shook his head. "Please move on. You're just making yourself miserable by holding on like this."

Months before, he had just wanted to push Lucas out of his life, letting him sink or swim in the debris of their relationship, but seeing Lucas's face in the shop, the strain around his mouth, the petty and hurt way he had approached Stephen about Rille, he couldn't do it. Whatever they were now, Lucas had meant too much to him in the past.

Lucas stopped at the entrance to the street-side pub, his back stiff and unyielding. "Is that why you invited me to dinner? For a pity farewell? If so, please count me out. I never deserved pity when you left me, and I certainly don't deserve that shit now."

"I'm not pitying you, Lucas. I just want to talk. Besides"—Stephen shouldered Lucas aside to go into the restaurant—"I'm starving."

Walking past the chalk-written sign at the restaurant's door that directed incoming customers to seat themselves, Stephen scanned the crowded pub for empty tables. He spotted some outside and led Lucas to the patio with its twin fireplaces at opposite ends crackling with heat to fend off the chill.

At a table not far from the metal railing separating the patio from the lazy evening traffic, they sat down. Lucas dropped the two menus he'd grabbed at the entrance on the table and put his suit jacket and briefcase in the empty chair.

"I don't understand why they light the fireplaces so late in the spring," Lucas said. "It's got to be seventy degrees out here."

He hadn't relaxed much since the store, only loosened his tie and rolled up the sleeves of his shirt, a parody of a carefree man. But they hadn't been alone in public in months, not since toward the end of their relationship. They'd had plenty of confrontations in Stephen's condo, but this somehow felt more intimate. Lucas, unusually vocal, obviously felt that too. His discomfort sparked a sympathetic ache in Stephen.

"People obviously aren't complaining," he said.

"True. Look at that woman. She's practically sitting inside the grate. If she gets any closer she'll catch fire." Lucas tilted his head toward the other side of the patio.

Stephen turned to look, surprised to recognize the lone figure. A bottle of white wine, nearly full, sat next to the remnants of her dinner while she drank from her glass and stared moodily into the fire. Should he go over there and say hello?

The question answered itself when a waitress drifted by her table. As she glanced up at her, her gaze caught Stephen's. She raised her glass to him in salute, briefly answered the waitress before looking back into the bright flames. In her pale blouse, tight dark jeans, and high-heeled black boots hugging her slim calves, she looked inviting, sexy. Nothing like how she had dressed for dinner a few weeks ago.

"Someone you know?" Lucas glanced at the woman again.

"Yes."

"She's attractive." Lucas opened his menu. "Doesn't seem like the type to ride a bike."

In his roundabout way, Lucas was trying to find out how Stephen knew her. The thought made him smile.

"She's Rille's girlfriend."

Lucas glanced up from the menu, an eyebrow raised. "You'll have to run that one by me again. And go slower this time. I don't think I heard you correctly."

"You did. She's Rille's..." Stephen searched for the term Rille used. "Primary partner."

Lucas absorbed the words with a slow nod. "I never figured you for one to settle for second place."

"Believe me," Stephen murmured, his voice rumbling deep and intentionally provocative, "I'm not settling."

At Lucas's abruptly shuttered face, Stephen regretted his words and the self-satisfied way he tossed them at Lucas. Despite their incompatibility, Lucas deserved better than this.

"I'm sorry. I shouldn't have said that."

"No. Say what you mean. That's one of the things I've always liked about you, Stephen. No bullshit. No matter how painful."

Pain. The only thing left from the relationship they once shared. Nothing but pain and the realization that the past two years had been only leading to this separation and drift.

Stephen cleared his throat. "Do you know what you want?"

Lucas looked at him. "Yes, I do."

Without saying anything else, Stephen closed his menu and signaled a waiter over. Maybe this impromptu meal hadn't been such a good idea, Stephen thought. But he shoved aside his regret and did what had to be done.

Over burger, beer, and fries, he slowly unwrapped his truth to Lucas. The truth that he'd realized through this new, amazing person in his life. Spending the last few weeks with Rille and snatching precious minutes with her on the phone, he had begun to solidify what he wanted from another person. With Lucas, he knew what he didn't want. With Rille, unlimited possibilities unveiled before his eyes every moment he was near her. With her strength, she challenged him to be a stronger, better person when dealing with others even while he submitted to her.

"Lucas. I love you."

Lucas sipped his beer. "But?"

"There's no but. There is more, though."

Lucas sighed. "Of course." His mouth twisted. "I told you before, I don't want your pity."

"You're not getting my pity. You don't deserve that. What you do deserve, is clarity."

"Clarity?" Lucas raised an eyebrow.

I'm not ready to be with you again.

The last time they talked, that's what Stephen said to Lucas. Those words were weak and unfair. He would *never* be ready to be with Lucas again. Saying it aloud was what Stephen owed him.

"Yes." Stephen thumbed the mouth of his Heineken bottle. "I love you. And because I do, I want to tell you that we'll never get back together. You know that and I've said it. But I know you still think there's a chance for us. I want to be absolutely clear with you. There's nothing between us. There will never be anything between us again. If Rille will have me, I'll be with her for a long time."

A spasm of pain crossed Lucas's face again. Stephen looked away from it, tipping his glance instead toward Sara. To his surprise, she wasn't alone anymore. A woman sat at the table with her. Long-haired. Velvety dark skin. A diamond flashing on her ring finger. He thought he heard Sara call her "Raven."

The woman reached for a lock of Sara's long, loose dreads and tasted the texture with her fingers. Sara laughed. There were two wine glasses on the table, and the bottle was nearly empty.

Stephen forced himself to look away. Lucas stared down at the table, not noticing his straying attentions. He took a careful bite of his cheeseburger to give himself a moment to consider what was happening at Sara's table. Who was that woman? They were obviously on very intimate terms.

"I suppose I should be grateful for your *clarity*," Lucas said. His teeth clenched around the last word. "But I'm not. After you didn't return my last few calls, I assumed, for you, it was really over."

They'd spoken on the phone once since that night Lucas came into his apartment uninvited. During that call, Stephen mentioned Rille in passing, as a woman he had met and wanted to get to know. He'd done that not to share information but to let Lucas know that he was moving on. But Lucas needed more from him than hints.

"I can't say I'm surprised you have someone new," Lucas continued. "But I am surprised that it's a woman like that."

"Like what? You don't even know her."

"I know enough for me to wonder. She's an academic. Her whoring around aside, I didn't think she'd be exciting enough for you. A physics professor? Really? I think you'll be bored in no time, just like you got bored with me."

Stephen's jaw tightened, but he let Lucas finish. From what he'd already seen from the window of his shop, Rille took full advantage of the freedoms Sara allowed in their relationship. But that didn't mean she was a whore.

"She is *not* whoring around," Stephen said, forcing himself to speak without anger. The matter of him being bored with Lucas he let settle into the silence. It didn't matter why they weren't together anymore. "I didn't invite you here for you to attack her character," he said. "She's a good woman."

"As long as you say so. She only has to show that to you..." Lucas paused. "And her other lover."

They both turned to look at Sara. She had settled into quiet conversation with her drinking companion, both women with their knees turned toward the fire, the bottle of wine between them now empty.

"If that's the person you want to love, I can't stop you. I wish I could. You know that I love you, with no conditions, no buts. I'm not going to chase after you like some desperate twink, though."

"I never asked—"

"I know. I know. You never do." Lucas sighed. "She doesn't deserve you, Stephen." He put the beer bottle to his lips. "You should hear what they say about her on campus. She's a grown woman who messes with young kids."

Stephen's eyes narrowed. "The people I see her with aren't underage."

"But they don't know any better than children. You do, or at least I think you do. She's a slick bitch able to talk her way out of any shit she steps into. Nothing sticks to her."

"I don't know the person you're describing. And you don't either. All of that sounds like rumor and jealousy."

"Rumor and jealousy don't start lawsuits, Stephen."

He drew in a deep breath, pushing away the dart of irritation. "This is none of your business. It really isn't."

At Sara's table, the two women stood to leave, talking quietly as they gathered their purses and noisily shoved the chairs under the table.

I hope she had a better dinner than mine.

Across from him, Lucas shrugged. Stephen could see that it cost him a lot to give that simple, dismissive gesture.

"I have to go," Lucas said. He quickly drained the last of his beer. "I have a long day ahead of me tomorrow." He plucked a twenty from his wallet and put it on the table. "This should cover my part of the bill. Leave the rest as tip." He stood and his thick Adam's apple bobbed heavily in his throat. "Take care, Stephen. I'll see you around."

He grabbed his briefcase and jacket then he left. By the time Stephen paid the bill and walked out of the restaurant, Lucas had already disappeared. He sighed.

Despite the hurtful things Lucas said, he was just trying to take care of Stephen. Even with Stephen telling him over and over again that he didn't need a replacement father. He didn't need someone to take care of him, especially someone he didn't ask to take on that responsibility. When his parents died, Lucas was there. Holding him during the worst of his night terrors. Understanding his coldness during the endless days. Eventually, Stephen had become numb and even Lucas's loving strength hadn't been enough.

He crossed the street, pausing in the middle of the crosswalk for a tiny green VW Beetle to turn left in front of him. The night hummed with evening traffic, music from the outdoor restaurant and live band on the next block, conversation from the bums and street kids on the street corners. As he approached the white brick façade of his building, a shadow moved near the doorway. He stopped and dropped a hand inside his pocket. His other hand tightened on the strap of his messenger bag.

A few months ago, a customer from one of the neighborhood bars had been mugged, shot and killed for nothing more than the thirty-seven dollars in his wallet. Since then, Stephen didn't take safety for granted. In his pocket, he gripped the box cutter he kept with him just in case.

"What can I do for you?" he asked the shadow.

It stood up from the steps, unwrapping itself from the darkness, and moved toward him.

"Hey," Sara said.

Stephen stared. He thought she'd be well on her way back to Rille's arms by now after her cozy dinner with that other woman. And a married woman at that. Sara dusted off the bottoms of her jeans and stared up at him from under the thick fall of dark, curling dreadlocks. The white blouse glowed against her dark skin.

"What's going on?" he asked.

"Not much. I wanted to stop by and speak with you for a moment." She glanced toward the red door at the top of the stairs leading into this building. "Can I come up?"

Why? But he couldn't think of any reason to refuse her.

"Ah, sure." He let himself in with his key and walked quickly up the short flight of stairs to the condo. He opened the door. "Come in."

Once inside, he turned on the light and dropped his keys in the bowl by the door and his bag on the couch. Sara came in behind him into the spacious living room, peering around the condo with curiosity. He was suddenly conscious of not cleaning up before he left that morning. The hardwoods needed sweeping, an empty drinking glass still sat on the coffee table from the night before, a couple of plants on the windowsill drooped from lack of care.

Stephen cleared his throat.

"Can I get you something to drink?"

"Water, please. Sparkling, if you have it." She settled into the sofa, an arm draped across its back, stretching her neck slowly this way and that as if forcing herself to relax.

He got a bottle of Perrier for her—one of Lucas's leftovers—and poured himself a glass of water from the tap. With an apologetic noise, he whisked away the old empty glass from the coaster in front of her and replaced it with the green bottle. He sat in the armchair across from her and waited.

The last time he saw her was weeks before when all three of them met at a restaurant then went home together. The night was a blur of skin and sensation and the hot glow of Rille's happiness at finally having them both in bed with her. He spent the night but woke up to only Rille's warm skin in the bed beside him and sunlight spilling across their bare bodies. Sara was already gone. Out of the bed, out of the house. For a jog, Rille said.

On the sofa, Sara slowly twisted the cap from the bottle, watching her own movements as if there was some peril in it. Stephen swallowed his impatience.

"What can I do for you?" he finally asked.

She finally unscrewed the top from the Perrier bottle and put it on the table beside the coaster. Sara took a long sip.

"I don't want to fight you for her," she said.

Stephen kept the surprise behind his face. "I don't want to fight. Period."

Sara dipped her head. "Very diplomatic."

"Not really. Listen. I like Rille. A lot. I think you already know that. The day I met her she told me she was involved with someone else. She said it wasn't a problem. The last thing I want to do is step on your toes or make you uncomfortable—"

Sara laughed harshly. "Now you're just telling lies. The real truth is you don't give a shit about me. All you care about is being with her. If anything, you *want* me to be uncomfortable. You *want* me to go away."

Stephen looked at her. "Isn't that what you feel, too?"

"I'm trying to care about my self-respect. Sometimes it's not an easy thing to do with her." Sara looked down at the bottle in her lap then lifted her eyes to him. "I want to let you know how things will be with us. I can't afford to let circumstances carry me along just because Rille wants them to." Her eyes hardened.

"Rille wants you. I don't. When we're in bed together, you don't touch me. Ever. I've never been with a man and I have absolutely no curiosity about what it's like."

When they had been making love with Rille, there was no connection between him and Sara. Except for that brief moment when she sat up in the bed and examined him with clinical and curious hands, they never deliberately touched. Rille was disappointed. Sara didn't care.

In one moment, with Rille's body soft and liquid under his, she had reached out blindly for Sara, called her name. But Sara had withdrawn her beautiful body to the other side of the bed. Even with the frantic rush of desire pulsing through him, Stephen understood. Despite the fact of them lying in a bed together naked and making love to the same woman, he and Sara felt like hostile strangers. He didn't want to imagine touching her.

"Okay," Stephen said. "I have no problem with that."

"And even if you did have a problem, it wouldn't matter."

His jaw tightened. He nodded.

"I don't want to fight for her and I'm not going to. I'm letting you know now. If you have a problem with that, you can leave. If you don't want me in the house when you and Rille are there, you can leave. If you want to bring another man into this relationship, you can leave."

Stephen's mouth twisted. "Basically, you want me to just leave right now?"

Sara didn't see the humor in it. "That's what I would prefer, but we both know that's not going to happen."

"I'm not going anywhere."

She stood. "Thanks for the water."

"You're welcome." He followed her to the door.

Her heels tapped solidly against the floor as she walked, hips rocking in the tight jeans, spine held absolutely straight. She didn't look back.

"I'll be seeing you soon," Stephen called out as she walked down the stairs and out the door leading to the street.

The red door clicked shut with a soft finality behind her.

Nostalgia

Sara/Atlanta

Night had closed in on the house, leaving its insides a dark cocoon. Sara sat before the flickering gray light of the television barely paying attention to the nature channel's special on predators of the Sahara desert. The sound was muted leaving only the softness of her quiet breathing. Stephen lay upstairs, supposedly asleep after a long day at his shop. And she was alone, in the near dark. Thinking.

A sound at the door pulled her attention from the television and its closed-captioned text giving away the juicy details of a spider's seduction and conquer technique.

Rille stepped into the living room and dropped her small purse on the sofa table. "I'm surprised you're up," she said.

The light moved over Rille's face, into the hollows of her cheekbones, creating shadows between her chin and slender neck, the shallow groove between her prominent collarbones.

"I don't know why." Sara had had insomnia for years now. Ever since college. She couldn't even remember the last time she'd gotten more than four hours of sleep.

Rille made a noise, a laugh maybe. "Just something to say."

"Hm." Sara hummed in response. Sometimes it seemed as if Rille didn't even know her. Fourteen years be damned. "How was the party?"

"The usual. Nothing unexpected." Rille sank into the sofa at Sara's side. The white slacks and ice green lace blouse looked too big for her body. Sara did mental calculations. The outfit was nearly five years old. When they'd bought it together, the soft cotton had fit Rille like a second skin, clinging to her slim legs and rounded thighs, the blouse's web-like lace a tattoo on her breasts and shoulders.

"Why go to the party then?"

Rille's finger conjured a caress along Sara's jaw line. "Sometimes, I like the expected." She smelled like gin and lime.

"You shouldn't be drinking."

Rille drew her hand away, made a sound of annoyance. "I'm tired of being told what I can and can't do."

And that had always been her issue, the words that she fell back on. Rille wanted to do what Rille wanted to do. Nothing else. If someone offered her sky, she'd take earth. Over the years, she hadn't changed much in that regard. Selfish. Seeking. Willful. Weren't those the things Sara saw in her at Vreeland all those years ago? Weren't those the things Sara had run to for destruction's sake?

With a slow sigh, Rille kicked off her high-heeled sandals and stretched full body like an animal in the sun. Toes out and off the floor, hands smoothing down her thighs then sweeping up to hover in the air above her head, as if shrugging off whatever made her brows wrinkle. Sara's concern. She curled back into the sofa, close to Sara again.

"I wish you had come with me to the party."

Sara didn't look at her. "You know how I feel about those kinds of things."

On the TV screen, a sand fox with wide ears and a long, graceful body swiped at a pale lizard. With a flick of its tail, the reptile disappeared into a hole, barely disturbing the sand around it.

"You didn't mind in college." Rille's after-dark voice dipped even lower, effortlessly evoking the first party, their first time as lovers.

"That was college. I'd like to think I've outgrown the naïveté that made me pretend to enjoy those things."

"Do you still enjoy me?"

Now Sara did look at her. At veiled eyes. Petulant mouth. All of her waiting for admiration.

"Not everything is about you, Merille."

Rille flinched at Sara's use of her full name. Spiky lashes flickered as her gaze moved over Sara's face, searching for something. "I didn't say that it was."

Right. "Anyway, tell me about your party. You're back early. It's not even two o'clock."

Rille drew back. "I think I need a drink before I talk about that." She looked at Sara as if expecting her to say something, but when nothing came, she went to the small granite topped bar near the window. Moments later, she sat down again with a glass of red wine.

Sometimes it was pathetic how Rille always seemed to need something to rebel against, no matter how trivial or inconsequential. Even when the rebellion endangered her own health. After a recent car accident that left her with severe neck pain, Rille had been taking Demerol to ease her discomfort. The drug didn't mix well with alcohol.

Sara moved the remote from the light blanket spread over her lap to the small coffee table. And waited.

The words came a few minutes later, sulky and reluctant, between sips of wine.

Marjani, a friend of Rille's from graduate school, had invited her to a birthday party in her big house in Marietta. The internist invited her every year, and sometimes she went but never stayed long. This time, she made an exception. Like her, Marjani was very liberal in her attitudes about sex and sexuality. Every year after each party, Rille's friends told her about what an amazing time they had, that she should hang around afterward because it was just her kind of scene.

Over the years, Rille had gone to a few of the parties but always left before the main event, going out to drink or dance with a few other self-described prudes then heading back home. But tonight it was different.

"I decided to stay," Rille said.

In her face, Sara could see everything. The night had yielded all Rille had both hoped for and feared. In the brightly lit bedrooms and corridors of Marjani's immense house, people had come together like animals. Eager and unselfconscious. Clothes fell away and hands reached out. Pleasure taken and given in a way Rille had experienced in college and now missed. Naked flesh gleamed under lights, sweat-soaked and ecstatic. Bodies moving over each other in a spectacle of raw fucking that begged the voyeur's participation, made envy tug at the flesh, and tossed inhibitions out the nearest window.

It was nothing like her encounters with the naïve students she'd occasionally indulged in before. In those situations, she could control herself; she could control her partners. When she took them, it was as if to prove she could still catch someone young, desirable, and healthy. What Rille really wanted—and what Marjani's group sessions offered—was a complete abandonment to sensation and pleasure. Multiple hands, tongues, penises, and pussies that could take her completely away from herself.

But Rille's blood kept her away, led her slinking to a dark corner where she touched herself in furtive and quick strokes, caught herself crying quiet tears even as one orgasm after another ripped through her over-stimulated body.

Staying to watch had been worse than leaving. With the misery squeezing at Rille's mouth, Sara almost felt sorry for her.

"I thought I could just watch them, just once, and remember what it was like to be free."

"You're hardly imprisoned now," Sara murmured.

"I am. Don't you see?" Rille slammed her wineglass down on the coffee table. Miraculously, it didn't break. "I'm trapped by this body and this damn disease." Her chin jutted forward, stubborn and belligerent. Loosened hair trembled around her face. "I'm tired of living like a victim of HIV. I'm sick of being sick. For once, I want to live my life like a woman, not as a woman with HIV."

Sara tamped down on the surge of worry that shot through her belly. During the past few weeks, Rille appeared to be teetering on the edge of discontent. Nothing pleased her. She sulked more, ate less, and was often gone from home. Sara had tried to find out what was wrong but only got snarled responses and a demand to be left alone. So she left Rille alone. She forced herself to dismiss Rille's new behavior as normal mood swings. And as the recklessness and cruelty of Rille's actions increased, so had Sara's apathy.

After one shallow breath, then another, Sara finally spoke. "In most situations, you do live that life, and it's a great one. Most people would kill to have what you do. But there's also the reality of your disease." She lowered her voice. "You *are* sick and you can't pretend that you're not."

"Why the fuck can't I pretend? Why can't I be like you? Or Stephen?" Rille abruptly fell back into the sofa, her anger gone. "I just want to do what I want," she said.

"If what you want is to have unprotected and indiscriminate sex, not even the most free of us can do that anymore." Sara paused. "It wouldn't be the wisest thing."

"Fuck being wise."

But there was no heat in Rille's words. It was as if she'd had this conversation with Sara in her head long before this moment. As if she knew the outcome to her desire to be free.

"I think you've managed to fuck that already." Sara picked up the remote and turned it over in her hands, resisting the urge to turn up the television's volume and drown out the familiar sounds of Rille's self-absorption. She felt like she'd just wasted her breath talking with Rille.

"Who's fucking who?"

Stephen's sleep-roughened voice sounded from just beyond the doorway before he appeared in the threshold, scratching his bare chest. His rough hair, plaited for sleep, hung down his ears and curled away from his neck, giving him a slightly thuggish look. A jaw-splitting yawn ruined the effect. His loose drawstring pants drooped from his narrow hipbones and fluttered around his thighs as he moved. He dropped into the loveseat and blinked sleepily at them.

"Not Rille. That's the problem."

The words spilled from Sara's lips into Stephen's ears. She saw him perk up, shake his head as if his senses misled him.

"You're not getting enough attention at home?" Stephen asked.

But he knew better than to ask that. A full day rarely went by without one or both of them making love with Rille. Sometimes twice or three times. Once, when conversation had been scarce, Stephen and Sara shared how neither had ever had such an insatiable lover as Rille.

"Then you must want someone else." There was surprise, puzzlement, in his voice. "Why?"

"Familiar fruit is not always the sweetest," Rille said, her words poetic garbage.

Sara put the remote control down and cupped her palms together in her lap. "You're just being greedy. As usual." She turned to Stephen. "What we should do is find other lovers of our own. Then she'd want us again. Rille only wants something because someone else does." Her mouth tightened scornfully. "We apparently need to raise our worth."

Stephen said nothing.

He'd never seen this side of Rille before, Sara realized. Stephen had told her how he managed to capture Rille, that bright and seemingly unattainable butterfly fluttering past the windows of his shop with a different and younger companion each weekend. When he told her that story, Sara had never stopped to ask herself if Rille had slept with any of those people, undoubtedly all students. She knew Rille. Had accepted most of what was good and bad about her. Most. She'd stepped back into Rille's world knowing fully what she was. What Rille could offer, and what she could only mimic.

"Would you have cheated on us or..." His eyes caught Sara's in the darkness then released them in pursuit of Rille.

Or offer the two of them the same deal she had offered Sara two years before. I need another lover to be happy. Take it or leave it.

Looking at him now, Sara realized he must have known how much Rille's inclusion of him in their relationship had hurt. He realized all those years ago and did not care. Sara glanced down at her lap, wondering how much of a revelation this was. Hadn't she always known? Wasn't that what she held against him all this time?

"I don't cheat," Rille said, tipsy and self-righteous.

Not anymore, Sara thought.

Rille looked at each of them. "I would have told you."

"But afterward." Stephen leaned forward in the sofa.

"You knew where I was going. You know what happens at those parties."

"So it would be our fault, *my* fault, for expecting you to control yourself like you've done over the years?" Sara tilted her head in question.

"Shut up." Rille's voice snapped cold and hard. The generous drunk abruptly gone. "You are not my mother. Don't speak to me like you are."

Sara clenched her teeth. "I'm treating you like my partner, not my child."

At her silence, Stephen looked at her more intently. "You are my partner, aren't you? You are our partner."

"I am myself." Rille's tone was final.

She picked up the remote again. "So your sickness was the only thing that stopped you from enjoying yourself at that party, right? Not any notions of partnership or honesty?"

"Yes." Rille dismissed Stephen from her gaze.

Sara released a sigh, silently grateful for the truth. Although she knew Stephen was not. "Thank you," she said.

The television's sound came back on with a press of her finger. A commercial flickered on. The sound of African drums and musical wailing. An advertisement for group vacations to the unspoiled heart of Kenya. Sara wondered if that even existed anymore. She didn't look up when Rille got up from the sofa, pausing for a half a dozen heartbeats' worth of silence, before padding barefoot, silently, from the living room.

Stephen's breath was slow and measured. He said nothing. Sara said nothing. When the golden barrenness of the Sahara desert reappeared on the television screen, they both sat in the dark and watched.

REUNION
SARA/2002

Sara dropped her father's letter in her attaché and snapped the black alligator case shut. A flick of her wrist to confirm the time, and she was out of her condo, slamming the self locking door behind her before sailing down the stairs and to her car in the underground parking lot. Although she'd only given her father's latest missive a quick glance, she gathered that things were still the same with him.

Retired from the seafood factory with a middling pension spent on the necessities like envelopes, stamps, and a subscription to *National Geographic*, her father lived a peaceful life. In cheerful rebellion against Sara's frequent though brief e-mails that he received on the computer she'd bought for his house in Tampa, Daniel Chambers diligently wrote his daughter once a month. In lengthy letters, he detailed the minutiae of his days and shared feelings on everything from the tedium of Florida retirement to his heartache behind the reason Sara didn't visit him more often.

His vivid and emotion-laden words strongly evoked the Tampa house Sara hadn't set foot in since her mother chased her out with words that pelted and stung her tender skin. Eight years. Sara pressed harder on the gas, pushing the silver Volvo faster up the highway.

In her eleventh floor Buckhead office building, she stepped through the heavy steel double doors of Winthrop, Baines, and Associates.

"Good morning, Anthea." She greeted the receptionist with her customary smile and Anthea nodded and smiled, apparently occupied with the voice chirping from the headset sitting neatly on her dark, upswept hair.

In her office, Sara put her briefcase beside the desk and booted up her computer. A knock sounded abruptly at her door before her boss's graying dark head peeked in. Today, like most days, he looked ready for the cover of *GQ*. Three piece pinstriped navy suit. Purple paisley tie. Iron gray eyes.

"Sara, can I see you in my office for a moment?" Lloyd Baines looked at Sara as if there was only one possible answer to that question.

She checked her watch to make sure she had enough time to spare before her first morning appointment.

"Sure."

She plucked her BlackBerry from her purse and followed him out the door and into his brightly lit corner office. As he shut them into the large room, she noted with surprise the other figure sitting in one of the two large leather chairs in front of his desk.

"Have a seat," Lloyd said.

She sat.

Lloyd moved behind his desk, glancing once at the other man sitting across from him before giving his full attention to Sara.

"This is a little short notice," he said, "but Derrick here is in need of a pinch hitter."

Sara crossed her legs. Lloyd's habit of talking in sports metaphors had always annoyed her. When she'd first started at the firm, she tried to learn every metaphor, analogy, and term that could possibly trip off her boss's lips. But by the second year, she'd grown fed up with his "good old boys' club"-speak and merely asked him to clarify if she didn't understand something.

She pursed her lips. "What's the situation?"

In the seat next to her, Derrick Wainwright gave her an apologetic glance. Newly clean-shaven after a recent divorce, his face held a smooth, boyish quality that was taking Sara some time to get used to. The mountain-man lawyer of the office was no more.

Derrick smoothed his houndstooth pant leg. "My client is a professor at Emory University being sued by a student for sexual harassment and breach of promise. The student has no proof so we're going for a dismissal of all charges."

"Did he harass the girl?"

"Not he. She." Derrick glanced at a spot just to the left of Sara's ear before looking her again in the face. "And it's a matter of perspective."

Meaning the two of them did have an affair, but after being dropped, the student got angry. And vengeful. Not Sara's kind of thing. "Ah…I'm not sure about this one. There isn't anyone else in the office who can take the case?"

"I think you'd be better suited for this, Sara," Lloyd got up from behind his desk and cracked his knuckles. "I'm going to take an early lunch and leave you two to work this one out, but I'd really like for you to take the case. This Thompson woman isn't just some sour-faced academic who can't stop putting her puck where it doesn't belong." He paused as if to let that metaphor sink in. "Her people are well-connected in Atlanta. If the firm makes this thing go away, the family will be very grateful. They're shopping around for a firm to keep on retainer."

Lloyd gave Sara one last meaningful look before closing her inside his office with Derrick.

She unclenched her back teeth before facing Derrick again. "I guess that's that then."

"Sorry about this, Sara. But she—I just can't continue to represent her."

Realization slowly began to dawn. "Is she that bad, or that good?"

A blush worked its way up Derrick's handsome face. Before, his neatly clipped beard would have hid most of that color, given him some privacy instead of baring his emotions for Sara to see. She felt embarrassed for him.

"Ms. Thompson is very attractive," he said.

"And you're very divorced." Which meant that once off the case, he'd be free to pursue the woman. God save her from men and their hormones. Because this one couldn't keep his dick in his pants, she'd have to take on another client when her current caseload was more than enough to keep her in the office past six every night. "No problem," she murmured, her tone conveying just the opposite. "Do you have her file with you?"

Without saying a word, he pulled a thick manila folder from the briefcase at his feet and handed it over. Sara's mouth tightened. Derrick and Lloyd had both been so sure that she would take the case. Trying not to show her annoyance, she flipped the file open and skimmed the first page. The client's full name caught her eyes. And held them.

Sara looked up at Derrick. *Was the world really this small?*

"What? Did I forget to include something?" He frowned and leaned close to look at the papers in her lap.

"No," she said, her voice echoing dully in her ears. "There's more than enough here." Sara cleared her throat and closed the folder. "If I need anything else, I'll get it from her." She stood, holding the file and her life's newest earthquake, loosely in her hand. "Tell me, why did you ask me to take on this case? The woman is bisexual. Aren't you and Lloyd worried that she'll seduce me too?"

Derrick's mouth twitched. "No." As if it were the most ridiculous thing in the world that she would be ruled by emotions. "You're actually the only one in the office who I think would be immune to her seduction."

She didn't have to ask why. Sara knew that the others in the office thought of her as cold and remote. Although what Lloyd would refer to as a "team player," she didn't play with her coworkers outside of the office. At the Christmas parties, she drank and chatted, obligingly bought a secret Santa gift, sometimes even showed up with a pretty woman on her arm. But that was all. They didn't know any more about her life than they had to, and she preferred it that way.

"I'm disappointed that it wasn't my brilliant legal mind that had you and Lloyd knocking at my door." Sara made her tone deliberately neutral.

"If the boss didn't think you could win this, hard-ass or not, he wouldn't have suggested you for the case. He wants her family's business." Derrick gestured for her to precede him.

Sara nodded then stepped through the door that he held open for her. "I'll do my best."

"That's all we can ask for. Thank you." He gave another one of his naked smiles before walking in the opposite direction toward his office.

Sara watched him stride away, a hand in his pocket, the tailored black suit shifting over his lean but broad-shouldered frame as he moved. Did the Merille Thompson of the thick legal file and pending lawsuit return any of his affection? And if so, what did that mean when Sara finally saw her again?

❖

Sara walked briskly down the Emory University hallway, high heels rapping against the newly installed marble floor, her attaché gripped firmly in her hand. *This should be just like any other case.* The thought swirled in her head as she walked past closed doors, the lingering smell of dry erase markers and teenage hormones. With each step, her loosened dreadlocs bounced against her shoulders.

Near the end of the hall, she stopped before a frosted glass door. The words "Conference Room" etched across the glass assured her she was in the right place. Sara put her hand on the knob, turned it. Startled clear eyes leapt to her face, but she only raised an eyebrow before taking a chair at the head of the small rectangular table.

At twenty-eight, Rille looked…healthy. Thick blond and dark curls pulled up in a twist left a few wisps of hair framing a brown face still unlined around its aggressive bones. A pale green sweater and camisole twin-set brought out the color in her eyes, skimmed her slender yet softly rounded body. Rille was just as Sara remembered. She didn't look sick.

"Good morning," she said to her ex-lover, as if it had been only a few hours instead of eight years since they'd last seen each other.

After Rille's breakdown on the stairs in front of Sara's room, they'd never spoken again. For the first couple of weeks, it was as if Rille disappeared from the campus altogether. All attempts that Sara made to contact her were met with silence. Rille's roommate had nothing for her but a blank stare, a gentle closing of the dormitory room door in her face. No one knew where Rille had disappeared to. No one wanted to talk. Then a month later, Sara saw her, a ghostly presence near the student affairs office who did not turn when Sara called her name. But that bright hair and dark skin were unmistakable.

Then much later, Sara found out through Devi that Rille had finished up the semester at Vreeland in near-seclusion and had successfully defended her thesis. She then enrolled in a PhD program in her hometown instead of at MIT with Devi as she'd originally planned. The news had left Sara reeling. Her first lust. Gone, just like that. No explanation. No closure. Although Rille had been the one to cheat on her, to lie to her, to endanger her health, Sara felt she was the one being punished.

"Sara? Sara Chambers?"

Merille Thompson's disbelieving voice pulled Sara abruptly back to the present.

"I should feel flattered that you remember my name." The bitter words spilled from her lips, unbidden. So much for a cool and unaffected front.

Rille blinked, visibly pulling herself together. She leaned forward in her chair, a frown still hovering on her brow. "What are you doing here?"

"Working for you. I'll be your attorney from now on. Derrick felt he could no longer properly represent you."

"I didn't know you were at Winthrop and Morris." Rille crossed her arms on the table, head tilted. Hidden meanings simmered behind the opaque glass of her gaze. Sara felt the weight of that look, its undisguised appraisal. "If you'd rather I didn't work on your case, then I'm sure someone else from the firm would be happy to step into my shoes."

Rille shook her head. "Why did he abandon me?"

Sara's mouth quirked at the drama of Rille's question. "He felt it would be a conflict of interest given his *interest* in you."

Rille threw back her bright head and laughed.

"Are you serious?" She laughed again, all her equilibrium apparently regained. "A big strong man like that can't handle a little flirtation without it getting in the way of business?" She made a contemptuous noise, propped her chin in a loose fist on the conference table. "Maybe it's for the best."

"I can't see how. Derrick is a very good attorney. I've seen him win impossible cases."

"You think my case is impossible?"

"Did you sleep with that girl?"

Rille's mouth twitched. "What do you think?"

"Did you sleep with that girl?" Sara repeated, holding back a sigh. This was eight years later. There was no reason to play games with this woman.

"I don't want to talk about this here. Let's go somewhere we can have a more private conversation."

But wasn't Rille the one who suggested Derrick meet her here at the university so she could get back to her office hours afterward? She'd never stopped playing games, Sara thought. Although perhaps meeting in this atmosphere was meant to discourage Derrick's infatuation. Only Rille could say for sure.

"All right." Sara leaned back in her seat, waiting for Rille to make the next move.

Rille stood. "Let me get my things. I'll be right back."

Before Sara had a chance to register that she was waiting for her ex-lover to whisk her off to who knows where, Rille came back clutching a slim designer bag that matched her brown leather shoes. She held the conference room door open for Sara. "I'll drive," she said.

❖

Spring in Atlanta was a sinful time. In Rille's open convertible, Sara became more aware of it than ever. The air, intimate with perfume and pollen of a thousand fertile plants, pressed against her face and the sensitive whirl of her ears. Blossom-swollen crape myrtle trees reached over them to tangle the tips of their branches together turning the small back road they traveled into a semi-private arbor.

"It's a surprise to see you in Atlanta, Sara. I thought for sure you'd end up somewhere like California or New Mexico."

"Why did you think that?"

The jazz station crooned Sade and the speedometer barely moved above thirty, a gentle enough speed not to blow their attempts at conversation out the window. Rille skillfully handled the burgundy four-seater Mercedes, glancing over at Sara as she spoke.

"You always talked about warm places, remember? Whenever we were in my room, you wanted to pull the drapes around the bed and turn the heater on." Rille laughed. "Even though it was, I swear, no less than seventy degrees outside."

At the sound of Rille's uninhibited laughter, a reluctant smile tugged at Sara's mouth. Yes, she had wanted the heat when they were in college. Heat loosened Rille's tongue. Made her share herself. Sara had learned more about Rille closed up inside that thin velvet cocoon than she had anywhere else.

And Rille gave Sara her heat, although she must have been miserable. Instead of complaining, Rille insisted on being naked in the room, whether or not her roommate was there with them, crawling into the velvet-canopied bed, her skin glistening with sweat as she brought fruit or ice cream or some bit of food to sweeten her palate.

Sara's smile faded. Was this the sort of innocent flirtation Rille had indulged in with Derrick, so much so that he lost his mind and was now probably out buying an engagement ring?

"That was the past," Sara said coolly enough that it brought Rille's gaze back to her face.

Rille nodded slowly, consideringly. "Yes. So what's going on in the present then, Ms. Chambers? What are you up to these days?"

"Why don't we talk about the case? You are paying for this, after all."

"I *am* paying for this. Once we get to the restaurant, we can have a proper impersonal discussion of what your firm is getting paid for. But right now, I want to talk about you."

Sara shook wind-tossed curls out of her face. "The last time I saw you, we both thought you were going to die. Now, you seem to have recovered enough to seduce more foolish coeds. Instead of talking about me, can you tell me what changed in you between then and now?"

At first, Rille said nothing. She only pursed and unpursed her lips, staring straight ahead. "You're grown hard, little Sara. I'm not sure it suits you."

The car turned abruptly off the small road and into thicker traffic. Craftsman style homes disappeared. As they drove, the houses became older, more run down, three- and four-level apartment buildings interspersed them. A coffee shop. Then a dingy-looking bar next to a credit union. A clothing store with tie-dyed cotton dresses in the window. Gone was middle-class banality. Spring in this neighborhood had edges and teeth. They passed utility boxes grafittied with bleeding flowers and crude drawings of genitalia. A couple pressed together in an alley, making earnest love next to an overflowing Dumpster. Pierced, pale, and poor looking people strolled the sidewalks with good will in their steps. Rille pulled the car into the parking lot of a British-style pub.

"Here we are."

Rille climbed out, leaving Sara no choice but to follow. She brought her briefcase, stepping gingerly over the paved but potholed lot. Inside the pub, the black-clad server gave them two menus then indicated with a wave that they should seat themselves. Rille led Sara out to the patio, a wide-open space with wrought iron tables and chairs and a close-up view of the street. Only a short fence and the grace of four feet of sidewalk separated them from passing cars.

Rille opened the menu, and a girl appeared at the table. She wore a silver ring through her bottom lip and her entire left arm was livid with a tattoo of a blossoming cherry tree.

"Can I get you anything?" The girl's voice held traces of some sort of Irish or Welsh accent.

Rille ordered a taco salad, a side of onion rings, and an iced tea with two straws.

"Nothing for me, thanks." Sara shook her head.

"Order something. It's on me, of course."

"Of course." Sara pointedly gave the menu to the girl. "Nothing for me, thanks."

The waitress left and came back a few moments later with Rille's iced tea and a glass of water that she placed at Sara's elbow. Her perky, black-covered bottom disappeared before Sara could say a word.

While Sara watched, Rille took a pillbox from her purse and shook two tablets into her palm. She dropped the straws in her iced tea and took a long drink, swallowing nearly half the glass along with the pills. She sighed with satisfaction. "Now that you've proven that you can be difficult, we can talk about my case."

"I'm not sure if that's wise here." Sara glanced around them for emphasis. This wasn't the sort of restaurant she'd expected.

Although most of the patrons of the roadside pub looked very much caught up in their own affairs, drinking beer, exchanging loud conversation over large plates of food, or watching the wall-mounted television that showed a lively soccer game, this was as far from private as one could get.

"Can I get you to come to my office sometime this week?" she asked Rille.

"If I do, will you tell me what you've been doing over the past eight years?"

Sara raised an eyebrow. "Will you?"

Rille made a noise of disgust low in her throat, but she was smiling. "I have a feeling that my new attorney will drive me to drink."

"As long as you're drinking iced tea, I don't mind."

Rille looked away from Sara, her smile widening as the waitress reappeared with her food. "Perfect timing. I'm starved."

The girl echoed her grin, a blush working its way from her pierced lip into her pale cheeks. "I hope you enjoy it."

"I'm sure I will," Rille murmured.

Sara stared at her in amazement. *She just can't help herself.*

"I'm sick," Rille said, with a rueful smile. "Not dead."

Sara's eyes flew to her face. Did Rille just tell her—

The confirmation of it hit Sara sharply in the chest, and she opened her mouth to pull in more oxygen, suddenly breathless.

"Don't look so tragic. This can't be a surprise to you, not the way we left things. I don't want to die any sooner than the next idiot, so I do what my doctors say. I take my pills, exercise occasionally, and stay away from the really hard drugs." Rille shrugged. "That's my life."

Sara closed her mouth and swallowed hard.

"Anyway, it's good to see you." Rille mixed up the taco salad with her fork, blending the lettuce, cheese, black beans, and salsa. "I hadn't thought about college in years until you walked through that conference room door. God! That was such a long time ago."

It *was* a long time. Over the years, Sara had wondered what had happened to her. She watched the news, seeing all those reports of AIDS victims being abandoned by their families, in denial about their condition until it was too late to get medical help, spreading their infection through the community like a bullet. And she'd thought of Rille. Hoping that Rille had somehow dodged that fate and was alive and whole somewhere, living the kind of life she always wanted.

Sara watched her, at a loss for words.

Rille, not at all discomfited by her silence, took a bite of the salad, frowned, then picked up an onion ring, pried the limp vegetable from its beer batter shell, and tossed it aside. With languid motions, she tore the batter into pieces and sprinkled it over her salad. Rille did this a few more times before she tasted her salad again. She nodded in approval.

"By the way, you look stunning." She licked the oil from her lips. "At Vreeland you were cute, but now you're easily the most beautiful woman I've seen in a long time." Rille tore into another onion ring, using her teeth to separate the batter from the worm-like onion. "This is *so* good," Rille murmured around a mouthful of fried dough. "You sure you don't want to try some?"

Sara shook her head. She wanted to remain untouched by the reality of Rille's illness. Untouched by her compliments. And for the most part, she was. More than anything, those lines of Rille's seemed cheap and rehearsed, something she'd tweak depending on which woman she delivered them to. But while the words were trite and easily dismissed, Rille's eyes...They watched Sara as if she were the most important thing in that moment. Independent from the cheap seducer's trick of a mouth, those eyes took her apart piece by piece, they were grave and tender and begging to be believed.

"Listen. I have to get back to the office." Sara glanced at Rille's barely touched salad and the rubble of naked onions on her plate. "Take your time and enjoy your lunch. I'll take a cab back to the university."

"No, don't do that. Just give me a minute to get this wrapped up to go and I'll take you to your car."

"It's fine. You're obviously enjoying your meal. Don't put yourself out on my account." Before Rille could say anything else, Sara plucked her phone out of her purse, pressed the speed dial button for her usual cab company, and put the cell to her ear. When the operator picked up, she made her request. When Sara was done, she turned to Rille, briefcase in hand. She pushed back her chair and stood. "Call my assistant and make an appointment for next week. We'll talk more then."

Then she walked away. Attaché gripped firmly in her hand. Heart knocking like an exile against her chest.

To: retiredJAman@tampamail.com
From: chambers@winthrop_morris.com

Daddy, it was good to get your last letter. I miss you. Maybe some day I'll get to see the irises you planted in the backyard after I left. If I send a plane ticket, will you come see me?

Before she could second-guess herself, Sara tapped her mouse, sending the e-mail on its way. She'd never asked him to visit before, content (she thought) with their exchanged e-mails, letters, and gifts through the mail. But now something in her needed to reconnect with family more than ever. Although her life in Atlanta was financially and professionally successful, she was lonely. And that feeling of loneliness pressed in on her with each passing day.

The phone on her desk beeped, interrupting her thoughts. She pressed the intercom button.

"Yes?"

"Your eleven o'clock is here."

The computer clock said it was barely quarter to eleven. Sara toyed with the idea of making Rille wait, then rejected it as childish. "Thanks, Anthea. Send her in."

Sara dismissed her open programs from the computer screen and retrieved her legal pad and a pen. Her paralegal had already conducted interviews at the university as well as at the student's apartment and job. From Derrick's thorough notes and the paralegal's previous work, Sara had a pretty good idea how she would proceed with Rille's case. There was an excellent chance of it being dismissed.

After a single knock, Rille breezed in, smiling. A shock of loosened curls, a green body-skimming sweater dress, and high heels. Sara leaned back in her chair as Rille closed the door, tossed her purse in an empty chair, and sat on the other side of the desk.

"Your office is much nicer than Derrick's."

Sara, caught off balance, fidgeted with her pen. She hadn't thought about Derrick one way or another since taking the case from him. And she especially hadn't thought about her office versus his. What he liked, what she didn't. They both had the same furniture. The same window that ran the length of the wall showing off a sun-drenched view of the Atlanta skyline.

"I like the fern hanging in front of the window." Rille stood to get a closer view of one of the three potted plants suspended from the ceiling, the delicate green fronds moving languidly in the air-conditioned breeze. She reached up. "They're maidenhair, right?"

"Yes." Sara's hand tightened on the pen.

Rille stood before the window, silhouetted in sunlight. The sight of her body was an ache.

"Please," Sara murmured. "Sit."

A smile played with Rille's mouth. Her look challenged Sara before she slowly brought her arm back to her side and returned to her chair.

Sara laced her fingers over her lap and crossed her legs. "So tell me about this girl. How did the affair start?"

"This girl." Rille made a mocking face. "Clarissa was in one of my classes during her senior year."

An undergraduate? Sara's fingers twitched, but she said nothing.

"She applied to the PhD program in physics for the next year, and I gave her the proper and deserved encouragement. Without any exaggeration, Clarissa is a brilliant girl. During the summer when she didn't have classes, she started coming around the department, just to get a feel for what graduate school was like. At least that's what she told me." Rille paused, tapping a long, blunt-tipped finger against her chin as if considering what to say next. "That's when it started."

Sara could imagine that Rille didn't try very hard to put the brakes on the relationship. First of all, the girl wasn't even technically a student when the affair started. And second, from her photo, Clarissa Wilson was gorgeous.

"Did you promise her the position as your graduate assistant?"

"In the heat of the moment, yes, but—"

"Does she have proof?"

"No. Not unless she taped us having sex."

"And can you be sure she didn't do that?"

"Positive. I always had her at my place. Or public places that she had no control over."

Really? Sara jotted down a note.

Rille tucked a curl behind her ear. "I know you want to know if there have been others."

"As a matter of fact, I don't. We already have several people willing to testify that this girl actively pursued you. She talked about you to anyone who would listen, even published a short story in an underground magazine about her fantasy of having sex with you in the physics lab."

A delighted laugh exploded from Rille. "You're joking!"

"She may be brilliant, but she's not particularly smart." *Fortunately*. Sara tapped her pencil against the pad. "I want to set up a meeting with her attorney. Preferably next week. What dates are good for you?"

Rille fixed her with a look of growing respect. "Maybe it's a good thing Derrick was frightened off. He definitely wasn't moving this fast on the case."

Ah, Derrick. Sara held up a hand to stem the rush of enthusiasm. "This thing isn't resolved yet. We're just meeting with her and her attorney to put things on the table."

"Still, I'll remain cautiously optimistic." Rille pulled a datebook from her purse. "Clarissa is costing me too much damn money for this to drag on."

Sara pursed her lips, already regretting what she was going to ask. "Speaking of Derrick, has he contacted you recently?"

"Yes." Rille's eyes caught hers between the chiaroscuro curls.

Sara bit the inside of her cheek. Waited.

Rille spoke before Sara's teeth broke flesh. "He called and asked me to dinner, but I declined. He's not who I'm interested in."

Sara nodded once. "I'm sure he was disappointed, but he'll get past it." She picked up her calendar. "Now, about that appointment for next week."

After they found dates that would work for them, Sara called up Clarissa Wilson's attorney. While Rille sat and listened silently to the telephone conversation, Sara and the gruff-voiced attorney settled on a date to meet for the following Thursday.

"Wonderful, I'll see you and your client in my office then, Mark."

"Sounds good, Sara. See you Thursday."

She hung up the phone. "That's done."

Rille grinned. "Great!" Then at Sara's cautioning look, she toned it down to a smile. "But I won't celebrate yet."

Sara nodded and slid her notepad in the desk drawer. Although she couldn't say it to Rille yet, this was almost over. She waited for a feeling of relief, but it never came. *Damn.*

Rille picked up her purse. Slid her datebook inside. "Even though we haven't won yet, can I talk you into having drinks with me tonight?"

"No. You can't."

"Not even to catch up on old times?"

Sara felt her fingers twitch again. "Especially *not* to catch up on old times."

"What are you afraid of?" Rille's clear green gaze was quiet. Penetrating.

Not you. "What we have between us here and now is a working relationship. Don't try to make this something it's not. Don't bring up the past. Don't force me to drop your case, because if you keep pushing me, I will."

Rille's eyebrows went up. Her lips pursed tight. "All right. I think you've made things very clear." She rose to her feet. "Thank you, Ms. Chambers, for all you've done. I look forward to concluding our business."

After Rille left, Sara sank into her chair and turned to drown her thoughts in the city skyline. She hadn't lied to Rille. It wasn't Rille who frightened her. Sara was afraid of herself. Even after eight years and over a dozen other lovers, most of them *better* lovers, her reaction to Rille was still powerful.

The longer Rille sat across from her—shifting in the chair, crossing and uncrossing her legs, the rough voice an undeniable aural caress while flashes of arrogance transformed the curve of her lips—the deeper Sara fell. It was more than memories of the past. More even than the resurrection of feelings she hadn't felt before or since Vreeland. It was because she felt Rille moving into that empty space creating itself inside Sara over the past few years. Because of that, she knew she was in trouble.

❖

"*Now* is it okay for me to celebrate?"

Rille smiled at Sara from across the conference room table, a wicked grin fanning small lines from the corners of her eyes.

"I think so," Sara conceded, sliding her files into her briefcase.

She looked up again at the complainant's lawyer, Mark Reynolds, an old classmate of hers. He tipped his imaginary hat to Sara then turned to escort the unhappy young woman from the room, his hand firm on the small of her back. Clarissa Wilson was even prettier in person, tall and fleshy with a shaved head and big gold circles dangling from ears shaped like question marks. Throughout the meeting, her eyes kept moving restlessly over Rille as if searching for the thing Rille had promised but never delivered. It was obvious she was devastated by the outcome of her relationship with Rille.

Clarissa had decided to settle the suit without going to court, letting her grudge go for what amounted to an apology from Rille and a piddling amount of money that Rille's family gladly paid.

"You were absolutely brilliant," Rille said. "Thank you for everything."

"Don't thank me, pay the firm. Lloyd's been angling after your family's business. But I'm sure you know that."

"I do."

"The firm is a good one. The Thompsons could do a lot worse."

"I'll let Mummy know that." Rille picked up her purse from where it lay on the table then stepped close to shake Sara's hand. "Thank you again. I appreciate that you gave this your best." Her touch was cool and firm.

"I wouldn't have given anything else."

As Rille turned and headed out the door, Sara tried to hide her amazement at how differently Rille had acted from the last time they met. Throughout the meeting, she'd been perfectly professional. No innuendoes, no offer to go for drinks, dancing, or otherwise. Disappointment was too strong a word for what Sara felt. But it was close.

Behind her closed office door, she relaxed with a glass of coconut water and a casual glance through her calendar. It was barely eleven o'clock. She didn't have another appointment until her three o'clock court date with one of her less interesting clients, an accountant yoked in on fraud charges.

Sara looked up from the calendar as someone knocked on her door. "Come in."

A burst of yellow entered first. Roses. Then Anthea's smiling face. "Look what the delivery guy just dropped off for you."

"Ah..." Sara wrinkled her brow. "For me? Are you sure?"

"Unless there's another Sara Chambers in the office I don't know about." The assistant arranged the flowers in their clear vase on the small bistro table near the window. "There's an envelope." Anthea plucked it out of the nest of roses and gave it to Sara, then stood back, smiling, waiting for her to open it.

Sara waved the white envelope under her nose, smelling nothing but roses. She looked at Anthea with a wry twist of her mouth. "If it's anything good, I'll let you know."

Anthea didn't hide her disappointment. She turned, dignified once again, and walked out of Sara's office, closing the door behind her. Sara chuckled. Of anyone in the office, only Anthea dared to tease her. Sometimes it was nice.

The card inside the envelope was thick and plain.

"For a job well done," it said, signed with Rille's flowing signature. Also in the envelope, two tickets to something called Dinner & Jazz Under the Stars scheduled for nearly two weeks from that night. Sara glanced over at the flowers, bursting with vitality even as they slowly died in their little glass prison. Yellow roses, she'd read somewhere, could be a symbol of happiness. Or deceit.

She tucked the tickets and card back into the envelope. Dropped it face down in her desk drawer. It was still there when she turned off the lights that evening, closed the door, and walked down the darkened corridor heading home for a long weekend of rest.

❖

Sara leaned against the railing, the crystal and amber lights of her adopted city spread out before her. Standing seventy stories above Atlanta, it was easy to fool herself into believing that despite the hushed conversations taking place behind her, she stood alone on the terrace of the glass covered restaurant on top of one of the tallest buildings in the city, and that the jazz quartet on the stage played only for her pleasure. Sara closed her eyes.

"I wasn't sure you'd come."

Rille's low words tapped her lightly on the shoulder.

"Up until about a couple of hours ago, I wasn't sure either." Sara straightened and turned around.

Rille stood close enough to pinch. Hair pulled up into a simple knot this time, diamond earrings and a tiny bag in her hand. A fitted white cocktail dress with a bow at its high waist made Rille's skin glow under the lights.

Behind her, the rest of the restaurant lay spread out like a glass enclosed fairy tale complete with glittering princes and queens. The band wove its sultry sounds throughout the room, while waiters promenaded between tables with their trays of sumptuous foods and drinks.

"Whatever the reason you came out, I'm glad. Now that I'm not your client anymore, I wanted to enjoy your company without you thinking too hard about it."

"It would be foolish not to think around you."

Rille chuckled. "Do you have a table yet?"

"Yes, actually. We got one as soon as we came."

"We?"

"Of course. You did give me two tickets." Sara smiled in the face of Rille's discomfort. "Was I supposed to save one for you?"

Rille's gaze skittered away. "No. No. Obviously, I got in on my own."

But the second ticket had been a decoy. An expensive distraction meant for Sara to think that Rille expected her to take someone else. It was rare enough to catch Rille off her game that Sara relished it, feeling warmth in her chest long after her smile faded. A dark-suited figure coming from the sliding glass doors to the patio where she stood caught her eye.

"Oh, good. Here's my date now." She waved.

Rille turned around, checking out the other women in the spacious restaurant, most of them wreathed in diamonds and laughter, looking as if they belonged here at the glass covered oasis in the sky. The tall man with salt and pepper hair obviously caught her by surprise.

"Rille, this is my father, Neville Chambers." Her father, debonair in his dark blazer, open necked white shirt, and slacks, smiled and clasped Rille's hand. "Daddy, this is Rille Thompson, an old friend of mine from college."

"Good evening, sir." Rille's discomfort gave way to a glow of real pleasure.

"My dear." His Jamaican accent enveloped the few words in melody. "Always good to meet the people in my Sara's life. I don't get to see too many of you since I'm down in Florida and she seems set on making a life up here."

"Daddy!" Sara squeezed his elbow.

He grinned down at her. "Shall I escort you ladies to the table or leave you to your private conversation?"

"Our table, please." Rille said. "I can talk to Sara anytime."

She threw a smirk over her shoulder and tucked her hand into the crook of his elbow, maneuvering Sara to take his other arm. They made their way back into the restaurant and to their table. He pulled out each of their seats before taking his own.

"In my retirement, I've been reading up on the role of a gentleman in America." He winked at Rille as he arranged his napkin over his lap. "It's a complex business, but I'll enjoy fumbling my way through it during this visit."

A waiter materialized at their small table. "Would you care for anything?" he asked.

Startled at the abrupt appearance, Sara blinked up at him in surprise. But Rille didn't miss a beat.

"Oh, yes," she said with one of her laughing looks, and grabbed the menu.

They ordered their entrees and agreed on a bottle of white wine to share. Sara, mindful of her low tolerance to alcohol, urged the waiter to keep the water carafe full even though she might be the only one drinking from it.

When the waiter left, Rille continued as if there had been no interruption.

"You don't look old enough to be retired, Mr. Chambers."

"Call me Neville. When Sara was in college, you girls could 'Mr. Chambers' me all day long. These days my vanity needs the help."

Rille laughed, a thrilling, full-bodied sound that attracted the attention of people nearby. "Neville it is then."

Two weeks before when Sara's father had accepted her invitation to come to Atlanta for a few days, she was so surprised that she nearly forgot to be happy. Had it been that easy all these years? Just ask and he would come? In Tampa, he didn't maintain much of a social life, only preferred to stay at home with his garden, and his wife who'd decided against retiring and continued to work at the seafood factory. He'd never been to Atlanta before, and Sara wanted to make sure he relaxed and had a good time on his visit.

Rille's invitation had lain in her desk up until that afternoon when her father asked about Atlanta's famous nightlife. When she mentioned the concert, his eyes lit up. He didn't even complain about shopping for the new coat and slacks before they had to rush back to the condo for a shower and change of clothes.

"This is a nice place," he said. "The music isn't bad. They could use a steel drum in that band, but not everything can be perfect." He flashed Rille a smile. "And the view of the skyline is impressive."

"I'm glad you like it, Daddy." *I'm glad you came.*

They shared a warm look.

This was his first night in Atlanta after having arrived that afternoon. Sara took the day off to pick him up from the airport and take him out to a long and leisurely lunch. Once back at her condo they'd talked around things, only touching on the biggest issue on both their minds. But he would be with her for a week. They had time.

"So how long have you been in town, Neville?" Rille asked. "Has Sara been showing you a good time?"

"I just got in today, my dear. I don't want to wear out my experience in this grand city too soon."

"Never that. There's much more to see in Atlanta than most could imagine. I was born here and still haven't exhausted its possibilities."

"I'm surprised at that," Sara murmured, sipping her water. "In school, I remember you getting bored very easily."

Rille glanced at her. "Back then I was a child. Now I have a renewed appreciation for things I'd put aside."

The food arrived then, knocking whatever Sara was going to say back down her throat. With a flourish, like a magician debuting his greatest trick, their tuxedoed waiter placed the steaming plates on the table. Sara's pan-seared salmon with a pomegranate glaze and a sprinkle of black sesame seeds. For Rille, garlic sautéed scallops arranged with a perfect hillock of lobster mashed potatoes. And her father's braised short ribs with baby carrots and tiny onions masquerading as pearls.

"Gorgeous!" Rille breathed, reaching for her fork even before the waiter drifted away.

Sara had to agree. Her father reached for her hand and they quietly began to say grace, forcing Rille, who already had a piece of scallop in her mouth, to drop her fork and join in. The succulent food sweetened their tongues too much for conversation. Instead of talking, they ate, content to listen to the tinkling melody of the piano climbing and falling in perfect harmony with the velvet voice of the woman dressed in a fitted tuxedo and tails. With her thick black hair moving like a live thing around her face and shoulders, the singer moved gracefully among her band mates on the small stage. Her red, red lips pursed as she crooned a song about delicious heartbreak, seeming to make love to the 1940s style chrome microphone.

As she ate, Sara's eyes flitted between Rille and the woman on stage. Something told her that Rille was performing too, trying to make a good impression with Sara and with her father. There was no point; soon they would be out of each other's lives again. A sudden sadness at the thought caught Sara by surprise. She looked away from her and focused on the food before her.

When dinner was little more than smears on the white plates, conversation resumed and Rille became a glimmering butterfly again. If nothing else, Sara mused, Rille was fun to watch.

"Do you mind if I ask your daughter to dance, Neville?"

Sara put her wine glass down. "Ah…"

"Not at all," Sara's father said, surprising her.

Swift heat came into her face when he squeezed her hand.

"It would be good to see my Sara have a little fun," he continued. The corners of his eyes crinkled as he smiled.

They'd never directly addressed the issue of Sara's sexuality. From what she gathered the one and only time it came up in conversation, he'd always known about her preference for women. And supported her in a way that her mother never had.

Rille held out her hand. "Will you do me the honor?"

She kept Sara's hand in hers all the way to the dance floor, ignoring the looks they attracted.

"You know that people are staring," Sara murmured as Rille held her close for the band's rendition of Johnny Hartman's "Easy Living."

"Stop caring so much what they think. Relax." Her hand settled on the small of Sara's back. Lightly. Respectfully.

They moved in perfect rhythm with each other among the sprinkling of other dancers. Cheek to cheek. Rille's subtly spiced perfume—ginger?—distracting Sara's nose. This was a new experience for her, being out with someone so…out. What if her father had no idea that she was gay? What if she wasn't comfortable holding a woman this close in public?

"You're very presumptuous," she said without heat.

"Isn't that what you liked about me in college?"

Ah. Had she been that obvious as a school girl? She laughed at her teenaged self. Poor Sara. So easy to read.

"College was a long time ago," she said.

"That we already established." Rille twirled her and pulled her back in. "You're not as cold as you pretend, Sara. Not at all."

"Why can't I be?"

"Because in my arms, you burn." Rille's breath touched her neck. "I remember."

Sara released a sigh. "Leave the past behind, Rille. We're both different women. We have different lives now."

"Absolutely correct. But I'd still like to get to know you better. I'm no longer your client so that excuse is out the window."

As the song ended, Sara pulled her hand free of Rille's and turned to walk back to the table and her father. But he wasn't where they left him.

She spun around. "I wonder where—"

"Relax, he's at the bar." Rille gestured to where her father sat talking with the bartender and another man. A barely touched whiskey sat in front of him.

"After all this cosmopolitan exposure, I wonder if your father will be able to go back to a normal life in Tampa?" Rille's words, gently teasing, surprised a smile out of Sara.

"Daddy is adaptable. I think he'll do fine."

"I think you're right about that." Rille sat at the table, then, after a slight hesitation, picked up the drink menu. Within moments, a waiter appeared.

"Very prompt service," Rille said, approval lighting her voice.

"There always seems to be when you're around."

"Ha!" She ordered a Dewar's on ice and, after Sara indicated she wanted nothing, sent the waiter on his way.

Rille cleared her throat and clasped her thin hands. "You know, I think I owe you some truth."

"Oh, you've been lying to me already?" The acid in Sara's tone splashed up between them.

"Ouch." Rille toyed with a loosened curl at the back of her neck. "The person I was in college may very well deserve that, but the one sitting in front of you doesn't. I'm not the same."

"Why should I believe that?" *Why should I believe anything you say?*

Rille must have seen beyond the disbelief in her face to the nearly decade old feelings of resentment for past actions.

"Sara, that day you told me that I might be sick, I lost my mind. Even after I spoke with that RA and he tried to get me to calm down and take things logically. I'd seen the truth of it in your face. And I couldn't look at you anymore."

Sara glanced over at the bar to her father. He laughed at something the thick-middled man behind the bar said and took a sip of his drink. Her eyes moved back to Rille.

"Jason, the RA, went to the doctor with me a few days later to take the test," Rille continued. "When the results came back, I had another breakdown. They confirmed the worst, and all I wanted to do was curl up and die. But I didn't. I managed to finish the semester, finish my thesis, and because I didn't know what to expect, I gave up my place at

MIT and enrolled in a program here in Atlanta." Rille paused when the waiter reappeared with her drink. She put her mouth to the glass. "As you can expect, my parents were surprised, but glad, I think, to have me home. I found a regular doctor near the school and lived with Mummy and Daddy while I finished my degree."

"Did they help you deal with your illness?" Sara knew that both Rille's parents were doctors and might have access to more advanced information or medicine than was available to the general public.

"I never told them. They don't know." Rille shrugged. "Anyway, as the years passed, I figured I wasn't going to die, so I just made adjustments. And here I am." She toyed with the rim of her glass, circling it with the tips of her fingers.

Watching her, Sara remembered what those fingers could do. She took a long sip of her water.

"I still don't understand how you can live in the same city as your parents, move in the same circles—I assume—and they haven't noticed anything different about you or your habits."

"They don't pay that close attention to me," Rille said. "Unless my doctor came out point-blank and told them, there would be nothing for them to notice. They're not the most attentive people."

Sara clamped down on the impulse to pity her, and instead made a noncommittal motion. Rille appeared to have survived it all intact and was even more herself than ever.

"Not to sound unsympathetic or anything, but why are you telling me this?"

"Because I think you deserve my honesty. Over the last few days, I've had the chance to think a lot about the past. Even with what I'm going through now with this tainted blood, my lies are what I regret the most."

"You're just trying to tell me whatever I want to hear to get in my pants."

Rille dipped her head low to peek at Sara through a fan of lashes. She smiled. "Is it working?"

It was. Too late, she realized she had been leaning toward Rille, her body a pliant and attentive slope.

"Daddy's been gone a long time," she said, feeling her face grow hot with guilt. She'd been more interested in the words in Rille's mouth than what her father was up to. That guilt brought her to her feet and to the bar where her father still sat.

"Hey, Daddy. Why so far away?"

"I wanted to get myself a real drink." He glanced over his shoulder to the table with Rille's solitary figure. "Besides, I thought you ladies needed some time to talk." He put a finger under her chin and lifted it, forcing her gaze to meet his just like he used to when she was a child. "You know, the music sounds just as good from here as it did from the table."

She batted his hand away, grinning.

"I hope we didn't drive you away, Neville." Rille came up behind them, her hand warm on Sara's shoulder. "These days it's hard to get me to shut up, especially when I'm with your beautiful daughter."

Sara twitched under Rille's palm.

"Trust me, I understand. I was infatuated once." He laughed, tickled at his own joke.

A loud crash jerked Sara's attention from her father.

"Slippery bottle." Behind the bar, the bartender shrugged in feigned nonchalance before glancing around to see who else had noticed his accident. He knelt to sweep up the glass fragments at his feet.

"And I think that's a sign for us to return to the table. The unexpected arrival of such beautiful company is making my new friend nervous." Her father dropped a ten-dollar bill on the bar and nodded at the bartender before standing up. "Shall we?"

They moved back to the table where they shared dessert—bread pudding made with croissants infused with bands of dark chocolate and pistachios—and a bottle of port. With the music from the quartet falling as background to their conversation, Rille and Sara's father charmed each other, exchanging compliments and laughter while Sara half participated, watching Rille's ease with her father and feeling bewildered by the turn of events. But she should have remembered that Rille could be very charismatic when she wanted to be. And tonight, she apparently wanted just that.

The sweet wine that spilled over her tongue helped Rille to enchant her senses. Sara relaxed into the evening, allowing herself to be charmed too. She didn't shrug Rille's surreptitious hand from her thigh. Instead, she stayed laughing at the table until the waiters glanced meaningfully around the otherwise empty restaurant where even the band stood packing up their equipment and a tall boy with a mop lurked, waiting to clean the floors.

In the underground parking deck, Sara's father and Rille exchanged a warm good-bye hug.

"I like this woman," he said, eyes dancing between Rille and Sara. "Hopefully, when I come back to Atlanta I'll see you two together again."

"I'm sure we can get together for dinner again or something like that."

"Or something," Rille said, conspiracy plain in the smile she gave Sara's father. "Enjoy the rest of your visit, Neville. It was truly a pleasure to meet you." She squeezed his arm then kissed Sara briefly on the cheek before getting into her car.

Sara didn't watch her drive away. Only opened the door for her father before getting behind the wheel. Thankfully, her buzz from the wine had worn off and she could navigate the well-lit streets without worrying about attracting police attention.

"She's a really nice girl." Her father leaned back against the seat watching the city lights pass by the car window.

"Rille can be."

"And you like her."

"I'm trying not to."

Her father chuckled before his face settled into grave lines. "Life is too short to waste it on futile things, my Sara."

Life is too short.

Sometimes it did seem that way. Things happening too soon. Friends passing in, then out of her life. Five years, then ten, gone. In the blink of an eye, twenty.

"She's not always a good person, Daddy. In college, that tortured me."

But with the flavor of their shared port still on her tongue, the music from the band still echoing in her ears, it was difficult to recall those old hurts. Oh, she remembered the infidelities and lies all too clearly. Yet the sting of them had eased. Despite everything, she wanted that old madness. The vertigo-inducing high of being with Rille. She wanted to be the center of her gaze, her touch, her smile.

It was dangerous loving that woman. If nothing else, Sara knew that. Rille's coldness. Her often self-serving nature. And that damn

HIV. Since Rille came back into her life, even in the face of her earlier denial that she wanted Rille again, Sara had been doing research into the disease, called clinics to find out the likelihood of female-to-female transmission. Slight, but not impossible, they told her. Then she asked what steps she could take to lower risk. Yes, she was afraid, but she was also ready.

"Are you trying to talk yourself out of a decision you've already made, my Sara?" her father asked.

"Maybe." A smile pricked at her lips. But she already knew.

He laughed and squeezed her hand.

At the condo, her father only yawned, signaling with a kiss on her cheek that it was well past his bedtime and he wanted to rest. After the lights flickered off in the spare bedroom, Sara changed her clothes, left a note in the kitchen for the next day, then got back into her car.

The Atlanta landscape again. Distant stars glinting beyond her sunroof as she stopped at the red light. But no second thoughts.

When she knocked at the house with the ruthlessly manicured lawn, visible even in the glow from the far-off streetlamp, Sara invited those seconds thoughts, waited for them to rush and overpower her, for them to shove her back down the cobbled path and to her car sitting ghostlike in the driveway. Those thoughts didn't come.

Instead, the door opened.

Her breath rushed out. "Don't say anything."

Rille's surprised mouth fell shut, her eyes blinked once, but she obeyed Sara's hushed command and opened the door wider. Sara came in and closed it with the weight of her body, pulling Rille forward while she fell back against the sturdy wood, hand hooked in the burnished curls at the nape of her neck. Those curls, rougher than they seemed, clung immediately to her fingers. The mouth under hers opened. And kissed back.

ALL GOOD THINGS...
SARA/ATLANTA

I think you're bored." Sara put the last plate in the dishwasher and closed it. "Bored and self destructive." She programmed the machine, stabbing at the buttons, then turned it on.

"*Self*-destructive? I don't think so." Rille turned from the refrigerator, a sandwich in her hand. Looking at Sara, she peeled off its plastic wrap and bit into the neat stack of bread, vegetables, and meat. She crumpled the plastic in her hand.

"Jesus." Sara left the kitchen, shaking her head.

It had been days, or maybe just a few hours, since Rille confessed there was a girl at the university she had a very unprofessor-like crush on. "She reminds me of myself when I was in college," she'd said, a smirk tugging at her lips. "Fearless."

Fury erupted in Sara's belly. But she held it in. Instead of letting it explode, she said, "Oh, really?" before getting up and walking out of the house. Hours passed before she was able to return home. Hours of walking around the neighborhood and along the paved paths of the university campus, her mind flooded with what had brought her to this place. On the way back home, she held on to herself, hugging her torso against the bite of spring breeze that already nipped at her bare shoulders and arms. Was this girl the reason for Rille's moods and emotional distance? The reason that it felt Sara was getting less and less attention from Rille? It was *bullshit*.

With Rille trailing behind her from the kitchen, Sara treaded heavily up the stairs and into the bedroom. Near the bed, she turned.

"You know I don't like anyone eating in here."

Rille walked in anyway, but she moved the sandwich away from her mouth, still chewing. "Is this because of what I said yesterday?"

Was it just yesterday? "What the fuck do you think?"

Rille's jaw stopped moving. She gulped, swallowing the bit of sandwich as if also digesting the fact that Sara just cursed at her. Sara never cursed.

"You're angry with me."

"Do you have any idea what I've given up to be with you? No—" Sara abruptly shook her head. "Do you even care that I've given up things to be with you?"

Rille stared at her. Speechless for the first time since Sara had known her.

Why did I even ask? She turned, stumbled around the bedroom, unable to recall what she was doing in the bedroom in the first place. "Dammit." She raked fingers through her hair. Pressed palms against her hot cheeks.

Rille's eyes darted around the room, flitting over then past Sara. She put the sandwich to her mouth and took a bite. Lettuce crunched between her teeth. Crumbs from the whole grain bread tumbled down the front of her blouse and scattered across the hardwood floor. Yesterday's submerged rage bubbled to Sara's surface.

"Get the fuck out of my goddamn bedroom with that piece of shit, motherfucking sandwich!"

Rille startled. The sandwich fell from her hand and tumbled to the floor in its separate pieces.

"You know what?" Sara threw her hands up. "Never mind. I'll leave. You can have all this to yourself. All your lies. All your promises. Your *crumbs*."

Sara grabbed a suitcase from the top of the closet, jerked open the drawers of her dresser, tossed in her clothes. Bits of small things—panties, bras, stockings, a purple blindfold—tumbled to the floor in the uncertain transition between the drawer and suitcase.

"Wait! What are you doing?" Rille wrestled the suitcase away. More silken flotsam against the cherry hardwoods. She dragged it to the other side of the bed, out of Sara's reach.

"I'm tired," Sara said, her voice soft. She held out her hand. "Please give me my suitcase."

"No. I can't let you do this."

"Let?" Sara's eyes narrowed.

Rille immediately backpedaled. "No, what I mean to say is—"

"I've *let* you get away with everything. You brought a man into my bed, into my life, and all I said was 'okay.' You wanted me to move from my condo in town to this little suburb with higher property taxes." She ground her back teeth. "And I gave in. All that nonsense is done." Sara felt as if her blood bubbled just under the skin, threatening to incinerate her. "Right now the only thing that I'll allow you to do is let me go."

"Sara." Rille dragged the suitcase even farther away, her voice a low lull. She moved toward Sara, arms held out. "Sara." Smells from her recent meal—of mustard, cold bread, and turkey—brushed Sara's nose. Her hands moved in languid circles on Sara's arms. Rille hummed her name again.

She allowed Rille to pull her close, allowed her anger to be tucked away again. Her head fell forward. "Please," Rille said.

The turbulent breath inside her eased. Rille pulled her closer then down onto the unmade bed that still smelled like the three of them. "Don't be hasty. I know you're angry."

Yes, Sara was angry. It felt like she had been angry for so long. Angry and impotent and dragged along on a tide not of her choosing. And now after having let go of many of her life's possibilities—for Rille—Rille was abandoning her, giving everything Sara had sacrificed for to that girl. On the bed, she rolled onto her side, away from Rille but felt her move to follow, adjusting herself to tuck Sara into her body's shallow cup. Beyond the bedroom window, the sky was an empty blue.

"Don't be angry," Rille murmured, lips a moist apology against Sara's neck.

Sara flinched and turned over. But not away. Not this time. That's what she would do if there were more time. She pressed her lips to Rille's and Rille made a low sound in her throat, one of victory, and opened her mouth. Slid her hands down to pull Sara against her.

Their lovemaking had come a long way. Before Rille had taken her virginity in college, Sara had no idea what to expect from sex. Or perhaps she expected too much—a miraculous transformation into womanhood, into realizing the sensual person she was meant to be. But now she knew sex as animal. Every beast for herself.

Some days, it meant pleasure; wanting hunger to claw at Rille until Rille surrendered herself completely, until the words she spoke weren't her own, until she'd do anything Sara asked. Beg. Cry. Bleed. Just for the storm of orgasm to decimate that need and wash her clean.

Some days, sex was surrender. To a lover's touch. Not a particularly gentle one, but a knowing one. This surrender came from giving Rille the satisfaction of knowing that she could make Sara come as many times in one night as she had fingers.

Today, though, sex meant good-bye.

Under her, Rille smiled. Offering herself, ready to be pleased. Sara pushed aside Rille's clothes, not needing the full revelation of body to appreciate the supple skin, the curve of breasts, to slip her hand between thighs that loosened around the assertive musk. She loved the way Rille groaned her name, how she bit her lip, turning her eyes away so she wouldn't have to face the one making her lose control. Hips thrust against Sara's hand, provoking the humid scratch of pubic hairs into her palm. Her breasts, dotted with sweat, trembled.

Sara devoured those breasts, pressed her face into the musky sweat between them. Sighed in the smell of Rille's desire. For her.

"Oh! God!"

Rille bucked against the sheets and tore her gaze wide open. She didn't wait to recover; instead, she pounced on Sara, mouth open and ferocious. Kissing everywhere. While Sara fought for pleasure under the firm grip of Rille's hands, water leaked from her tightly closed eyes. Rille stole her senses twice, leaving her thrashing like a hooked fish in the bed.

Her body quieted. Her breath steadied. The minute aftershocks released their hold on her sensitized nerves. Rille watched her, a smile on her damp mouth.

"You know," Rille murmured, her hand stroking Sara's bare hip. "Six years ago when we came together again, I thought I had been given another chance." At Sara's attentive silence, she continued. "A chance to do what, I didn't know. But I knew I had to take it. Those first few months were so…transforming. I thought I could become someone else with you. Someone better."

"Then what happened?"

"Life, I guess."

"Reality, you mean." Sara blinked at the blurring image of sky and light beyond Rille's shoulder. "The first months *were* incredible," she said, refocusing on Rille. Lashes fluttered against Rille's cheek as Sara traced a sharp cheekbone, the low dip of her nose.

Six years ago, she thought she had been handed a renewed universe. With Rille, she had night after night of explosive, getting-to-know-you-again sex. The feeling of opening herself emotionally for the first time in years. Of falling free of disguises and pretense. Yes, those first months were paradise. Rille had given her everything she'd ever dreamed of in a lover and a potential partner.

"You're at your best when you want something," Sara said quietly. "But once you have it, your life is meaningless again and you start to treat people as if they're meaningless too."

Rille flinched under her touch. The dark eyes snapped open.

"I've never treated you like that. You mean everything to me."

Sara smiled at the lie. So dramatic. "That's such an ordinary and sweet thing to say. I'm tempted to believe you."

"You should just believe me. Don't doubt."

"I can't. You're a liar." Sara tapped Rille's mouth. Gently. "A pretty and sincere liar." She whispered the last like an endearment. A love word.

"And because of this you're still going to leave me?" Rille sat up, brows lowering.

"Yes. Yes, I am." Sara lay on her back below Rille's looming height, slim torso, the stalk of a neck, jaw firm with the beginnings of anger.

Rille's stare sharpened. "Until I saw you again after college, I never saw myself as ordinary. Never. But over the years, you made me that way. Feeling love, wanting validation, even a fucking house in the suburbs. I found myself protecting your feelings," Rille spat this last as if it was the worst. "Now that you've made me into this ordinary *thing*, you want to leave?" She pushed herself off the bed and yanked her clothes into some semblance of order. The curls loosened from their earlier tussle crackled with electricity around her face. "Fuck you, Sara Chambers."

Her footsteps hurried across the floor. The door slammed.

Cotton sheets shifted under Sara as she turned to the window. The Japanese maple waved its banner red leaves, bowed its head to the strengthening wind. Could she really do it? Was this really the end of them? Her throat felt dry and torn. Breath rasped through her open mouth.

A loud curse and a series of laddering bumps jerked Sara's attention from herself. She sat up. "Rille?"

Without waiting for an answer, she dashed to the bedroom door, flung it open, and ran down the short hallway. "Everything okay?"

A groan and another thump drew her to the stairs.

"My God…"

Rille lay on her back, a twisted doll, at the bottom of the stairs. Her head moved slowly from side to side as if searching for something she'd lost. Naked, Sara rushed down the stairs, careful to hold on to the railing.

"Don't move!"

But Rille didn't listen. Before Sara could reach her, she fumbled up for the banister, trying to drag herself up, but slipped and toppled backward, smashing her head into the bottom step. Blood exploded through the blond curls, spread across the cherry hardwood stair. Her eyes fell closed. She didn't move again.

"Rille!"

The pulse in Rille's neck beat sluggishly, but it was there. Sara grabbed the cordless phone from its stand near the banister and called 911. "There's been an accident," she gasped to the woman who answered the phone. "Please tell me what to do."

ALL GOOD THINGS...

STEPHEN/ATLANTA

There's someone on the phone for you." Manny poked his newly shaved head into the office.

"Thanks." Stephen absently picked up the phone, his mind still on the compact bike pumps he was thinking of carrying in the store. They weren't as good quality as the ones they now sold, but students and bikers on a budget would appreciate them. "Stephen here. What can I do for you?"

"There's been an accident." Sara's vibrato voice seized him in the throat.

He was halfway out of his chair even as the questions tumbled out of him. "What happened? Where are you?"

"It's not me. Rille fell." A rough breath distorted her voice. "We're at Emory University Hospital."

He drew a breath of his own. "Okay."

It took him twenty minutes to get to the hospital, find a parking space, and run down the hall through sharp medicinal smells to grab a pacing Sara by the arms.

"Tell me."

He felt the eyes of the other people in the waiting room on him. Through their coughs and specific sounds of pain, through the noise of the television, he focused on Sara.

"She fell down the stairs." The skin around Sara's mouth was pinched and tight as she spoke. "We had an argument."

Did you push her? He wanted to ask, but as soon as the thought burst into his brain, he knew it couldn't have happened that way. Sara was not impulsive. No matter how much Rille pushed and pushed, Sara would never push back. Not like this. Between his hands, she shivered as if cold and Stephen impulsively pulled her against his chest. She didn't pull away.

"I prayed for her," Sara whispered. "She needs to be all right."

"She will be. Don't worry." Stephen said the words into her hair, wanting to believe them himself. "Have the doctors said anything yet?"

"No. They just took her away." Sara plucked at the front of his shirt. "She was so still."

Stephen walked with her to the nearly empty row of padded chairs, tugging her down beside him to wait. But after a moment, she shrugged him off to pace the carpeted floor again. In her oversized T-shirt, yoga pants, and tennis shoes, she looked very young, like one of Rille's students. Her curling locks spilled around her face and down her back. She pushed them away and behind her ears as she paced, looking at the wall clock after each complete circuit of the room.

More than an hour passed before someone finally came in with news for them.

"Sara Chambers?"

Stephen dropped the magazine he'd picked up in desperation for something to take his mind off their unknown. Sara whirled to face him, her eyes wide. She held out her hand to him and he took it. The slim brown doctor in green scrubs introduced himself as Dr. Benipal, shifting the clipboard he carried to shake Sara's hand.

"This is Stephen," she said to the doctor. "He's also listed on the paperwork I gave the nurse as family."

Dr. Benipal shook his hand too, wrinkled forehead giving him a look of gravity and concern. "It's not good news," he said. "I'm afraid that Ms. Thompson is in a coma."

The horror of the doctor's words abruptly washed over Stephen. *A coma? How hard had she fallen?* He felt Sara sag against him. "What does that mean?" he asked.

"Her condition is serious but stable. She could wake up at any time or…" Dr. Benipal paused, looking at them with regret in his large round eyes. "…no time soon. We've made her comfortable, but that's all we can do."

Sara swallowed audibly. "What about her HIV? Will the coma make it worse, or could she stay asleep longer because of the virus?"

"We're managing the HIV with medication while she is in the comatose state. One condition shouldn't adversely affect the other."

Sara's hand tightened on Stephen's arm. She sighed. "Okay."

"Can we see her?" The question jerked out of Stephen's mouth.

The doctor nodded. He led them through the automatic double doors and down a long, brightly lit hallway, past the blip of machines, curtained off rooms, faceless men and women in scrubs glancing down at charts as they rushed in attendance to the sick and dying. A voice rang over the intercom: "Paging Dr. Madden. Pick up extension seven seven one. Dr. Madden. Extension seven seven one."

Dr. Benipal paused before a closed door. "We've already moved her to a private room so this is where she'll be from now until she recovers enough to go home." He pushed the door open.

Rille looked diminished. Lying in the small bed under a steadily beeping machine and with an I.V. feeding fluid into her arm, she was the smallest Stephen had ever seen her. Her face was turned away from them to the wall, showing clearly where they had shaved nearly half of the back of her head to clean and bandage a wound. Up close, her features were still and ashen.

"Her hair!" Sara lurched away from him toward the bed. But she didn't touch Rille. Her hands only hovered above Rille's face, above the eyelashes that seemed as if they would lift at any moment to reveal that familiar teasing gaze.

"All we can do at this point is hope for the best," the doctor said from Stephen's side. "Like I said, she could wake up very soon."

Or never. Stephen bowed his head at the unsaid words. "Thank you, doctor."

Dr. Benipal squeezed Stephen's shoulder. "Stay with her as long as you like. When you're ready to leave, see someone at the nurse's station and they'll let you know about regular visiting hours and answer any questions you might have."

He looked at Sara who stood on the other side of Rille's bed, her arms crossed over her belly as if in pain. After a moment's hesitation, the doctor pulled a card from his breast pocket. "Here's my contact information in case you need to speak with me directly."

Stephen thanked him again. After another glance at Sara, the doctor left them alone with Rille. Stephen sank into the chair at Rille's bedside, unable to stay on his feet any longer.

"How did this happen?"

This morning when he had left them for the bike shop, everything was the same as usual. They made love as the sun rose above the horizon and crept into their bedroom. Rille was particularly attentive to Sara, whispering into her throat, taking her with a rough tenderness that Stephen hadn't seen in a long time. Afterward, he made breakfast, fruit topped waffles dusted with powdered sugar, that they ate in the kitchen while reading their various newspapers. When he kissed Sara's indifferent cheek then Rille's mouth before getting in his car for work, Stephen sensed nothing out of the ordinary. Nothing.

Sara straightened over Rille's bed. "There was a fight. A misunderstanding. While we were talking in the bedroom, I told her something she didn't want to hear. She ran out the door and fell. I guess she was in too much of a hurry to get away from me." Her hands clenched around the bed rails.

"Was it about that girl at the school?"

Sara flinched but did not look away from Rille's still face. "She told you about that?"

"Yes."

"And you don't care?"

He weighed his words carefully. "I wouldn't say that I don't care, but if she's determined to have this girl, what can I do about it?"

Sara made a noise of disgust and turned away from the bed. "Do you really feel that way?"

"Don't you?"

Her look speared him. "I felt that way four years ago. But not now."

He wanted to ask her what changed, but the look on her face stopped him cold. "Are you going to spend the rest of the day here?" he asked instead.

Before she could answer, the door opened.

"Merille, oh my God!" Rille's mother burst through the door, followed closely by her father.

Beverly Thompson pinned him and Sara with a single poisonous stare before nearly falling into Rille's narrow bed. Sara scuttled out of her way.

"What the devil happened here?" Beverly stared down at Rille, but her cold voice broadcast to the entire room. The cascade of malachite crystals against her throat and chest clattered as she leaned down to caress Rille's face. Her green dress, Stephen noticed idly, matched her eyes.

Her husband quietly closed the door behind him. "The doctor already told us it was an accidental fall, Bev."

Short and thin, with a crest of silver hair surrounding his dignified bald crown, Fletcher Thompson seemed the very opposite of his wife. He walked slowly into the room. As if taking in the feel of the air, making sure he was in the right place. Making sure that it was Merille Thompson in the bed, his daughter, and not some stranger. Making sure this wasn't some terrible mistake. He nodded at Stephen, offered a stiff smile to Sara as he moved past them to hover at the foot of Rille's bed. His already narrow face crumbled in on itself.

Stephen had only met the Thompsons a few times since he'd been with Rille, and he was surprised at how much they loved their daughter, yet did not know her. Theirs was a love fostered by willful ignorance of their child's personality and needs. As long as Rille performed well in school, her profession, and in public, they were pleased to acknowledge her as their own.

"Merille? Baby?" Beverly's voice dropped to a whisper. She pressed her palms against Rille's cheeks as silent tears rushed down her face.

The misery in Sara's eyes jerked Stephen out of his stupor. He stood and moved toward the door. He felt Sara follow behind him.

"Thank you for calling us, Sara." Mr. Thompson's voice reached out. He stood at his wife's side with a hand on her back.

Sara made a low noise, cleared her throat. "I couldn't have done anything else, sir," she said.

Beverly's necklace rattled again. "I'm sure you did this." She straightened over the bed. "The doctor told us about her sickness. It's because of how you live. That's why she's HIV positive. That's why."

"Darling, please," Mr. Thompson said. As a doctor, he knew what Beverly said wasn't true. Even she should know better. She who was a pediatrician and no stranger to illness.

But his wife wouldn't be stopped. "I know one of you did this to my baby.

Sara shook her head and crossed her arms. "It was an accident." The steel behind her words surprised Stephen. "I'm sorry that this happened," she said steadily, reaching for Stephen's hand. "Stephen and I both are."

They walked out of the room.

"What's wrong with that woman?" Sara hissed under her breath. "Can't she see we're all suffering here?"

In the parking lot, she and Stephen looked at each other, lost, not quite knowing what to do. Like her, Stephen didn't want to leave the hospital, but with Rille's parents in the room, it didn't make sense for them to stay.

"Go home, clean up. Come back later." He squeezed her hand. "If they're not gone by then, hopefully Beverly will have calmed down at least."

"Yeah, right."

Still, Sara got into her car and pulled out of the hospital parking lot toward home. As she disappeared out of sight, Stephen sagged against his car, the thin façade of control abruptly falling away. His body throbbed dimly on the inside, a thudding pulse of worry, fear, and foreboding that he didn't know what to do with. He didn't want that feeling again. The drowning under a tide of uncertainty, being pulled away from the safe haven he'd gestated in for the past four years.

Looking back at that time, he'd never prepared himself for loss. Even with Rille being HIV positive, he never thought his time with her would end. He'd prepared himself to stay in her orbit forever. With or without Sara.

It wasn't fair. The thought drummed in his head like a migraine. *It wasn't fucking fair.*

Approaching voices and footsteps roused him from his thoughts. He shoved away from the car, fumbled for his keys in his pockets, and got in. At the store, he ignored Manny's look of curiosity and worry and buried himself in work for the rest of the day. By the time he got home after ten that night, Sara was back at the hospital. The note she left in the kitchen near the plastic containers of take-out Italian told him she'd be home in time for bed then work the next day. Stephen turned over the note in his hand, her clear, looping handwriting blurring before his eyes. The hospital.

At work, he hoped it had all been some unthinkable dream, that when he pulled his car into the driveway, Sara and Rille would be home, talking quietly on the couch while their favorite jazz station played in the background, or sitting at the dinner table waiting in front of empty plates for him to join them. But this bagged food from a strange restaurant. This note. All unthinkable, but not a dream.

He put the food in the fridge and went upstairs to bed. The hospital could wait. Tonight, he would slip between their sheets, find Rille's scent in them, and perhaps dream of her. Awake.

"She's still the same."

Sara's voice, the light settling of her weight in the bed, pulled Stephen from his tentative slumber.

"I know." His words were thick with the tears he'd only been able to release in sleep. "You would have called otherwise."

"Yes."

In the gray shrouded room, he watched her pull the covers over her bare shoulders and snuggle into her favorite pillow, the Temperpedic memory foam that Rille had bought for herself but surrendered to Sara when Sara started having neck pains.

"I'm going to work for a couple of hours tomorrow, but I'm heading straight to the hospital afterward." She turned to face him, maintaining a perfect Rille-sized distance between them. Her hand drifted into the empty space. She closed her eyes. "Good night."

"Good night," he echoed, but knew sleep wouldn't come for him again.

By the end of the week, they'd drifted into a routine of sorts with Sara and Stephen leaving for work at roughly the same time in the mornings on his days to open the bike shop. After Manny came in, he grabbed lunch near the hospital then went to sit at Rille's bedside, always hoping for a change. By seven o'clock, Sara arrived with dinner she picked up on the way. They ate together in the small park nearby, with Stephen forcing himself to pick through the meal while Sara only rearranged hers in the Styrofoam container, face blank as she talked about a case or something or other, anything but the reason they were sitting there. After eating, they hovered near Rille in the room, both watching until deep into the night for a flicker of an eyelash, a twitch of a finger. Something. He and Sara held vigil until eleven o'clock or until one of them grew tired or the Thompsons swept into the room to drive them off.

Sara, he knew, was slowly coming apart. He walked into the kitchen to find her at the counter, staring down at a thick pile of mail.

Scattered envelopes. Bills. Sales circulars. A flyer about the next neighborhood watch meeting.

"Rille usually picks up the mail," she said, as if explaining something he didn't know.

With her hair twisted into a tight bun, long-sleeved white shirt tucked into navy slacks, high heels braced against the tile floor, it could have been Sara after any day at work. But tears ran unchecked down her face. Breath hitched at the back of her throat like a too-quick metronome. She was wrecked.

Stephen put the mail in the basket and urged Sara to sit at the kitchen table. He made her a cup of hot chocolate and sat with her until the tears dried and she was in control of herself again.

On Friday evening, seven days after the accident, Stephen came near the end of his own breaking point. He leaned over Rille's bed, terrified by the absolute stillness in her face.

What if this was all there was? He looked around the cool hospital room. What if she never recovered? Could he spend the rest of his life in this room, watching and waiting?

"Wake up, dammit!" He shook her. "Stop being so goddamned selfish."

She was nothing but meat in his hands, flopping and loose-limbed. Her face stayed slack. The monitor beeped its relentlessly even rhythm.

"What are you doing?"

Sara's voice jerked him upright over the bed.

"I'm trying to do *something*." He swung to face her. "If it wasn't for you we wouldn't be here. She wouldn't be here."

Sara's face slammed shut. All emotion, the worry in her voice, dropped away as if they had never been. She became stone. "Do you think you're telling me something I haven't thought of myself?"

He felt the scorn of her eyes on him, a single searing glance that pushed him back into the chair at Rille's bedside. Sara walked deeper into the room, looking Rille over as if checking for some damage that Stephen might have done. Then she sat in the chair farthest away from the bed. Not bothering to look at him, she threw the brown paper bag she carried into the trash can and dug into her purse, emerging with the day's paper. It rustled angrily as she opened it in front of her face.

Stephen sat, regret sitting hard on his chest. *I'm sorry.* The words hovered just beyond his lips, but he couldn't make himself say them.

He felt them. He knew Sara wasn't to blame. There was nothing to blame except maybe fate and unfortunate circumstances, but he needed this anger. He needed something to burn away the yawning ache in him. He needed it.

"Sara..."

The newspaper before her face slowly lowered. Tears. Tears dripped away from the wide misery of her eyes.

"Oh fuck." He moved toward her.

The newspaper crumpled in her hands then fell to the floor as she stood. Sara backed away from him and out the door. He followed.

"Sara!"

But she didn't stop, only hurried down the brightly lit corridor, ignoring the curious stares of nurses and patients she shot past.

"Sara," someone else called out.

Farther down the hall, a tall gray-haired man Stephen didn't immediately recognize walked toward Sara. A slender figure followed behind like a ghost.

"Daddy?" Sara stopped, hands flying to her mouth. "Daddy." She sagged where she stood, like a puppet with its strings abruptly cut. Then started running and didn't stop until the sturdy figure caught her against his chest. Sara's father wrapped his arms around her, pressed his cheek into her hair, hugged her as she released deep, heaving sobs into his shirtfront.

Stephen shoved his hands in his pockets and slowly approached them until he stood mere inches away from the woman he used to think was the most controlled person he'd ever known. Her cries drowned the sound of his pounding heart.

Sara lifted herself from her father's chest, palming away tears.

"What are you doing here, Daddy?"

His forehead rippled as he rubbed a soothing hand down her back. "I never got a response from Merille to my last letter so I got a little worried." From him, Rille's full name had cadence of comfort and familiarity to it, unlike when her mother, Beverly, said it. Neville Chambers continued. "A few days ago, I called the house and Stephen told me what happened. We got on the first flight we could."

"We?" Sara looked past her father.

Stephen felt the shock in her from where he stood. She took a step forward, as if pulled against her will toward the slim woman behind

Neville Chambers. But she reeled herself in and held fast to her father's arm instead.

"Mama?" She looked confused. Wary.

"We were both worried. We still are." Neville shook her arm, gently, bringing her eyes back to him. "How is Merille?"

"The same. She's the same." She looked at her mother, then away.

"Take us," her father said.

Stephen stepped up. "Neville, I'm glad you could come." Sara's father shook his hand and smiled gratefully at him.

"Stephen. Thanks for everything."

A few days before when Stephen had answered the phone call from Sara's father, he had been shaken from the routine of grief. It never occurred to him to call Neville Chambers and let him know that his daughter's girlfriend was in the hospital. He didn't even know that Sara's father and Rille were close. But apart from that, he knew that Sara was hurting and needed her father's support.

Without hesitation, he made the arrangements to fly Sara's parents to Atlanta to be there for her.

"It's the least I could do, sir, for both of you." Stephen made sure his smile included Mrs. Chambers. She wavered at her husband's side, not with uncertainty but with a reserve born from years of practice. Stephen had never met Millicent Chambers before now but had heard her husband and daughter talk enough about her to form his own opinion. He'd never shared those opinions with Sara. "Rille is just down the hall."

In the room, Neville stood at Rille's bedside. "Oh my Jesus." He touched her face. "She didn't deserve this." He closed his eyes.

Uncomfortable with any show of religiosity, Stephen wanted to leave the room. But for Sara, he stayed. Still hidden in his pockets, his fists clenched. He backed up until the wall supported him.

Sara's mother, once she came all the way into the room, kept glancing between Rille's body in the bed and Sara who stood pressed tight to her father's side with clasped hands pressed to her chest, as if Neville's mere presence in the room would make Rille better.

Neville put his hand to Rille's forehead. He offered his prayers. But Rille didn't rise and walk. She did nothing but lay there and play dead. Stephen stood apart from them, his emotions clenched in his fists, and hoped anyway.

At the end of visiting hours, they piled into Sara's car and went home. While she showed her parents to the guest room and gave them a tour of the house, Stephen made a simple dinner. Black beans and rice with steamed broccoli on the side. Mechanically, he set four places at the table and sat down with a cold beer, waiting for them to finish upstairs.

Neville and Millicent Chambers' presence in the house banished the sense of emptiness that had lived in it since Rille went into the hospital. Their soft voiced conversations. Sara's uncertain almost girlish tone. The way she leaned on her parents the way she had never done with him. Even on the mother who had abandoned her. But why should he expect her to rely on him? He'd been the one to encroach on her relationship with Rille. He knew what he was doing four years ago. He knew she hated what he had become to Rille.

Over the years, he'd simply hoped that she would get used to the idea and the reality of him. Of him being in their shared bed and in Rille's heart. Rille was too big of a personality, too magnanimous of a lover to have just one lover of her own. Sara was too selfish to see that. This had been his rationale. And now? He sipped his beer, the bottle a cool, wet slide between his lips. The sound of footsteps against the hardwoods approached the dining room. Three voices moving seamlessly together in a delicate wave, moving closer.

After dinner, Stephen slipped away to the workout room to give Sara and her parents privacy. Breaths. Muscles burning. Mind numb. He dead-lifted the seventy-five pound weighted barbell, grunting as it tugged at his forearms, the muscles in his ass, legs and back. One. Two. Three. Pungent sweat, his own, snaked into his nose, conjuring the last time he was in this room.

Rille slipping in to watch him, watch him sweat. Her mouth curved up, but there was no humor in her face, only a coveting, a naked craving that made him feel worthwhile and bursting, the clear control of her gaze on his straining body, that gaze that became like a touch on his heated skin until all of his body, flush with arousal, cock hard as his back pressed into the weight bench, the fifty-pound stacked barbell trembling above his head, his body working as much against the weight as Rille's eyes on him, pressing into him like a fist.

And only when he was done, when the hour was up and his body was a twitching, adrenaline-infused mass, did she come to him. Eyes and cunt greedy, body dry against his wet, mouth drinking his salt. And after, always after, she kissed him gently, sipping his breath, rolling his lower lip between her teeth, feeding him her love.

A moan jerked the weight from his hands. The barbell slammed into the floor with a thud and rolled once. Stephen dropped to his knees, his breath coming rapidly, as if he'd run a useless distance only to end up at the same place. He doubled over, squeezed his hot face into the mat that smelled thickly of sweat and effort and Rille. Oh God. Oh God. He couldn't bear it again. He couldn't. Sound tore out of him in a grating howl that he pressed into the mat. The plastic was bitter and salty under his tongue.

He gathered himself. He gathered himself slowly. Stood, wiped his face, and shrugged off the sadness. With steady hands, he retrieved the errant barbell and replaced it on the stand before leaving the room, not looking back into its emptiness as he headed for the shower. Wet comfort. Tile against his palms. His tears hidden in the hot stream over his head and face. As he dressed, he listened for Sara and her parents, that whispering closeness that excluded him. That whispering closeness that he'd had with his own parents so long ago.

The house sat quiet and still as he crept through its dim corridors, bare-chested. Barefooted. Loose pants an indifferent caress against his thighs and legs. He settled into the sitting room, stretching his body into one of the chairs before the naked bay window, resting his feet on the sill framing their lamp-lit front yard and the dark street beyond. His loneliness was utter. This is how it begins, he thought, his mind drifting to his life before Rille had appeared to take its reins into her hands. A desert.

He felt Sara's presence in the room before he heard it. The shifting indecision in her once she saw that he already claimed space there. But after that hesitation, she came and sat near him, keeping the empty chair—Rille's chair—between them.

"I'm sorry about earlier." Stephen offered the apology before the tension could lengthen. "This thing has been hard on me, but I know it's been hard on you too. I was out of line."

Sara nodded. She curled into the plush armchair, her tall body in tights and T-shirt morphing into a child's. "I don't know what my mother is doing here," she said.

It took him a moment to shift the focus of his thoughts.

"Did you ask her?" Stephen asked.

"No."

"You should." When she focused her intent gaze his way, Stephen nearly flinched. "I'm just guessing, but I think she's here to support you through this. Not do anything sinister."

"But why? She doesn't know who I am, and I sure as hell don't know her." Sara steadily watched Stephen. "Rille is my lesbian lover. Mama threw me out because I'm a dyke. Rille is in the hospital, but I'm still a dyke. Nothing's changed."

"But maybe she has."

"Hm." The chair creaked as she moved again. Silence descended between them. Another creak of the chair. "Do you think she'll die?"

Stephen blinked against a sudden sting at the back of his eyes. He drew a silent breath before answering. "I don't want to think."

Instead of thinking, he wanted to wait and sit in his hope. Make dinner and go to work and take care of their family until Rille came home again. But he wasn't taking care of things. In the wake of Rille's accident, Sara was diminished. Her façade of icy control that he'd recognized from the very beginning as just that, lay around her in pieces. Hurt lingered just at the corners of her eyes. Her mouth seemed always on the verge of a tremor. It shouldn't be like this. He never wanted to break her. He never wanted Rille to break her. Even with her death.

Beside him, Sara lay unmoving in her chair, head leaned back, her knees tucked into her chest. Despite her vulnerable pose, he knew she wouldn't welcome any pitying words from him.

"I met Rille's new girl," he said, deciding to follow her random pattern of conversation. "Nazrin."

A soft sound left Sara's throat. She lifted her head in surprise, and he felt the steady weight of her eyes.

"And?"

And he'd been struck by how young she was. None of her qualities that Rille had gushed about afterward had been apparent to him. The girl, like a guppy, was unformed and uninteresting. Did she even have any sort of personality to fall in love with? Her body was spectacular, and probably that was the thing that had lured Rille so effectively.

"I called Rille a dirty old bitch."

A smile ghosted across Sara's face. "She's that young, huh?"

"Very. I doubt she's even twenty." And a young twenty, at that, Stephen thought, recalling the pretty girl who'd seemed tough, but overwhelmed by Rille's attentions.

"That's too young, though." Sara frowned. "A girl that age has her whole life in front of her. It wouldn't be fair of Rille to pull her into this with us."

"Do you think it's that serious?"

"You know it is. She's working her up to moving that girl in. I can feel it." Sara paused. "Rille wants to invite Nazrin to dinner here at the house. The other day she asked me about it."

Stephen couldn't help but notice Sara's words. *She's working. Rille wants.* As if she didn't believe for a moment that Rille wouldn't wake up from her coma. Would not continue her life as it had been before the accident.

"Do you think she told Nazrin about her HIV?" Sara asked softly.

"I honestly don't know," Stephen replied after a surprised breath. "With me—" He cleared his throat, overcome by memories of that night Rille revealed herself to him in the deliberately bright bedroom of his old condo. She, already naked, with her voice low and serious as she shared her condition. Stephen, too far gone to care less. "With me," he continued, "she was honest, but not until four months after we started seeing each other. At Sara's shocked look, he shook his head. "She told me before we slept together."

"Jesus! After four months of cock-teasing I'm sure you would have fucked a dead chicken by that point."

Stephen flushed, unable to deny it. He hadn't had such a bad case of blue balls since high school. Although with Rille it had been more than the promise of sex. Her unshakable confidence, the idea that he could both lose and find himself in her. Those things had kept him at her feet after she told him about the HIV.

He pushed the subject away from him. "Nazrin is young enough for her youth to be an advantage in more ways than the obvious. Most people under twenty-five don't think of HIV and AIDS as any big deal these days. If and when Rille tells her, she'll probably dismiss it as just another thing to live with, like herpes or hereditary baldness."

"Neither of which we have any experience with," Sara said dryly.

"Thank God," Stephen said, running a hand over his thick hair.

A weak laugh trickled from Sara's lips.

Then her smile disappeared. "You know, I think Rille is trying to capture college again. Back when she was the big girl on campus and all the little freshers tossed their panties after her." She made a noise of disgust. The old Sara coming back.

"Was it really like that for her?"

"Yes. I was one of those freshers. So eager to have a taste of her." She spat a laugh, the opposite of amusement. "I got a taste all right. It almost killed me."

"But you survived."

"Did I?" Her eyes lifted. "Rille's going around searching for a repeat of her college experience. Unfortunately, she resurrected mine in the process. I'd rather have left all that uncertainty in the past. But here it is again, and that feeling of death looming. And my mother." She glanced quickly at him in embarrassment. She'd shared too much, her gaze said.

Stephen shrugged. "But it's not like before," he said, fumbling his way toward reassurance. "This is nothing like college, despite all the surface shit. You don't see a beer bong or naked frat pledges around here, do you?"

That faint smile came again. The beginnings of an arch look. "I have no idea *what* you have hidden up there in your so-called workout room."

Stephen chuckled, glad for the bit of unexpected humor between them. There hadn't been much throughout the years, he shamefully realized. At least not without Rille initiating it. The reminder of Sara sent a lance of sadness tearing through him. He peered briefly toward Sara's face, but she had turned away.

Her chair creaked. "I'm heading up to bed." Sara rose to her feet, squeezing his shoulder as she brushed past.

"Good night," Stephen murmured.

Alone in the darkness, he listened to the unique silence of a house asleep. Noises he barely paid attention to during his waking hours. From the kitchen, the faint hum of the refrigerator. Rille's antique clock ticking above the fireplace. Somewhere close, a dog barking.

Was he the one responsible for all this?

He had come fully into Rille's life knowing that Sara already existed in it. Knowing that she would be hurt by his presence. If he said no to Rille four years ago and told her he wanted no part of what she already had with Sara, maybe they wouldn't be at this point. No Rille in that hospital bed. No tears.

In the women's conversation before Rille fell, he imagined Sara's frustration rising to the surface after four dormant years. Had she threatened to leave Rille? There had been many times throughout the years he saw the need for distance in her face, a need for self-preservation that disappeared all too easily when Rille poured attention and kisses on her.

He had been the one to enable all this. His presence gave her the permission to have and suggest additional lovers. He was the one to feed Rille's hunger for more.

Still, even he was taken off guard when Rille suggested Nazrin. Stephen clenched his eyes shut.

Rille came to the shop one afternoon, bringing her smile and a rare invitation to have lunch at the place where they'd had their first date. The faint chemical scent from her morning at school drifted up from her hair and her skin. She wore jeans and a lace bra that showed through her long-sleeved green sweater. At one thirty in the afternoon, the store was full of customers. Manny was pissed. But Stephen left with her. He followed after her, mesmerized by the swaying beacon of her hips. The laughter in her voice.

At the restaurant, they sat on the patio and ordered drinks, her favorite taco salad and his standby burger since he never knew what to order at that place anyway. The idea of a British pub and its menu with things like toad-in-the-hole, bangers and mash, and Guinness pie, vaguely repulsed him and pushed him toward the familiar. Burgers, fries, and a beer. Between plucking at her salad and sipping iced tea that was mostly ice, Rille complemented his store, the way he dressed, trailing teasing fingers through his closely clipped goatee.

"I like you with facial hair," she said, chewing on her straw.

Two weeks before, she couldn't stand to look at it and had stopped kissing him. Only Sara's passingly uttered, "nice" and his desire for something of his own had stopped him from shaving it off.

"You don't like it," he said to her.

But she leaned across the table, traced his lips with her cool tongue, nibbled his mouth until he opened, grateful and eager like a puppy, to her kiss.

She sat back in her chair, scratching the corner of her top lip with her tongue. "Rough, but nice."

He shook his head and smiled. "What were you expecting, a Brillo pad?"

"I've never had a boy with a hairy face." She tilted her head, looked at him through her lashes. "Maybe it's something I should have done before now."

"That's what I'm here for, to open you up to new things."

She laughed and stole one of his fries.

Something over his shoulder captured her attention. She followed whatever it was with her gaze before looking back at him. *Must be a pretty girl,* he thought but didn't bother looking since the best looking woman in the place already sat across from him. But Rille's lips pursed as if tasting a decision. Then she looked past his shoulder again, this time smiling at someone. When she stood, Stephen turned in his chair to look.

A girl wove her way through the restaurant patio, attracting stares of both masculine and feminine appreciation in her low rider jeans and a yellow tube top with the university's logo scrawled across the breast.

"Nazrin."

"Hey," she said breathlessly, fanning at her face with one hand. "Sorry I'm late. I couldn't find parking."

Late? Stephen looked at Rille. She reached across the table for his hand, squeezed it, and let go. On the table, his fingers closed on nothing, still reaching out for hers.

"I'm glad you could make it," she said to the girl, stretching up to kiss her cheek. "Sit."

They both sat down.

"This is Nazrin," she said to him, with a possessive arm on the girl's that could only mean one thing.

Unease squirmed in Stephen's belly. "Is she?" He glanced from Rille to Nazrin. "I'm Stephen," he said. "But I think you already know that."

The way the girl looked at him, as if she had already determined who he was, was proof enough of that. Rille had told her about him, and about Sara. He looked down at his plate, suddenly nauseated at the thought of food.

Stephen signaled their server. It was time for him to go.

At the shop, Manny asked about his abrupt return and Stephen only shrugged. He could say that for the first time, he knew how Sara must have felt when Rille brought him into her home. He wondered where it would stop, how far Rille would go. Would their house swell to accommodate one more lover? Two? Twenty? Did she ever think about them and how they might feel being dropped further and further down the totem pole? At the end of all his questions, he realized that it didn't matter. As long as they tolerated it, Rille would do exactly what she wanted to.

Stephen stared after Sara in the gray half-light of the house. He imagined her climbing into their empty bed. Imagined Rille's hospital bed and its different kind of emptiness. The pain throbbed in the center of his chest again, threatening to suck him in. He pushed it away. *None of us deserve this.*

Stephen got to his feet and followed Sara into the dark.

Touching Base

Stephen/Atlanta

Leaned back in the reclined driver's seat of the car, Stephen lightly tapped his jean-clad thigh, keeping time with Creedence Clearwater Revival's "Green River." As far as he could tell, his was the only occupied car in the nearly full parking lot, the other vehicles waiting for their drivers in the pregnant pre-five o'clock moment just before the squat glass building in front of him emptied of its corporate slaves.

Stephen tapped fingers against his thigh. Waiting.

At 5:09, the first of the escapees came rushing out, clutching briefcases and laptop bags as they swarmed toward the parking lot where Stephen sat. Watching them, he felt a renewed sense of relief for opting out of the corporate rat race and running his own slow-paced business instead. His eyes pecked at each dark face and tall figure.

When "I Put a Spell on You" replaced "Green River" on the stereo, he stretched to turn up the volume. It wasn't his favorite version of the song; Nina Simone sang it much better, but Fogarty's unique and rough voice still managed to do the lyrics justice.

"I thought it was you sitting there."

Shit! Stephen nearly jumped out of his skin at the sound of the voice so close to him although he'd been waiting for it, and the body it belonged to, for nearly an hour.

Stephen smiled briefly up at Lucas's tall form, briefcased and dark-suited, standing just outside his car window. He turned down the music.

"It didn't have to be me sitting out here," he said. "I'm sure there's another black man in Atlanta driving a bright yellow Smart Car."

"I'm sure there is, but I haven't seen him yet." Lucas switched his briefcase to the other hand and leaned against the car's roof. "What's up?"

"Nothing. I just wanted to see you."

And Stephen did see him. Still slim and pretty, his skin like the bark of a cypress tree in shade. Eyes hooded and knowing. A gold ring on his left hand.

"Oh, come on. You haven't sought me out in almost two years." Lucas's striped orange tie fluttered in the breeze. He looked over his shoulder as someone called his name, a passing co-worker. After a friendly wave, he turned his attention back to Stephen.

Stephen stretched his mouth again. Two years. They'd exchanged holiday cards and the occasional phone call, but that was about it for deliberate contact. Occasionally, they saw each other when Stephen went out to one of the local bars with Rille and Sara. He'd heard through the grapevine that Lucas had gotten promoted to manager at the telecommunications company and now had his own office near the top floor of the twelve-story building.

"You look good," Stephen said.

Lucas grinned. "I know." He tipped his chin and seemed to make a decision. "Get out of that midget car. Come on. Let's go for a drink. You can wait out traffic with me."

Stephen made his words light. "Why are you trying to boss me around?"

"Don't pretend you don't like it." Lucas stepped away from the car. "I'm parked over there."

They climbed into his two-seater black Honda still carrying its new car smell, and Lucas put the car in motion, quickly catching the tail end of the mass exodus from the parking lot. As he changed gears, veins stood out against his muscled forearm in sharp relief. Stephen looked away.

Things had been so easy with them. Everything that Lucas wanted was what Stephen wanted—except for those last days when Lucas tried to push him to get therapy after his parents died. Lucas's assertiveness had manifested itself unexpectedly, but by then it was too late for them.

"Where we heading?" Stephen asked.

"This place down the road that has great wings. The beer isn't bad either."

Stephen forced a chuckle. "Beer and chicken wings. Is that what after-hours corporate life is all about?"

Lucas tossed him a glance. "Could be worse."

Traffic sailed past the car's tinted windows. Stephen tried to remember what his and Lucas's after-hours had been about when they were together. After Different Spokes closed at night, Lucas often came down to walk him home. Along the way, they'd stop for a drink with friends. Other times, they'd go straight home, play foosball or air hockey in the building's basement game room, pretending to compete with each other before heading upstairs to the condo where Stephen would soak in the tub while Lucas read aloud from the day's paper. It hadn't been a bad life.

"So is that how you and your new man spend the evenings, then?" Stephen asked. "Beer bellies and greasy fingers?"

Lucas laughed and glanced quickly down at his flat stomach before putting his eyes back on the road. "Sometimes greasy fingers. But not from fried chicken."

Naughty, naughty.

Lucas's laugh sparked a smile from Stephen, a real one this time. He was glad to see Lucas happy, although when he'd left three years ago, he couldn't have cared less. Stephen was glad Lucas had survived despite him.

Lucas looked at him again. "Is the current state of my domestic life the reason you tracked me down on a Wednesday evening?"

A dart of pain. Stephen swallowed and licked his lips before speaking. "Let's talk about that when I have a drink in front of me. Okay?"

After a pause, Lucas nodded. "Okay."

Cars packed the restaurant's parking lot. They circled the building twice before Lucas, with a frustrated curse, finally made his own parking spot at the back of the restaurant, squeezing the small Honda between a Dumpster and the curb. They had to press their bodies through a tight alley to get to the front door.

Inside, Stephen and Lucas waited in a short line before being seated in a corner booth with a view of the front parking lot and the street. The waiter gave them menus, water, and a few minutes to decide what they wanted. When he came back, Lucas ordered for both of them, surprising Stephen.

"With that deep line between your eyes, you could only be in the mood for the Ass-kick Teaser." The corner of Lucas's mouth tipped up.

"Things change, you know," Stephen said.

"Yeah, *some* things."

When the waiter came back with Lucas's mug of amber beer and Stephen's shot of Patrón Silver with a bottle of honey ale, aka the Ass-kick Teaser, Lucas nodded his head once. "Drink," he said and took a sip from his mug.

Stephen knocked back the tequila and leaned into the leather booth. Heat from the alcohol spread through his chest, drifted to settle in his belly. His shoulders loosened. A sigh rolled out of his mouth and he closed his eyes, allowing his head to fall back. It felt good to be back here again, he thought. Under Lucas's gaze, knowing that whatever happened, he was safe. Lucas would not abandon him to himself, no matter what had passed between them before. When he opened his eyes, another glass of tequila sat in front of him. Stephen picked up the clear shot glass, held its cool weight between his thumb and forefinger.

"So what's going on?" Lucas asked. "You look like someone died."

Stephen shook his head. *No. Never that.* He couldn't answer that question yet. "Did you have any regrets when we broke up?" he asked instead.

A snort of laughter from Lucas. "Other than the fact we did break up, you mean?"

"Yes. Was there anything you wished you had gotten the chance to do, that *we* had gotten the chance to do, before it all just…disintegrated?"

"No. I said everything I wanted to say when we were together." Lucas studied the bottom of his glass. "Even when things were good between us, I never took any of it for granted. Life had proven to me over and over again that nothing is promised. Either do and say something now, or risk never getting the chance again."

A shriek just outside the window, a car alarm, pulled Stephen's attention from Lucas. Seconds later, a man jogged to a silver Lexus, circling the car to check for damages as he frantically deactivated the alarm. Beyond him, streetlights flickered on. Dusk was approaching.

"Now I know why I could never get you to shut up about love and life and everything else." Stephen smiled, though it was an effort.

Lucas gripped his mug, leveled a cool stare at him. "Well, after you left, I found someone who could appreciate that quality in me."

"No." Stephen reached out across the table to squeeze his wrist. "I didn't mean it in a bad way, it's just that—"

"You're in pain and you have to kick back at someone."

He quickly downed the second shot of Patrón. It burned as beautifully going down as the first.

With the alcohol in his belly, Stephen could admit that he was in pain. The days stumbling between home and work and the hospital had left a gnawing ache in him. Existence boiled down to those three places, to waiting for Rille to fall on the side of death or life and out of the uncertainty of her coma. The waiting was agony.

Earlier, after leaving the shop and Manny's clumsy attempts to cheer him up—first with an unwanted barbeque sandwich brought back from lunch, then with a chattering parade of all the sick or dying people Manny knew and how most of them survived their illness or painlessly "crossed to the other side"—Stephen climbed in his car and put himself on autopilot. He hadn't been surprised when he ended up on Lucas's doorstep.

Lucas had always represented peace to him. A lulling sea that was only unappealing when presented as Stephen's sole alternative. A few times over the years he'd caught himself wondering what would have happened if he'd offered Lucas the same deal that Rille gave Sara when she brought Stephen into their lives. The best of both worlds: Rille's strength. Lucas's calm. But he would have needed Rille-sized balls to do such a thing.

The booth creaked under Stephen as he shifted, his body suddenly restless at the thought of Rille.

"The woman I live with," he said, "I've never told her that I love her."

"Why not tell her now?" A note of impatience crept into Lucas's voice. "Better late than never?"

Stephen sucked air between his teeth and dropped his eyes to the table. "She—she's in the hospital. In a coma."

"Oh. I'm sorry."

"What for? You didn't put her there."

Lucas slid his half empty glass across the table. Backward. Forward. In and out of Stephen's field of vision. "Sometimes I used to wish that you'd lose everything."

The words jerked Stephen's head up.

"That was a long time ago." An embarrassed look spasmed across Lucas's face. "After you left." He drank from the glass, wiped a thumb across his mouth, looked everywhere but at Stephen. "I wished that you'd lose everything and come running back to me. Not very noble, I know. But I was a mess after we broke up."

Stephen knew he was staring but couldn't stop himself. The Lucas he'd known would never wish a thing like that on him. Would never allow himself to be "a mess" no matter how badly Stephen had treated him. This had to be a lie, some sort of weird mind game.

"You didn't act messed up," Stephen said.

"I suppose I didn't. But would it have made any difference if I had? Would you have stayed with me?"

Stephen said nothing. Instead, his alcohol-slowed mind tried to imagine Lucas wrecked over him. But he only pulled up the image of Lucas as he'd always been—constant and stoic, his gentleness clothed in adult responsibilities and button-down striped shirts.

"I didn't think so." Lucas sighed into Stephen's silence.

"I—it wouldn't have worked out for us. You deserved more than I was ready to give you."

Lucas shrugged and choked up a bitter laugh. "Really?"

With his chest heavy under the press of regret, Stephen quietly watched the face opposite him. "Listen, I—"

"Hey, Lucas." A woman in a pinstriped suit paused at their table. She carried a stack of napkins and two bottles of sweating beer in her hands. "Good work on the Phoenix issue today. The whole group was stumped until you looked at it."

"Thanks, Rita." He smiled tiredly up at her. "I'm sure they would have figured it out eventually, though."

Her gaze moved to Stephen, who, after an initial smile, buried his attention in the bottom of his nearly empty beer bottle.

She flashed her capped teeth at Lucas again. "Well, keep up the good work. See you tomorrow."

"Take care."

After another brief look at Stephen, she drifted away. He tilted his head to watch her disappear into the thin crowd. Across from him, he felt Lucas do the same.

"I think I'm done with this place," Lucas muttered. "Let's get out of here."

"Okay." Stephen finished his beer in two gulps and reached for his wallet.

"No, it's cool. I got this." Lucas peeled thirty dollars from a billfold and dropped it on the table before standing, barely glancing Stephen's way, and weaving through the steady stream of customers to get out the door.

The brisk spring air needled through Stephen's thin shirt as he followed Lucas. He hunched his shoulders against the chill, wondering at the cause of Lucas's stiffened back and the sudden tension that had descended between them in the restaurant. They slipped through the narrow alley with the sound of Lucas's Bruno Magli dress shoes striking the pavement in time with the slow in and out of Stephen's breathing.

The car chirped as the alarm deactivated.

"You know—"

At Lucas's words, Stephen paused with his hand on the car's door handle. He looked up as Lucas walked over to his side of the car and stepped close.

"I think it's really fucked up how you came to me this evening." Lucas rested his hand on the car's roof, watching Stephen with a mild gaze.

"What?"

"I said—"

Stephen rushed to intercept and diffuse the anger he heard in the growled words. "I heard you. It's just—"

"Then why make me repeat myself?"

In the light from the distant streetlamp, Lucas's face was unreadable, hard and hugged in shadow. With a rush of fabric, he closed the space between them. Beer breath chuffing in Stephen's face, fingers knotting in the T-shirt, fists a hard push against Stephen's chest.

Caught off guard, Stephen simply reacted. He shoved back at Lucas. Palms slapping against muscled pecs, hard abs, ripping the cotton shirt out of pressed slacks. Lucas came back at him harder. They spun. Lucas banging against the car. Then Stephen. Both of them panting. Stephen tripped by deliberate feet, flailing back and smacking painfully into the car. He grunted. Lucas gripped his T-shirt again, trapped him between metal and his body. Stephen grabbed at his hands, but they wouldn't budge.

"What the hell are you doing?" Stephen gasped through the pressure against his chest.

The fists shook him, slammed him against the car, bruising. "When you left me, I took it," Lucas said. He thumped Stephen against the car again.

Stephen struggled, breath coming quickly, fighting against the instinct to punch Lucas in the face, the belly, anywhere to get Lucas to let him go.

"Stay still, damn you." Lucas shook him again. "Stay still and listen to me."

Through his own pounding heartbeat, Stephen heard the sound of grinding teeth. Not his.

"I sat in that damn restaurant and listened to your self-pitying bullshit for nearly two hours."

Stephen bucked against the tight grip. "If you didn't want to sit there all you had to do was get up and leave."

"No. I couldn't." Lucas took a breath and untwisted his hands from Stephen's shirt.

"What is it that makes you run so far and fast from unpleasant things? Hm?" Lucas's eyes snared his. "When your parents died, you buried your head in the sand. You turned away from the healthy things in your life and walked into whatever disaster was close by." With a low curse, Lucas backed away from him as if he couldn't stand to be near Stephen any longer. "And now that your escape is in a coma, you come running to me as if I'm nothing more than a toilet to throw your troubles in and flush them away. You owe me more than this, dammit. You owe me more!"

Lucas spun away, slammed his fist into the Dumpster's thick metal hide. A dull clang from the impact rang out. He clutched his fist, face contracting in pain. "Fuck!"

"You don't mean that." Stephen's face felt frozen. Numb.

"Get over yourself, Stephen. I mean every word of it." He held his bruised fist against his chest. Harsh breath whistled between his teeth.

Stephen backed away, his hands clenched into fists. "I'm going to leave now. I'll find my way back to my car."

They stared at each other, trapped in silence and darkness with the chasm of too many unresolved years between them.

"Don't be stupid." Lucas yanked open the car door and got in. "I'll drop you back there. Come on." He started the engine.

Stephen found himself sitting in the passenger seat, buckled in. The car took off. *Your escape is in a coma.* Lucas's words slashed through his thoughts. He had no idea. No idea that Lucas had been so hurt by the way they'd ended their relationship. None. Everything he thought he knew about Lucas was a lie. Lucas wasn't calm. He was the kind to leave bruises. And he knew how to hurt.

When Lucas's car came to a stop, Stephen fumbled for the door and opened it. As he pushed outside, his entire body seemed to ache. His chest. The small of his back that had struck the car. His knees popped like an old man's.

As he turned away, he heard the window being lowered.

"Stephen, I didn't—" Lucas stopped.

"You said what you had to." Stephen dropped heavily behind the wheel of his car, not bothering to face Lucas. "I hope you got what you needed out of this."

Lucas sighed. "Not exactly. But I didn't want to hurt you."

"Yes, you did want to hurt me. That's okay. All our motives can't be pure, right?" Stephen smiled weakly. "Thanks for the drinks."

He pulled his car door shut. Next to him, the dark Honda sat idling with the passenger window still gaping open. Across the leather seat, Lucas's grim features watched him. He said something, mouth moving to allow words to escape. Before, Stephen would have leaned in to catch those words. But not now. Not today. He started his car, and drove out of the parking lot.

Light, Unexpected

Sara/Atlanta

Sara felt Stephen when he came in from work. His bathroom noises were quiet, self-conscious, she thought. When he finished, he sank into the bed smelling of toothpaste and hand soap. She moved her hand across the sheets, letting him know that she was still awake. She didn't want to talk. Only wanted that certainty of knowing he was there and suffering like she was. Or maybe not like she was. But something close.

He sighed and rolled over, but did not speak. Only breathed deeply, slowly, as if trying to force himself asleep.

Sara's mind, normally running in smooth and logical waves, felt stalled. Having her mother near was stacking hurt on top of hurt. She felt as if she were huddled in a corner waiting for the next blow to fall. If her mother had wanted to hurt her even more, this was the perfect way to do it. By appearing out of nowhere.

Earlier in the evening, as they'd pulled up to the house, Sara noticed her mother's surprise. Millicent Chambers absorbed the size and details of the home Sara shared with Rille and Stephen with widened eyes. And Sara wondered why. Her father had taken pictures and told his wife about Sara's life in Atlanta. There were no surprises awaiting Millicent Chambers here. Not even the older contours of Sara's face should have brought a second look. But everything did.

As Sara swept them through the house—and Stephen disappeared to do whatever he needed to—her mother became more relaxed. With her big handbag clutched against her stomach, Millicent glanced around the house, peering into corners, and slowly began offering her opinion:

"That table is just like my grandmother's from England, you know, when she got married." Of the deep red floors: "Beautiful. It must have cost a lot of money. Much better than carpet for allergies, but oh, I'd hate to be the one to get on my knees and shine them." She tossed out all her pronouncements, seemingly at random, for them to land on anyone close. Nothing specifically to Sara. Her father often responded. It was as if they needed his presence as interpreter for every action or word between them.

It was with relief that Sara saw them climb the stairs to bed just after dinner.

❖

The next morning, Stephen was already up and gone. Sara felt the emptiness in the bed without turning to see. Through the closed bedroom door, she heard the faint traces of morning. Plates. Low conversation. A lawnmower moving across a neighbor's grass. Sara forced herself to climb from the bed and to the shower.

Clean but no more refreshed than before, she walked into the kitchen and stopped short at the sight of her mother at the dining table.

"Where's everybody?" she asked.

Her mother smiled weakly and lifted a teacup to her lips. "Neville went with Stephen to the shop. They said we should stop by for lunch later before we go on to the hospital."

Oh, Daddy. You're not being fair. But she put on her own smile and went for the refrigerator. Although she had been about to sit at the kitchen table with the Saturday paper, she needed something to do with her hands. Getting grapefruit juice from the fridge seemed the safest thing.

"I made breakfast," her mother said softly. "Would you like some?"

"Ah. Sure." She poured a glass of juice, ignoring the slight tremor in her hand as she shoved the carafe back into the fridge. Sara sat at the table. In the opposite chair, her mother made no move toward the stove and the offered food. Again, Sara was caught off guard by how little her mother had changed over the past thirteen years. Even though she'd seen her father more frequently, Sara could trace the changes on his face. Around his mouth, the deepening lines. The gray in his hair that had spiked just over his forehead while she was in college and now took over his whole head. And the teeth he'd had pulled from the sides of his mouth and not bothered to get bridges to replace.

The woman across from her had the same slenderness, the same salted and permed black hair worn in a bun at the back of her head. She had the same frail body that took its strength from her will alone. Her face was smooth, expressionless. No laugh lines around her mouth. No frown lines between her eyes.

"I'm sorry about your friend, Sara. Neville says she is a good person."

"Thank you. She is." Sara pressed her palms around the cool glass, not bringing it to her lips. Her throat felt itchy, demanding that she drink. But doing something as ordinary as drinking in front of her mother felt strange. It felt more correct, more right, that she suffered through her thirst while this near stranger looked on. She swallowed.

"I'll get the food," her mother said, finally getting up from the table.

Sara lifted her glass and finished half the juice in two hasty gulps. Behind her, her mother puttered at the stove and rummaged through the cupboards for plates. She didn't turn to help or look. Only stared at the abandoned cup across from her. The string attached to the immersed teabag had a small map of Jamaica on it surrounding a piece of ginger root. Her mother must have brought the tea with her from home. Sara drank more of her grapefruit juice.

When a plate of callaloo and saltfish appeared under her nose, Sara blinked. "Thank you."

She poked at the food, remembering the last time she ate something her mother cooked. Mackerel and boiled bananas. The plates had shattered in the sink as her mother dropped them in one after the other, still holding their load of food.

Sara put down her fork. "Why are you here?" When her mother said nothing, only looked at her with dark and inscrutable eyes, she lost her patience. "Is it easy for you to sit in my house as if the last thirteen years never happened?"

Her mother drew a deep breath. "I lost my son—"

"I lost Syrus, too!" Sara's clenched fist slammed into the table.

Her mother began again. "I lost my son to something I had no control over. Sometimes I look around the house and it's like he was never there." Lines appeared briefly on her forehead. "After twenty years of having my life filled by another person, how is it possible that in the twenty-first year there's nothing left?"

Pain on top of pain. Sara felt it coil high in her throat, threatening to choke her. "There is something left," she said. "I feel him close to me every day. Not a moment goes by that I don't remember and thank God that I had a brother. He loved me. He encouraged me. I don't see why you sit there using him as an excuse for what you did to me."

"I'm not using him as—" Her mother stopped and looked down into her teacup. "Since you left, your father's been telling me about everything you've done. I haven't approved of all of it. Especially not what you have going on here." She sighed through a halfhearted sneer. "You with another woman, and a man. It's not normal. But Neville keeps reminding me this is what you've chosen for yourself.

Sara twisted her fingers in her lap. "What does this have to do with Syrus?"

"My son traveled all over the world to dangerous places. He put himself in the path of harm, but I closed my mouth and allowed him to do whatever he wanted." The chair creaked as she leaned toward Sara. "I loved him. I *loved* him." Her body sagged back into the seat.

Watching the brittle body across from her, Sara realized what she was trying to say. In her mother's eyes, when Sara came out, she had been stepping into something dangerous. A region fraught with disappointment and perils that Millicent could only foresee, not prevent. But this time, she decided not to close her mouth. This time, she acted, and that act was to expel Sara from her life. If she didn't see her child putting herself in harm's way, then it wouldn't hurt as much as it did the first time. With Syrus.

"But that doesn't make sense!" Sara whispered.

"Everything got away from me," her mother said, her voice rusty and low. "I never planned for the pain to go on like this." She stretched her hands across the table, palms up and empty. "Your father thinks this should end, and I agree with him."

Sara felt the wetness against her face. Tears splashed onto her hands twisted into painful knots in her lap.

She shook her head, unable to take the hands reached out to her. "It's been thirteen years." Her words came muffled and liquid.

In the years since she'd left her parents' house, Sara had only survived. She finished school with only her father at the graduation ceremony; she'd avoided planes, treating them like flying death machines. Each Mother's Day sneered at her from the calendar, a mocking and constant reminder.

For years, she felt herself a walking wound, suppurating and infected. And now her mother thought she could erase the damage with a few words over tea.

"Sara. I didn't come here for you to push me away," she said quietly, insistently, gaze steady on Sara's face.

Sara could only stare at her mother with the unasked question clenched behind her teeth.

"I want to fix things between us."

Sara pushed away from the table and shoved her hands in the pockets of her slacks. "Just to let you know, there's nothing dangerous about how I choose to live my life." She stared down at her mother, trembling. "I drive a Volvo, for God's sake!"

Her throat burned with uncontrolled emotion. She cleared it. "If you're done eating, we can go see Daddy and Stephen."

Her mother's head jerked. A nod. "Just let me get my purse."

As they drove to the bike shop, jazz and idle chatter from the radio filled the silence. At the store, Stephen took one look at her face before taking charge of the conversation, telling them where in the neighborhood to go on a mini sightseeing tour while he finished up in the next hour or so. It was far from lunchtime. He tried. Sara brushed his arm in thanks before walking past to latch on to her father. He kissed her forehead, blessing her with the crisp smell of his aftershave.

"What do you feel like for lunch, Daddy?"

❖

Lunch, like dinner the day before, was strained. When Stephen left the shop to join them, he, Sara, and her parents grabbed sandwiches and drinks to go and walked to the small park nearby mostly made up of a blue-surfaced basketball and tennis court, a small open area where a sprinkling of people already sat picnicking, and a few stadium style seats made out of dark unfinished logs. They sat down. The trees overhead rustled and parted with each brush of the breeze, covering and uncovering their heads with shadow.

Sara sat next to her father, watching a lone figure bounce up and down the basketball court while the conversation flowed over her.

She sipped her water. The uneaten sandwich sat next to her. From the opposite side of her parents, she felt Stephen's eyes on her but did not look up. He wanted to know what had happened at the house. She pushed him away. Denied him access to her thoughts.

"Are you okay, my Sara?" her father asked.

She shook her head, not looking away from the teenager practicing lay-ups. The girl's dark ponytail rebounded from her shoulders as she landed on her feet. "No, Daddy. But I will be. Later."

After lunch, the three of them went on to the hospital, leaving Stephen to finish up at the shop and meet them there later. The halls on Rille's floor were hushed as Sara and her parents moved through them. An unnerving quiet as if that part of the hospital itself was trapped in a coma too.

With her parents lagging behind her and talking softly about something she couldn't hear, Sara pushed open the door to Rille's room.

"Oh!" She stopped.

Beverly Thompson sat at Rille's bedside. With a bowed head, she leaned over Rille's hands with a bottle of nail polish, painting color into the tips of slack fingers.

She looked up at Sara. "I read in a journal that it's possible to stimulate patients out of a comatose state."

Rille's bare feet, ashen and thin, poked out from beneath the sheet. Each toe had been separated from the next with white tissue paper and painted a soft copper. Not a shade Rille would have chosen.

As she got closer, Sara noticed white headphones resting in Rille's ears and an iPod at her breast. She picked up the small blue device to look at what was playing. Tears pricked at Sara's eyes. Walter Russell's audiobook, *A New Concept of the Universe*. Rille had wanted to read it for a long time. She even had the paperback on the bedside table, saying she would get to it when she had more time. Sara glanced sideways at Beverly Thompson. She had no idea the woman knew Rille's tastes in books. Then again, in the last few years, she'd taken to coming back to the house with Rille after their biweekly brunches. Maybe she had seen the book in the bedroom or she and Rille talked about it over crepes and mimosas. Sara put the iPod back.

"If nail polish and books will bring Rille out of this thing, then I'm all for them," she said. She sat on the other side of Rille's bed.

"I haven't had my full two hours yet." Mrs. Thompson looked up from Rille's hand. "You should come back another time."

Embarrassed heat prickled Sara's cheeks. She stood and looked at her watch. "We'll come back after two o'clock."

"That's fine."

Just then, her parents stepped through the door, but she silently waved them back without introducing them to Rille's mother.

"She wants to spend time with Rille alone," Sara said. "Another hour."

By the time they returned at two thirty, the hospital room was empty except for Rille lying in the bed. Beverly Thompson had left the iPod, and Rille lay against the sheets with her freshly polished nails and new lace gown, looking sweetly asleep. Sara sat with her parents for another round of waiting.

Throughout the afternoon, Sara found herself watching her mother. Wondering what lay behind her smooth face. Behind the actions that spoke of concern—fluffing Rille's pillow, getting water for Sara and her father, reading to Rille from the day's paper. Sara wanted to scream at her to stop the charade. Stop pretending to care. Just go back to Florida and mourn her dead son. The living did not need her.

But Sara said nothing.

She leaned against her father as he read silently from his Bible.

In the background, night arrived, darkening the landscape outside the windows, switching on sharp overhead lights, ushering Stephen into the room. The day had been hard on him. He sagged on his feet, dragging himself across the floor with hesitation. Fear. His face, hanging over Rille's bed with sadness drooping at its contours, attracted her mother's soothing hands down his back. Something she hadn't done for Sara since she was a baby.

Millicent made gentling noises as she stood quietly behind him, watching Rille as her hand moved, as if searching for something in the still face that would offer an explanation for the depth of Stephen's misery. Or her daughter's loyalty. Sara turned away and pressed her face to her father's chest.

Collision

Sara & Stephen/Atlanta

"Good night, Daddy. Mama."

She and Stephen waited until her parents disappeared up the stairs toward the guest bedroom before getting up to clear the dishes. Stephen made a noise of frustration as Sara scraped the plates clean over the garbage can then moved to stack them in the dishwasher.

"I think your mother just wants to make things right," Stephen said, dragging a damp cloth over the kitchen counter. Though he looked at Sara, his eyes were distant, as if he didn't really see her. He'd been out of it since they came back from the hospital.

Sara shook her head, unable to deal with his issues on top of hers, and made her own escape. A searing shower. Under the water, she massaged exfoliating apricot scrub into her face and rubbed the stone pumice over the bottoms of her feet. She emerged from the bathroom's glass bubble with her newly exposed skin tingling and hot. Sara smoothed on lotion, lay naked between the covers. Could not sleep. Slept.

When Stephen came in, the bedside lamp still illuminated the room. Under its light, Sara lay sleeping, sprawled on her belly with the thin sheet pulled up to the middle of her back. He gently closed the bedroom door and slipped into the bathroom. After he finished, he turned off the light and climbed into the bed, under the sheet, sighing helplessly at the relief that wormed through his body. It had been a long day.

Sara popped up in the bed. "What—" She blinked, looking around the darkened room. "What's going on?"

He adjusted the pillow under his head. "Nothing. Relax. It's just me."

At his words, her body lost its stiffness and became liquid against the sheets.

"Are Mama and Daddy okay?" she asked, voice sleep-thick.

"Yeah. In the room watching TV. You don't have to worry about them. They're the ones worried about you, remember?"

She said nothing, only made a vague nodding motion, skimmed her hand across the empty space between them. "Yes. I remember."

And there was so much that she didn't want to remember. The relentlessness of this entire day, each word stirring up memories she thought she'd forgotten, bubbling emotions to the surface. She missed her brother. And as much as she had mourned him when he first left, she hadn't really said good-bye. Her reaction to her mother proved that. Sara had loved him for himself and felt her whole world shake and crumble at his loss. But he was also the chalice filled with her mother's love. Millicent Chambers put everything into Syrus. Anyone who'd seen her with her two children would know him as the favorite. Would hear it in the current flowing beneath her words, in the lingering and not-lingering of her gaze.

Through Syrus, Sara had captured her mother's love. Syrus loved her like he was the parent, always made provisions for her, always taught her new things. And old ones too. When he died, the chalice broke, and all of Millicent Chambers's love that Sara had felt by proxy spilled and disappeared into the earth. She remembered.

She grasped wordlessly across the space in the bed.

Earlier in the hospital, Sara's mother had touched him. Such a simple thing, but it undid Stephen for the rest of the night. What he had gone looking for from Lucas, he'd received instead, unasked, from a near stranger. He remembered what it was like to have a hand on his back in comfort. To hear a voice whispering nonsense, conveying care through vocal vibrations alone. And something inside him broke. Stephen had barely been able to hold himself together in the hospital. Within moments of that touch, he'd had to excuse himself to stumble, isolated, to a narrow and deserted hallway where he leaned, fingers gripping his knees, his breath chuffing from between dry lips. He couldn't remember how he made it home. To bed.

He rolled over onto his back to stare at the ceiling, his breath shallow. There were so many things he missed, so many words that had gone unsaid between him and his mother. He hadn't told her that he loved her on that last day. Sometimes he found himself wondering if she remembered that. Wherever she was.

A rustling movement on the sheets beside him. Sara's hand. She made a soft noise and he reached out to her.

"You all right?"

She clutched painfully at his skin. A groan scraped across the space between them. Did it come from him or her?

"Are you okay?" he asked again.

And he felt her mouth on his. He flinched back in surprise, but she followed him, her fingers gripping his arms. Stephen tasted her tears, desperation in her hot breath. And in that moment, it seemed that her desperation was his desperation and her actions were a result of his thoughts. Why had they left him? Had he done anything to deserve this isolation?

For too long, he had been drifting. His parents died and he was released into the atmosphere, an untethered balloon. A lost kite. But when he found Rille, he thought she would be his anchor. A connection to the world of feeling and security and family. But no.

"No." Sara chased him with her body, clinging and kissing. Her mouth clumsy on his. Body shaking and the harsh breath, the *no no no* clutch of her hands on his ass, pulling him between her legs, and her biting at his mouth and sobbing.

Sobbing. It infected him too, and his choked tears rose up. The powerful flexing of some internal muscle of sadness that nearly doubled him over in the bed, sent his forehead cracking into hers. She cried out in pain and flinched into him as he held onto her arms, pinning her quiet and away from him. His cock was ready. And he could bury his thoughts and grief and uncertainties this way, but even with his swimming thoughts and the warm gift of her body against his, some part of him knew that she would despise them both before the sweat dried.

He held her down. Held her tight. Tears and teeth sinking into his shoulder. Wetness hot against his face and in the curve of her neck where a frantic pulse hammered. Then slowed.

❖

She woke next to a deeply sleeping Stephen. On his back, he lay sprawled across his side of the bed and Rille's, sheets shoved away to bunch at his feet. The bedroom lay shrouded in shades of gray. And her thoughts, crystalline for the first time in nearly two weeks, prodded her to her feet where she dressed, quietly left the bedroom, walked down the stairs, and out the front door.

The air stung her face, and she breathed in the sugary scent of spring. She walked through the mist-shrouded early morning, hands buried in the pockets of her jacket, shoulders hunched against the cooling breeze. It wasn't lost on Sara how this walk echoed the one she'd taken two weeks ago after Rille told her about the girl. A hard smile flattened her face. It felt like a lifetime ago. The emotions that swirled in that damp evening—jealousy, anger, fear of losing what she had—seemed so far away and irrelevant.

Ahead, the dark gray line of the street stretched out, curved along the lawns of her neighbors, leading through and away from the life she'd known for the past six years. The houses, most with a single light burning on the front porch, were mindlessly alike even though the styles of architecture differed. Tudor. Craftsman. Three-story colonial. Prison. Prison. Prison. Sara drew the crisp air deeply into her lungs, padded on sneakered feet along the sidewalk, felt the concrete through the rubber soles like the first and last time. A thick-leafed tree brushed her face, leaving dew behind.

Syrus's death had created this moment. Just as his death had created every moment she'd lived since that afternoon she watched pieces of his plane float on the television screen in her mother's kitchen. Sometimes she imagined Syrus still alive, and one day he would walk into her house—no matter where it was—and sweep her up into a brother-sized hug with that big puffy hair of his moving in its own breeze as he grinned and said, "Sara! I'm back. You wouldn't believe where I've been."

She wanted to be brave, like she had imagined him to be, and so she lived her life in this way. And in the damp pre-dawn morning, Sara realized that Syrus had simply been living his life. He wasn't being brave. He was just being himself. In Stephen's arms she understood she didn't have to hold on to bravery. It had been as simple as letting go of that need and wailing for the brother she'd lost, and for the life she could have had. She was ready to let go. In the fog-speckled air, she did.

Stephen would stay. Rille could die, or she could live. Sara absolved herself.

Sara felt light. The weight pressing against her chest disappeared.

She floated back to the house, up the front steps, and through the door. In the bedroom, Stephen still lay asleep. She sat on the bed's edge, her knee nudging his hip.

In the growing dawn, she finally saw what had both repulsed and attracted her to having Stephen in her home. His thick, African bush hair. The dark face, pale teeth, strong neck. The very image of a brother. She put her hand on his back and he slowly woke, blinking through sleep to look at her. His eyes were clear, too.

"It's time," she said softly. Joyful and sad. "I'm ready to leave now."

About the Author

Jamaican-born Fiona Zedde currently lives and writes in Miami, Florida. She is the author of several novellas and novels of lesbian love and desire, including the Lambda Literary Award finalists *Bliss* and *Every Dark Desire*. Her novel, *Dangerous Pleasures*, was winner of the About.com Readers' Choice Award for Best Lesbian Novel or Memoir of 2012. Find out more at www.fionazedde.com.

Books Available from Bold Strokes Books

Battle Axe by Carsen Taite. How close is too close? Bounty hunter Luca Bennett will soon find out. (978-1-60282-871-1)

Improvisation by Karis Walsh. High school geometry teacher Jan Carroll thinks she's figured out the shape of her life and her future, until graphic artist and fiddle player Tina Nelson comes along and teaches her to improvise. (978-1-60282-872-8)

For Want of a Fiend by Barbara Ann Wright. Without her Fiendish power, can Princess Katya and her consort Starbride stop a magic-wielding madman from sparking an uprising in the kingdom of Farraday? (978-1-60282-873-5)

Broken in Soft Places by Fiona Zedde. The instant Sara Chambers meets the seductive and sinful Merille Thompson, she falls hard, but knowing the difference between love and a dangerous, all-consuming desire is just one of the lessons Sara must learn before it's too late. (978-1-60282-876-6)

Healing Hearts by Donna K. Ford. Running from tragedy, the women of Willow Springs find that with friendship, there is hope, and with love, there is everything. (978-1-60282-877-3)

Desolation Point by Cari Hunter. When a storm strands Sarah Kent in the North Cascades, Alex Pascal is determined to find her. Neither imagines the dangers they will face when a ruthless criminal begins to hunt them down. (978-1-60282-865-0)

I Remember by Julie Cannon. What happens when you can never forget the first kiss, the first touch, the first taste of lips on skin? What happens when you know you will remember every single detail of a mysterious woman? (978-1-60282-866-7)

The Gemini Deception by Kim Baldwin and Xenia Alexiou. The truth, the whole truth, and nothing but lies. Book six in the Elite Operatives series. (978-1-60282-867-4)

Scarlet Revenge by Sheri Lewis Wohl. When faith alone isn't enough, will the love of one woman be strong enough to save a vampire from damnation? (978-1-60282-868-1)

Ghost Trio by Lillian Q. Irwin. When Lee Howe hears the voice of her dead lover singing to her, is it a hallucination, a ghost, or something more sinister? (978-1-60282-869-8)

The Princess Affair by Nell Stark. Rhodes Scholar Kerry Donovan arrives at Oxford ready to focus on her studies, but her life and her priorities are thrown into chaos when she catches the eye of Her Royal Highness Princess Sasha. (978-1-60282-858-2)

The Chase by Jesse J. Thoma. When Isabelle Rochat's life is threatened, she receives the unwelcome protection and attention of bounty hunter Holt Lasher who vows to keep Isabelle safe at all costs. (978-1-60282-859-9)

The Lone Hunt by L.L. Raand. In a world where humans and praeterns conspire for the ultimate power, violence is a way of life…and death. A Midnight Hunters novel. (978-1-60282-860-5)

The Supernatural Detective by Crin Claxton. Tony Carson sees dead people. With a drag queen for a spirit guide and a devastatingly attractive herbalist for a client, she's about to discover the spirit world can be a very dangerous world indeed. (978-1-60282-861-2)

Beloved Gomorrah by Justine Saracen. Undersea artists creating their own City on the Plain uncover the truth about Sodom and Gomorrah, whose "one righteous man" is a murderer, rapist, and conspirator in genocide. (978-1-60282-862-9)

Cut to the Chase by Lisa Girolami. Careful and methodical author Paige Cornish falls for brash and wild Hollywood actress Avalon Randolph, but can these opposites find a happy middle ground in a town that never lives in the middle? (978-1-60282-783-7)

More Than Friends by Erin Dutton. Evelyn Fisher thinks she has the perfect role model for a long-term relationship, until her best friends, Kendall and Melanie, split up and all three women must reevaluate their lives and their relationships. (978-1-60282-784-4)

Every Second Counts by D. Jackson Leigh. Every second counts in Bridgette LeRoy's desperate mission to protect her heart and stop Marc Ryder's suicidal return to riding rodeo bulls. (978-1-60282-785-1)

Dirty Money by Ashley Bartlett. Vivian Cooper and Reese DiGiovanni just found out that falling in love is hard. It's even harder when you're running for your life. (978-1-60282-786-8)

Sea Glass Inn by Karis Walsh. When Melinda Andrews commissions a series of mosaics by Pamela Whitford for her new inn, she doesn't expect to be more captivated by the artist than by the paintings. (978-1-60282-771-4)

The Awakening: A Sisters of Spirits novel by Yvonne Heidt. Sunny Skye has interacted with spirits her entire life, but when she runs into Officer Jordan Lawson during a ghost investigation, she discovers more than just facts in a missing girl's cold case file. (978-1-60282-772-1)

Murphy's Law by Yolanda Wallace. No matter how high you climb, you can't escape your past. (978-1-60282-773-8)

Blacker Than Blue by Rebekah Weatherspoon. Threatened with losing her first love to a powerful demon, vampire Cleo Jones is willing to break the ultimate law of the undead to rebuild the family she has lost. (978-1-60282-774-5)

Silver Collar by Gill McKnight. Werewolf Luc Garoul is outlawed and out of control, but can her family track her down before a sinister predator gets there first? Fourth in the Garoul series. (978-1-60282-764-6)

The Dragon Tree Legacy by Ali Vali. For Aubrey Tarver time hasn't dulled the pain of losing her first love Wiley Gremillion, but she has to set that aside when her choices put her life and her family's lives in real danger. (978-1-60282-765-3)

The Midnight Room by Ronica Black. After a chance encounter with the mysterious and brooding Lillian Gray in the "midnight room" of The Griffin, a local lesbian bar, confident and gorgeous Audrey McCarthy learns that her bad-girl behavior isn't bulletproof. (978-1-60282-766-0)

Dirty Sex by Ashley Bartlett. Vivian Cooper and twins Reese and Ryan DiGiovanni stole a lot of money and the guy they took it from wants it back. Like now. (978-1-60282-767-7)

The Storm by Shelley Thrasher. Rural East Texas. 1918. War-weary Jaq Bergeron and marriage-scarred musician Molly Russell try to salvage love from the devastation of the war abroad and natural disasters at home. (978-1-60282-780-6)

Crossroads by Radclyffe. Dr. Hollis Monroe specializes in short-term relationships but when she meets pregnant mother-to-be Annie Colfax, fate brings them together at a crossroads that will change their lives forever. (978-1-60282-756-1)

Beyond Innocence by Carsen Taite. When a life is on the line, love has to wait. Doesn't it? (978-1-60282-757-8)

Heart Block by Melissa Brayden. Socialite Emory Owen and struggling single mom Sarah Matamoros are perfectly suited for each other but face a difficult time when trying to merge their contrasting worlds and the people in them. If love truly exists, can it find a way? (978-1-60282-758-5)

Pride and Joy by M.L. Rice. Perfect Bryce Montgomery is her parents' pride and joy, but when they discover that their daughter is a lesbian, her world changes forever. (978-1-60282-759-2)

Ladyfish by Andrea Bramhall. Finn's escape to the Florida Keys leads her straight into the arms of scuba diving instructor Oz as she fights for her freedom, their blossoming love…and her life! (978-1-60282-747-9)

Spanish Heart by Rachel Spangler. While on a mission to find herself in Spain, Ren Molson runs the risk of losing her heart to her tour guide, Lina Montero. (978-1-60282-748-6)